DISENCHANTED

FEY CREATIONS BOOK 1

A.R. MILLER

Mass-Market Edition - 2016

ISBN-10: 9780991493333
ISBN-13: 978-0-9914933-3-3

The Fey Creations Series

Disenchanted
Unenchanted
Re-enchanted
Shadow Play

For Howard and Anna
Because...well, they know...

Chapter 1

Seven o'clock, on the dot, Lorelei Lee marches into my salon. That should've been my first clue something's up, she's usually at least fifteen minutes late. Her lack of incognito wear—scarf covering her hair, Jackie O glasses and upturned collar—clue number two.

Number three, no pause at the front desk, no breathy greeting, or follow–me–boys wiggle. Hel, not even a wink for the male clientele waiting their turn. She grabs me, making a beeline straight for my station and pulls out a copy of the Iowa Star.

I assume it's another rave review of her show at Moonlight Lake, the swankiest hotspot in The Meadows. The place is like stepping into a time warp. Think 1940's glam and glitz, a little dinner, a little dancing enhanced by the dulcet tones of sultry siren, Lorelei Lee. She abhors the title, continuously explaining to her employer that she is not one of those *bird–footed teases*.

Automatic praise reserved for such occasions dies on my tongue with her grim expression. The brain switches gears, but before I can start the *they're just jealous speech*, she hands me the paper.

"I'm so sorry, Keely." She gently squeezes my arm, then turns to follow Nyssa, my shampoo girl.

Calling Nyssa a shampoo girl is an understatement. What that water sprite can do by simply washing your hair is better than visiting any therapist. Her ability to unravel knots of tension, fear and unease is amazing. Although, nowhere near as amazing as her ability to lean over a client without suffocating them. To say she's overly endowed is another understatement. At less than five feet, it's all right up in your face when she leans over you.

Sorry? What in hel does Lorelei have to be sorry about?

Unfolding the paper, I read the headline not once, or even twice. It takes three times for it to register. *Prominent Physician Latest Victim of The Collector?* This is exactly why I rarely read the damn thing, nothing, but bad news and fluff. Right now, I'd prefer the fluff.

The muscles in my shoulders bunch, cold fingers dancing along my spine as I scan the article. The physician is a Healer, Dr. Karen Engle. I've known her for ten years.

Last week I'd given her a new look to go with her new position as Chief of Metaphysical Medicine. Gods only know if she'll be keeping it now that the bastard took her hands.

I can't even imagine how I would cope in that

situation. An En's Talents aren't just things we can do. They're a part of us, a very physical part. The focus of an En's Talent is concentrated in a portion of the body. Karen's healing ability is— was in her hands. Take her hands and it's gone. Tossing the paper in the trash, I grab my rollers as Nyssa finishes.

Lorelei is content to sit back, close her eyes and let me roll. Usually she chatters away about any old subject, especially those centered on her, but today it all seems moot. Karen's attack rings a little closer to home than the last two, both of us are more than casual acquaintances with her.

A little mindless conversation would be a welcome distraction from the clucking of the little old blue–hair at Rey's station. The cape flaps at her sides as his nimble fingers pluck the rollers from her bobbing head. I almost expect her to take off, but chickens don't fly.

"That actor was skinned alive and not even a week later that fortune teller had her eyes cut out. It's just horrible, those poor people."

Catching her reflection, I suppress a shudder, any sympathy in her tone contradicted by a mask of fascination and eagerness. It doesn't help that she's an Unchant, or that *those poor people* had their hair done here before they became *those poor people*.

That actor—the perfect occupation for a morph with his ability to change his appearance at the drop of a hat—was a referral for Dara. That fortune teller was a seer and one of Rey's clients. I have to commend his calm, cool grace as she rambles on; if it were one of my clients she was yammering about, I don't know I could hold it together.

"Hold still, darlin'." Hair slips from Rey's grasp with each bob of her head. "How am I supposed to tease you?"

She blushes and giggles, squirming a little in the chair. I would be sorely tempted to whack bloodthirsty chicken lady with a comb, but not Rey. He flirts his way out of every situation.

Employee and friend, or not, even I can see his abundant charms. The sharpness of his therian heritage keeps him from being too pretty with the long auburn hair and wide forest colored eyes. I'm not a fan of his facial hair experiment. The closely cropped, rigid lines are a little too sinister, sneaky looking even. I suppose it's fitting since he's a fox. Literally.

Securing the last roller in Lorelei's hair, I motion Nyssa to put her under the dryer and retreat to the break room, choking on laughter. None of what happened is funny, but it's one of those laugh, or cry situations.

Struggling to breathe, I grab a soda out of the fridge, gulping it down until my coughing subsides. Maybe its shock, but all I can picture is Rey in a hen house full of clucking blue chickens.

"Let the carnage begin," I mutter, setting off another round of laughter.

"You are in a better mood than I expected."

The scent of clove and spice—from the little brown cigarettes she favors—clings to her skin like perfume, usually alerting me to her presence. I missed it today. Dara—I guess you could call her my second in command, she prefers manager—sits at the table thumbing through a trade rag. Obviously, she's seen the paper.

"Fox. Blue chickens. Never mind."

Perfectly arched brows—I've never seen touched by wax, or tweezers—slip under heart shaped bangs. Molten gold eyes swirl hypnotically and I break contact. Even Ens shouldn't look a vamp in the eye. My only excuse for slipping is that I trust Dara. We've been friends for what seems forever, having worked together back in Sioux City, when I first started doing hair. Amazingly, we ended up working together again in Des Moines and she came along for the ride when I started Fey Creations.

Grabbing a tissue, I wipe my eyes, and nose. "Hey, what are you doing here so early? The sun's still up."

She shrugs turning her attention to the magazine. Before I can pursue the subject, Jenny leans in around the door.

"Keely, your next appointment is here."

The newest member of our team is easily overlooked, hiding behind a camouflage of average. Average height. Average features. Average brown eyes and hair. Her uniqueness lies in her parentage. It's rare that a union of Ens results in an Un, but it does happen.

"Thanks." I'd spaced the cut and style scheduled while Lorelei was under the dryer. Sighing, I follow Jenny, hoping it's something simple.

No such luck.

Chapter 2

In the reception area, Jenny nods in the direction of my next client. An over enthusiastic twenty–something with a folder barely containing the pictures it holds. This is going to be fun. Not!

I don't get a chance to introduce myself before a tidal wave of praise and absolute certainty slaps me. A steady stream of how she has to look like the pictures continues until she sits down in my chair, stopping long enough to hand me the folder.

All her words are a tumble of blah, blah, blah as I open it and study the collage of pages torn from various gossip rags. Hollywood's Flavor of the Month, Leesie, stares back at me.

There is no way this is ever going to work. For one thing, my client is an Unchant. Hey, nothing against Uns—my receptionist is one—but it's nearly impossible to make an Unchant look like an Enchant.

Something about being magical adds to how we look. I don't mean in a drop dead gorgeous way, we have our share of nightmares. Even with all the cosmetic augmentation in the world, Uns just become piss poor emulations when they try.

They lack that magic spark.

I have no problem with things like colored contacts, or hair color. Before The Unveiling I relied on both. I was too easily distracted and my Talents too wonky to hold a glamour for any length of time. So my California–girl–stuck–in–Iowa–look came out of bottles and boxes, turning my platinum hair golden and nearly colorless grey eyes, blue. Fake–baking turned my über pale skin lobster red so I had to perfect the use of tan in a bottle.

My problem is with those who take it too far, like going under the scalpel. The glassy–eyed girl sitting in my chair rambling about an appointment to receive her wings brings to mind a talented pop star, whose face was literally dissolving due to so many augmentations. Gods, this needs to be nipped in the bud.

"Kira,"—so obviously not her real name—"are you sure you want to go this short?"

I hold out one of the bigger photos, the faery's slender, elegant features framed by an extremely short—dare I say it? Pixie cut. Like the origins of the name weren't answered with The Unveiling.

I can always use my Talents to regrow the hair, but let's face facts. Who wants to lose time and money giving away a free service to fix something avoidable in the first place?

Kira nods enthusiastically, eyes becoming all

the more vacant. The girl definitely has it bad. Enchants call it Faery Fever—since faeries and elves are usually the En of choice—the insatiable need to be around, to touch, and ultimately become an En.

I suppose this is preferable to some of Dara's clients, who want fangs and eternal life. Or Rey's, who think being furry is the answer to their problems.

Either I convince this child to let me do what will look best on her, or turn her away. Leaning a picture against the mirror, I move behind her and begin combing the hair away from her face, hoping she will see what I see. Features far too round to withstand such a drastic cut and curls that will revolt in Iowa's humid summer air.

No such luck, she just stares in rapture at the picture, assuming she will end up looking like her idol. Clipping the shoulder length tresses tightly to her head, I reach for the picture.

"Kira, I want you to look at yourself." I feel like I'm talking down a jumper.

"But it's not all wispy." The bottom lip begins to protrude as she struggles with her folder for yet another image.

As gently as possible, I move all the photos out of reach and toy with her hair until it simulates the cut. The lip now quivers and even an idiot can tell the waterworks are on the way.

"You're not going to do it, are you?" Her voice rises with the high, squeaky pitch of a child about to throw a tantrum. Without even looking, I can tell all eyes are on us. Some in sympathy, others relishing a blowout.

"I didn't say that." Steeling myself against the possible floor show to come, I reach out and play with the curls already fighting what little I did. "It's going to take a lot of work to get your hair as smooth as Leesie's. See how your curls want their own way?"

"But if you cut it short enough..."

The whine is back, next will be the reassurance she can make it look like that, then the begging. All typical of the younger generation, thinking they can just make it so because society decreed they can do anything they want.

No one explains the forces that make them what they are don't just bend to their will. That's what we get to deal with now because the masses sugarcoat everything. Everyone gets a prize, just because they show up. Welcome to the age of entitlement.

I shake my head. "It doesn't work that way, the only way to cut it short enough to get rid of the curl would be to shave your head."

"I can use a flat iron and gel." She clasps hands below her chin, praying to the gods of hair to transform her.

"It's not just the curl. Your facial features are wrong for this cut. I'd be doing you a disservice by doing it."

"But I want it." Her voice is beginning to rise. "I want to look like Leesie!"

That's it. The admission I need. "I can cut your hair like hers, but I can't make you look like Leesie." Pulling the picture back out, I place my hand over the faery's face and show it to her. "Do you still want the cut?"

Kira's shoulders droop as she studies the picture, minus the famous face, then her own reflection. Sniffles commence and she shakes her head.

Carefully choosing my words as my fingers arrange her curls, I describe something that will work for, instead of against her. She nods, giving consent, still unhappy about not becoming a clone of her idol, but unwilling to leave without something done.

When I finish, staff and clients alike applaud and gush over the new Kira, whose real name is Tiffany. Leaving her in Jenny's capable hands, I head back to my first client, glad that Lorelei's hair takes forever to dry.

Curlers removed, I give her shoulder a touch and she flips her head forward so I can finger comb the curls. With another touch, she sits up flipping her head back, giving her that sensual come–take–me look. Turning the chair back to the mirror, I grab the hair spray and step behind her.

"You did wonders with that child."

All I can do is shrug, not wanting a mouth full of spray as I lock the 'do in place.

"You're too modest." Leaning toward the mirror as she stands, a red tipped finger coaxes a stray strand caught in her lashes back with the others. The usual Lorelei charm descends across her features as glossy red lips curl upward in appreciation of my work.

"Don't forget my solstice party," she says, wiggling her fingers before heading up front.

Lorelei's solstice party is the event that kicks off summer. Since it's on her houseboat it starts in swanky evening clothes and ends up in bathing suits or less. Not something I participate in—bathing or birthday suit—but to each his own. Even with all the scary shit going on, I'm looking forward to going.

※※※※

"Check this out." Rey pulls me into the huddle around Jenny's desk.

"The rich jewel–tone colors and warmth of the wood is comforting yet elegant, even under the harshness of the bright lights. Heavy, ornately–carved chairs and vanities give a unique historical twist to a modern salon.

"Ms. Fey and her expert staff cater to not only the Enchant community, but embrace Unchants as well. In a world obsessed with how we look, this salon shuns current trends, instead giving the client a look suited to their needs and features. No one leaves with a look they cannot reproduce on their own.

"You all know I do not give out five stars, feeling there is always room for improvement, but Fey Creations comes close. The scenic drive to The Meadows is well worth your time and I give it four and a half stars." Jenny's grin joins the others as she finishes reciting The Iowa Star's review.

"Whoa." It's all I can muster. Sure, I've worked hard and I'm proud of what we've accomplished here, but I never expected a review like this. I was nervous when the reporter contacted me. Not being a complete moron, I knew there was more to it than a simple appointment.

Word of mouth can make, or break a business and this woman held the power of the press. Lucky for me, she liked what she saw.

"This calls for a celebration. How about tomorrow night and maybe the gracious Ms. Fey can pay?" Rey wiggles his brow, clearly amused by the rhyme.

The others nod, all grinning ear to ear, even Dara.

"Sounds great, and I think the salon can pick

up the tab for dinner,"—I look directly at Rey—
"within reason. Now, I've got a four and a half
star salon to run, so back to work with all of you."

I check my watch, fifteen minutes until my
next appointment. Plenty of time for a little fizzy
caffeine and taking the weight off my three-inch
heels is an added benefit. I don't know what makes
me think wearing heels—when I'm on my feet for
at least eight hours—will get any easier.

Sinking into one of the break room chairs, I
crack open a soda and take a long swallow. The
delightful fizz burns its way down my throat. I
think that's the only reason I drink soda. The
carbonation. Love the bubbles. My bubble high
recedes into a blissful moment of relaxation, erased
by the tingle of curiosity and fear. I should have
checked to see if I was the only one booked with
new clients. They're crawling out of the woodwork
tonight. Wonder why. The review? No, that only
came out today. Word of mouth? Best possible
answer. It's not like we're a chain salon and we
are a bit off the beaten path.

Low voices outside the door snap me back to
reality. Unlike two of my co-workers, I don't have
super hearing, but from the timbre, one is obviously
Rey. One point for the home team, behind door
number one we find Rey and Dara.

"Keely, your next appointment is early." A
healthy dose of curiosity tempered with concern

lurks in his eyes, where his companion's hold contempt.

Well, isn't this interesting? Makes me want to know who, or what my next appointment is.

"Do you guys know if he's a request, or was I just open?"

A simple question that deserves more than a shrug and a raised eyebrow, but that's all they are able, or willing to give. Irritation rises, but asking for more isn't worth the effort. Easier to find out myself.

Chapter 3

Nyssa is giggling like a schoolgirl, every movement exaggerated as she towel dries a freshly shampooed client at my station. It dawns on me why everyone is acting a little off when I catch his reflection. Summer personified, a liosâlfar. If the darkly sun–kissed complexion and fair hair aren't enough of a clue, then the patrician features are a dead giveaway.

Liosâlfar and their cousins the döckâlfar are often confused. Most think dark would lead to darker skin and light to fair complexions. Not so. The döckâlfar's pale skin—as pale as I am, minus the strange greyish tint—is due to lack of sun exposure. They live underground for the most part and don't tolerate the sun well. The liosâlfar on the other hand, are sun worshippers, their realm existing in the sky, or so I'm told.

It's no big revelation that the âlfar would make Iowa their home. We have a sizable Germanic population. Dwarves dominate Madrid—not matadors, or flamenco dancers and yes, we know that according to Spain we pronounce it wrong—even with the coal mines closed down.

Then there's Lorelei, who claims the waterways

here remind her of home. I don't see the comparison between the Rheine and the Des Moines River, but she says it calls to her.

Âlfar rarely fraternize with other Enchants, holding positions in politics and the upper echelons of society with all the arrogance of royalty. In other words, the majority are snots. Yours truly an exception, but that's probably due to my supposed half–breed heritage.

Approaching the chair I hold out my hands, palms up, in greeting. "Hello, Mr. Brand. I'm Keely Fey and I'll be cutting your hair."

There is a clear look of surprise as he looks from my extended hands to the belt containing sharp implements around my hips. Okay, faux pas number one, I've given a greeting of no weapons while wearing things that can be considered such. Dumb, dumb, dumb.

I slowly lower my hands, clear my throat and force a smile before moving behind the chair. Usually, when greeting a new client I place my hands on their shoulders, probably not the wisest action now.

"How would you like your hair cut?" Some of my nervousness abates with the excitement of getting to work with such beautiful hair. Even wet the color is incredible, every shade of blond imaginable, all on one head. I can't wait to see it dry. Women pay big bucks for poorly done imitations and even more for decent attempts, none coming even close. Problem being, the short military style, doesn't look like it needs cut. Maybe he just wants it cleaned up around his ears and neckline.

He just sits there studying me, possibly deciding if I'm qualified for the job. Like 2100 hours of training, passing the state board, continuing education every other year, holding a license for over twenty years and oh yeah, owning a well–reviewed salon doesn't qualify me.

That haughty attitude may intimidate others, but I'm Queen here and in control of the shears, or so I tell myself. Pulling a comb from the drawer, I step behind the chair and wait.

"Just a trim." His tone matches his coloring, smooth and sweet, with a hint of German accent.

I feel a warming deep within that begs to hear him speak again. With that amber gaze of his, it's tough to lift the comb. I lower my head for a moment, pretending to study the work before me.

Just breathe. He's just a cut like any other.

Centering myself, I pull a pair of shears from my belt. Sectioning his hair, I feel my Talents rise. An annoying little itch that you can't reach.

Not since adolescence, when my Talents first became apparent, has my control slipped like this. There's nothing like short hair in first period and waist length by third, or hitting two keys in typing class because you envied the prom queen's nails.

Making the mistake of looking at him in the mirror, I see the crease between his brows. He feels it too. My control doesn't just slip, it fails.

The ends of his hair curl around my fingers, gripping them without any coaxing until it brushes his shoulders. I struggle to regain some sort of control, but everything goes all slow-mo on me. The comb slips from my fingers, the sound horrendously loud as it hits the ground.

Dropping the section of hair I back away, but not fast enough, the chair spins and my wrist is in his grasp. The growing pain in my wrist, his only show of emotion.

"How?" He asks a question, but his eyes hold an answer. One he's not sharing.

I just stand there, trapped, mouth moving, but nothing coming out.

A hand grips his wrist. "Let her go." The softness of Dara's tone can't hide the menace lacing her words.

Slowly, his fingers pry themselves from my wrist, leaving behind perfect red imprints against my ultra-pale skin. That's going to leave a mark. Dara stands a step away from us watching through narrowed eyes and nods, as if a question is answered. When is someone going to fill me in on what's going on?

"Perhaps I should finish Mr. Brand's cut."

"That won't be necessary." He studies her. A predatory gleam in his hooded eyes belies the calmness of his tone.

Dara turns to me questioningly and I shake my head, fear subsiding, leaving curiosity. I want to know the secret they seem to share along with what made my Talents override their shield. Kicking the comb out of my way, I reach for another, more than willing to try again. He settles back into the chair and I spin it to face the mirror.

"Just the ends, or shall I take off more?" I run my fingers through now shoulder length locks.

"Just the ends." A faint smile touches his lips.

Gods, he's breathtaking when he smiles. Ignoring my shaking hands, I sectioned his hair. His eyes are closed when I look into the mirror, which helps. Taking a deep breath, I start cutting and before I know it, I'm done. A sense of loss falls over me.

Looking up, I see him staring at me as I run the comb through his hair for the millionth time. I have to stop looking directly into his eyes. Nearly fumbling my shears I place them back in my belt and move to grab the dryer.

Panic escalates as the need to see him again overrides the need to get his disconcerting carcass out of my chair. Hel, out of my salon. Maybe he won't like the cut. Maybe he won't come back. I could only be so lucky.

His hair feels like silk between my fingers and I wonder if his skin is as smooth. The tingle in the pit of my stomach this time isn't from errant Talent as my fingers accidentally brush his neck. Try as I might I can't deny the physical attraction, at least not to myself. I could blame it on what he is, or that he is incredibly attractive, even the scar dissecting his left brow doesn't detract from that. It makes him seem less perfect, more attainable.

Snapping off the dryer, I feel the need to run upstairs and hop in a cold shower. Time for him to go. If not for the sake of my hormones and sanity, then because my next appointment has arrived.

Escorting him to reception, I thank him, careful to keep eyes averted and hands to myself. Before he can reply, I greet my next client and explain I'll be with her as soon as I prepare my station. Trails of goose bumps run the length of my spine as I hurry around the corner.

❧❧❧❦❧❦❧

The night from hel is finally over for me. Leaving the others to finish their clients and clean up, I head upstairs. Good ol' Captain Curiosity is waiting behind the door when I release the locks, both man–made and magical.

A constant stream of cateese, follows me through the apartment. All I want is to take off my heels, but I won't get a moment's peace until I feed the little pig. A screech resembling now echoes, when I don't move fast enough to satisfy him.

"Fine." Walking to the kitchen would be much easier if he wasn't trying to trip me, something about cats and heels just don't mix. He stuffs his head into the bowl before the kitty kibble has a chance to hit bottom.

Maybe eating something isn't such a bad idea. Opening the fridge, I grab a soda and realize that's all there is, besides a few unrecognizable leftovers. I could open a can of tuna and make a sandwich, but that sounds too much like work.

Listening to the crunch of kitty kibble to my right, I decide on a bowl of cereal. Pouring the last of the milk over fruit flavored rice; I make a mental note to visit the dairy tomorrow, or should I say today?

Technically, it's Saturday morning, the beginning of my weekend. Unlike conventional salons, we're only open in the evening, Monday through Friday. It's a pretty flexible schedule starting when your first appointment is due and staying until your last. Each of us has a key so if you have a client who wants, or needs to come before seven—like Rey and his little old ladies—I don't have to be there.

Taking the bowl into the living room, I plop

down on the window seat and kick off my shoes. When most communities are rolling up their sidewalks, The Meadows kicks it into high gear. Outside a stream of partiers trickle by. Friday and Saturday nights, the parties continue until sunrise. Sure, the bars have to obey the two a.m. last call, but it doesn't mean the party stops. Some move to private residences, or Midnite Expresso, others continue to hang at Atramentous, or Moonlight Lake literally dancing the night away. Even Basement Brews continues to serve food and homemade soda until five.

The hair on my neck rises. Across the street, a lone figure leans against the street lamp, his attention fixated on my building. I part the sheers a smidgen to get a clear view.

Looking like a modern day Phillip Marlow, minus the fedora and cigarette dangling from his lips, stands Alric Brand. A large black dog—if you can call it a dog, more like Shetland pony—wanders up bumping him with a huge head. No natural dog is that big; it must be a therian.

I see his lips move as he rests his hand on the dog's back, but his attention doesn't waver from my window.

Icy fingers play chopsticks along my spine. Drawing the curtains with a little more intensity than needed, I hear a seam give way. Damn, first the man sends my emotions into overload, then he peeps me, and now he's made me tear my curtains. Add ruining supper to that list. Dipping my spoon into the soggy mess, I lose my appetite. Nothing like going to bed angry, with a sour stomach.

Chapter 4

Disembodied hands, empty eye sockets, naked muscle and bone dominate my dreams mingled with visions of a yummy honey–toasted elf. All of this chased away by a shadowy figure hanging in the fringes, that never comes into complete focus.

Little Princess, you have grown into a queen.

A voice I haven't heard in over three decades reverberates across my skin, both chilling and sensual. Vereinen. I try to recall the face of my childhood friend, but it's just a fuzzy memory. He wasn't real anyway, just someone my imagination conjured to extinguish loneliness brought on by a lack of playmates my own age.

"It's kind of inevitable."

True, but I had hoped to watch the progression.

Is that regret I hear? Doesn't matter. The gaping loss I'd thought healed rips open and any sympathy I might feel is tossed into the chasm.

"Hey, you're the one who disappeared on me."

Not by choice. Now the anger is all his.

"Then why?"

I was...

His words fade as a piercing beep from my alarm

gains momentum coupled with the realization my lack of breath is due to twenty pounds of grey and white fur.

Disengaging myself from the cat and tangled sheets, I slap the alarm into silence. Flopping backward, I pull a pillow over my head. CC immediately takes this as an invitation to poke and prod me. For him the alarm means two things—get out of my bed and make sure you put food in my dish. For me it means another day—if you consider four in the afternoon the start of the day—one I'm not ready to face.

Remnants of the dream race just out of reach through my sleep–fogged brain. What was he trying to tell me? Something about not his choice. As if things aren't crazy enough, I'm chatting with a disembodied voice I'd filed under childhood delusions.

Unlike most children, my imaginary friend never took on any solid form. He was a shadow who clouded my mind at best, with a voice that resonated through my soul. The Sisters, my grandmother and great aunts, did their best to discourage this flight of fancy. Around the time of puberty, Einen disappeared. I was a little more than resentful about that, but had more important things to worry about.

Puberty for Unchants is difficult enough with that whole body changing thing. Enchants get the cherry on top of that little treat, emerging Talents. It's no wonder I'd filed my friend away when I'd hit high school. Question is, why is he invading my dreams after all these years?

Having had enough poking and prodding from the cat, I crawl out of bed. Maybe I can skip working out. The disarray of the bed and dampness of my skin, proof that I'd spent the night multitasking. Not something I recommend.

Padding into the kitchen, I start the coffee without thinking. I can drink it black, but prefer it with a little milk, or cream, so I have three choices. Force it down in its natural state, head over to Midnite Expresso, or go get some milk. Looking at a box of cereal on the counter, the growling of my stomach makes the choice for me. First, I have a date with the shower and a toothbrush so I feel slightly alive.

❧❧❧❦❦❦

I can't help wishing Rick would give up on Jessie's Girl and cast a glance my way. A girl never forgets her first crush. Cranking the dial on the 8–track. Yes, 8–track, my car is nearly as old as I am and equipped with the finest in late 60's technology. Thanks to a flea market, I found a little gadget allowing me to play my rather large cassette collection.

I've lived through numerous incarnations of music, from vinyl to 8–tracks, cassettes to CDs, and now MP3's. Don't forget music videos. I was there like the rest of America's youth, glued to the T.V., watching my favorite songs become mini movies. Gotta love American ingenuity.

Speaking of that ingenuity, I dare anyone not to feel instant empowerment behind the wheel of an American muscle car. Even the timid feel superhuman with all that power pulsating through them. Getting to put the top down and let in the Iowa sunshine is like the icing on the cake. Yeah, I know someone as pigmentally–challenged as I am shouldn't be running around in a convertible. Call it a guilty pleasure tempered with some heavy duty SPF.

The 390 horses under the hood beg to run free and I'm tempted to turn off onto the highway letting the Mustang gallop as fast as she can. My stomach growls, a nasty reminder, forcing me to obey the speed limit and press on to my destination.

I could have had toast and black coffee, then gone for a longer drive, but I need milk, and the thought of ice cream is a little too tempting. Who wants chain store variety with a dairy so close by?

Udder Cravings opened in the late nineties and the name says it all. You crave their dairy products after your first sample. Moocha Java, or a longer drive? Milk in my coffee, or a longer drive? My stomach growls again and my tongue can almost feel the cool, creamy goodness of their ice cream. Oh yeah, I made the right choice.

With the car giving that false sense of supremacy I picture Alric Brand, the encounter at the salon, his appearance outside my window and the dreams from the night before. The undeniable urges to either tell him off, or toss him down war within me. Maybe a combination of both would the answer to my problems.

Sure, that's the ticket. Scream at him for being a rude stalker then rip his clothes off and ride him until he screams. A nervous giggle bubbles up as I slowly turn off the paved road, wincing with each pebble that bounces from the tires. I hate taking the 'Stang down gravel, but it can't be helped, considering my destination is on a country road.

The combination of the rumble of the motor and a road that severely needs grading agitates the sensations triggered by my little fantasy. I can feel the heat rising in my cheeks and it has little to do with the sun. What am I doing thinking about ravaging some guy I barely know? Gods, maybe I do need one of those little battery operated toys Nyssa is always praising.

That's the best kind of fantasy, an evil little voice whispers in one ear.

You caught him staring at your window, says the voice of reason in the other, *he could be dangerous.*

Dangerous can be good, argues the devilish voice.

I groan, vanquishing the voices of temptation and reason as I pull into the drive, parking alongside a gorgeous Valkyrie. I wonder who it belongs to. No one in town I know owns one, not that I know everyone in town, but a bike like that leaves a lasting impression.

The bell jangles as I open the door, and my mouth nearly hits the floor. Alric Brand stands at the counter sampling ice cream with one of the owners.

"Keely," Eileen calls, waving me in. "We made up some of your favorite ice cream. I even packed a gallon for you."

With those words, Mr. Brand is all but forgotten, until I catch the smirk on his face. He's leaning against the counter, as if he owns the joint, laughing. Probably at the imaginary drool running down my chin as I picture a gallon of coffee ice cream. Definitely putting a bur in my shorts. Turning back to Eileen, I feel the tension as well as heat in my cheeks with the forced smile.

"Great, Eileen, I also need some milk and cream." I hope she will ring me up while I pull the items from the cooler. No such luck. She scoops up another sample for Alric. Maneuvering around him, I place them on the counter.

"You should try the chocolate milk. It comes from real chocolate cows." Part of me hopes he's not just a pretty face and smart enough to catch on to the sarcasm.

Eileen laughs and shakes her head. "Pardon Keely's manners Mr. Brand. Just a little joke we like to tell."

"It's Ric." His smile lights the room.

"Ric," Eileen says, with a girlish giggle.

Unjustified jealousy rises as I watch the two of them. Pulling out my wallet, I place the exact change on the counter and reach for my purchases.

"Thanks for the special ice cream Eileen, gotta run. Nice seeing you again, Mr. Brand." I try like hel not to dash for the door, only to find him holding it open for me.

"Thank you," I mumble, trying to push past him as he snatches the bags from my hands.

"Allow me."

"What a gentleman." I hear Eileen say as we step outside and almost lose the fight not to roll my eyes.

"I can manage." I motion to the bags, succeeding in bringing back that condescending little smirk.

"I seem to remember you having a problem holding onto a comb yesterday. These are considerably heavier and much messier if dropped."

Every muscle tightens. It was his fault I dropped my comb. Not that it matters to him. Taking a deep breath, I walk to my car and point to the back seat. "You can put them there."

With a low whistle, he stands back, taking in the car. There's a momentary flash of pride.

"She's something, isn't she?" I run my fingers across the hood, on the way around to the driver side.

He nods, carefully placing the bags in the nugget gold interior.

"1969, right?" he asks, a grin tugging at the corners of his mouth.

"Yep." I feel like a schoolgirl seeing him eye the license plate. I usually laugh at those who don't get it, but something about the way he stares, makes I LUV 69 churn up dirty little pictures. The kind that cause cheeks to burn and legs to turn to rubber. Clearing my throat, I turn toward his bike.

"You own some pretty impressive wheels yourself."

Tearing himself from my pale yellow ride, he nods, grasping one of the handlebars, a cross between fondness and excitement. Sleek and shapely, a deep, rich red, not burgundy, not blood red, somewhere in between. My stomach growls breaking the silence and we both laugh.

"I should get going, but it's nice seeing you again." I slide in behind the wheel.

He gives me one of those diamond-dust-dazzlers of a smile. "My pleasure as always."

I watch as he gracefully mounts that beautiful machine, only starting my own when he exits the driveway.

Chapter 5

The four and a half star celebration starts with dinner at Basement Brews, the local brewpub. Just as suggested by the name the beer is brewed in the basement.

Everyone is dressed to the nines. Even Jenny, clearly uncomfortable under all the hair spray and eyeliner—Nyssa's obvious influence—but too polite to say anything.

Nyssa can carry the look, or maybe we're just used to big hair, false lashes and thick eyeliner. According to Rey, she hasn't changed her look since the 60's, when she dated the King. Contrary to popular belief, it's rumored he fashioned his Un wife after Nyssa, not his mother.

With a bow and sweeping motion of his arm, Rey holds the door for us, the courtly gesture lost when he proclaims us his harem. His lowered head bounces off the door as Dara's elbow connects.

The hostess immediately escorts us to our table.

"That was fast, even with a reservation I expected to wait on a Saturday night." I slide into the booth next to Dara.

"Only the best for our four and a half star

salon," she says with a wink, passing out the menus. "The boss also said the first round is on him. Your server will be with you shortly."

Shortly? More like the snap of your fingers.

"Hi, my name is Tina and I'll be your server tonight."

"Hi Tina, I'm Rey and I'll be your customer tonight, and your date when you get off work."

A collective groan is released and Nyssa sticks a finger down her throat as we watch Rey grasp little Tina's hand and kiss it.

Tina swats him on the head with her pad and chuckles as he lets go. "I've already been warned about you by the other waitresses. Now what can I get you all to drink?"

She efficiently scribbles down our order and hustles to the bar. This girl probably rakes in the tips, turning over tables faster than I can decide what to order.

"Hey, check it out." Nyssa holds up the specials insert. "Fey Creations Mousse!"

Leave it to Nyssa to skip right to dessert. It is flattering to see an item named after you, or in this case your business.

The drinks arrive and once our orders are taken, I look around the room. People watching is a hobby of mine. I enjoy trying to figure out what they are like by how they dress, act and interact with others. Most of the time I'm correct in my assumptions, but there are the rare occasions I'm completely off the mark.

This time the mark isn't even in sight. In the far corner sits Alric Brand with two others. One that I can't identify with his back to me and one that I thought I'd never see up close.

Var Royd, the king of tabloid fodder, Iowa tabloids anyway. Pictures so do not do that svelte body, or his sand and sea coloring justice, but that's not what keeps me staring. It's his aura, it's blurry. Not glamour blurry, more like a cloaking spell. Maybe it's a purchased spell, or charm, but that begs the question, why would a supposed En–hater use magic?

Royd heads up one of the largest insurance companies in the country catering specifically to Unchants. According to the gossip rags, he is the driving force behind The Alliance for the Removal of Enchants, or AFROE for short. Trust me, the hair reference—totally lost on them—gives us a chuckle. Obviously, he's smart enough not to leave a paper trail so there's no concrete proof.

Of course, there is a counter group, The Brotherhood of Enchanted Purity, a group of Ens with the basic premise of keeping Ens and Uns separate. I guess you can categorize them as the KKK of the En community. And let us not forget The Coalition for a Magical Tomorrow, comprised of Ens and Uns. Kind of a hippy love fest for all living things, queue the Disney soundtrack. That one is a real eye roller.

I mean seriously, who in the hel comes up with these names? Then there are all the splinter groups, too numerous to remember, most with ideas too whacked out to make sense.

This all started with The Unveiling in the 80's. The Angels were pushed aside by the Vice. The Brat Pack graced the silver screen. Big hair and glittering makeup were the standard for both males and females. The Berlin Wall fell and the Cold War became lukewarm. The 80's were an age of excess, excitement and enchantment. Not to say, I, as well as other Ens, haven't embraced the new millennium. Trust me we all partied in 1999, the 80's just hold a special place in most of our hearts.

Enchants who lived and intermingled with humanity decided they didn't want to be the hidden people anymore. There's plenty of controversy about who took that first step and allowed Uns to see us as we are, without all the glamours and hiding. Check the history books and you'll find several conflicting theories in both the who and why. Even Ens are befuddled by whose brilliant idea it was to come out. I hate that term. Maybe dropping the veil would have been more appropriate. Or sticking with stupid names how about Glamourless Glamour?

I don't blame anyone's fear; I have plenty of my

own. If I were an Un confronted by En Talents, I'd be terrified. As an En, those fears terrify me. Look back at Salem if you wonder why, or even right here in The Meadows at the State Hospital. Not a hospital at all, but a containment facility that housed Ens, who either refused to, or couldn't control their talents. Run by Uns who knew and wanted us locked away and Ens, who helped them to keep others from finding out about us. It's still in use, still state–run, but no longer referred to as a hospital. Aptly renamed the Containment Unit, or C.U. for short. Housing convicted Ens as well as those who cannot control their Talents.

Not everything you read about us is true, be it history books, or tabloids. Many of the 'myths' were allowed to circulate to keep us safe. Take mirrors and vamps—even though technically vamps aren't Ens—if it were true, why would they frequent the salon? Kind of pointless, just like that myth in today's age.

I elbow Dara and nod in their general direction.

"Curious," she says softly, cocking her head to one side.

That one word sums it up. Well, almost. Stalker also comes to mind as I glance back at the very hot, Mr. Brand. I'm getting more than a feeling he's following me, it's like the fourth time in two days I've seen him. A little too cowinkydink for comfort.

Chapter 6

A wall of funky techno beat greets us as the door swings open, enveloping us when we step inside Atramentous. Caught in a wave of barely heard greetings and congratulations, I'm separated from the others. Rey and Nyssa scurry off to the dance floor, pulling a protesting Jenny along and Dara disappears into a group of her own kind.

Musical fingers caress and pull, begging me to join the writhing crowd under the multicolored lights, but my well–wishers pull me the opposite direction. Brad grins from behind the chrome and smoked glass bar, and begins mixing my usual as well as one for Dara.

The owners of Atramentous luckily chose the sleek, elegance of the black and white palette with chrome accents. I may long for the 80's, but things such as pastel décor should be left behind.

I jump as Dara's burgundy–tipped fingers curl around the glass before it touches the bar. With one tip, the glass is empty and another waiting for her.

Maybe it's mind reading, or a gesture too quick for me to detect. I'd like to think Brad is just good at his job, but it's probably that he knows us too well.

She stands next to me, elbows braced on the bar, surveying the room, the lightness of her earlier mood gone. Here, is where tactfulness comes into play. Should I ask what's bothering her? Should I just stand here supportively?

I'm her friend, but I also know better than to step on sensitive subjects. It's probably better to let it alone. She'll tell me if she wants me to know. She has a tendency to keep to herself, unlike me who goes running to her whenever something seems the slightest out of whack.

A couple of Uns stand on the threshold of coming toward us, probably assuming we'll be dazzled by their fashion sense. One pushing up the sleeves of his coordinated sport jacket and tee combo, the other checking his frosted hair in a mirrored pillar.

I nearly choke on an ice cube as their progression halts. One look from Dara and they can't get away fast enough, Frosty shivering as he looks over his shoulder. She gives me a sly grin.

Jenny, Nyssa and Rey make their way off the dance floor, laughing and fanning their faces. I motion to what's come to be known as our table, complete with reserve card announcing Fey Creations. Yep, we definitely spend too many weekends here.

Dara shrugs, shoulders tense, jaw clenched. Looking around I try to pinpoint what's bothering her. Nothing unusual, just the typical lack of common sense induced by alcohol, the opposite sex, and the proverbial letting down of hair at the end of the week.

An extremely tipsy Un fawning over a group of Ens, catches my eye. The scene is funny and sad at the same time. You just can't get it through their heads being with one of us won't make you one of us. You have to be born this way. It's also dangerous. Un bodies are much more fragile than En bodies.

At the other end of the scale is a fashion disaster. Again funny, yet sad. On vampires, romantic–poet looks good, or maybe we just expect it, but dwarves do not look good in flowing lace and velvet.

"What's up with the fanged one?" asks Rey, receiving a tiny fist to the arm from Nyssa.

"Look who's talking about fangs." Nyssa links arms with Jenny and heads to the table.

He just grins and rubs his arm as he follows.

"Check it out, talk about sagging opportunities." Nyssa giggles bobbing her head in the direction of the bar.

A rather well endowed—check that—overly endowed female in need of support leans against the bar.

"Obviously she hasn't discovered Victoria's little secret."

The three of us groan, but Jenny's puzzled look

is just the opening she needs. Sure, it was cute the first time, but now it's getting a little old.

"What, you don't know what Victoria's secret is?" we ask in unison.

"Expensive underwear," pops off Jenny.

"No," we say, beating Nyssa to her own punch line. "The secret is that it pushes everything back up where it belongs."

"Oh...oh!" Jenny flushes bright red after turning to look at the woman. "Now I get it."

Mumbling something uncomplimentary under her breath, Nyssa's lower lip extends and she crosses her arms over her own endowments. Can we say, Keely's jealous? Yep, those of us flat as a pancake have a right to be, no matter how often we hear "But clothes hang on you better." Who wants to be considered a hanger?

Rey drapes his arms around Nyssa and Jenny escorting them to the table. Even Dara's mood lightens briefly before fading back to dark.

It isn't until we are seated that I see the reason for her mood shift, or maybe feel is more appropriate. Tingles slither across my skin as I look across the room and meet the eyes of the oh, so lovely, Mr. Brand.

The tingles turn to a slow caress as his lips curl upward and he nods, lifting his drink in my direction. Breathing becomes less automatic, I have to remind myself in and out as the walls begin to crush. This has gone past the creeping me out stage, moving on to scared stiff. Why do I want him when it's beyond obvious that something isn't right with the whole situation? I mean, shit, besides the fact that he has beautiful hair, what do I know about him?   I don't know if Dara's claws digging into me, the chorus of my name repeated, or him breaking eye contact brings me back to the real world. Doesn't matter, I'm just glad to be back.

"Geez, Keely, way to pay attention," says Rey. "What could have been more interesting than us?"

"They are." Nyssa points toward Brand and his companion then fans herself. "I'd say they are way more interesting than us. So hot."

She's right, they are both damn good looking. Brand's friend is the photo negative of golden boy. With midnight hair and pale skin, he's a male Snow White in the form of a döckâlfar. He's far from dainty, or even wiry like Brand, a strange combination of pretty and muscle. Visions of the dog with Brand outside my window flash and I wonder if they are one and the same.

A slow creeping itch rides the surface of my skin, their chemistry pulling more than my attention toward them. Damn elves, I wish they'd dial back the sexual attraction. With as gorgeous as they are, they don't need to amp it up. Practically any woman in here would take them home, hate to admit it, myself included.

Rey snorts, "Sure, if all you want is eye candy. Why bother when you have me?"

"Oh sweetie, that's like comparing Hershey's with Godiva." Nyssa shakes her head.

"Everybody likes a Hershey bar."

Nyssa rolls her eyes. "Uh...yeah right...like anyone would pick that over fine chocolate?"

"I would," says Jenny. "I like Hershey bars."

"See?" Rey slips an arm around Jenny. "Thanks, darlin'."

"And Godiva is too expensive."

Nyssa laughs, slapping her hand against the table and Rey drops his arm.

"What?" The look on Jenny's face is beyond priceless.

I shake my head. "Do yourself a favor Jen, let it go."

"But..."

"Seriously, they aren't making fun of you. It's just the two of them playing with sexual innuendos."

"Oh, oh!"

Sometimes I can't believe she's that naïve. I mean really, in this day and age is it possible for anyone of her age to be that innocent?

"This next set is for my stylist and her crew," announces the DJ as the first strains of a song from my favorite band blare from the speakers.

A spotlight swings toward our table and we shield our eyes and wave. Damn, this is turning into a regular town celebration not to mention some awesome free advertising.

A path clears and I'm feeling the whole celebrity vibe as we enter the dance floor to a flood of applause and cheers. Little flashes twinkle around us as cell phone cameras snap unflattering pictures. I mean really, those things are not only an annoyance, but take the worst photos ever. I'd rather a phone do what it's meant to do, make and receive calls.

"Ladies and gentlemen, I give you The Meadow's one and only four and a half star salon, Fey Creations," he announces before cranking the volume.

The adoration fades into the beat of the music. We're all, but forgotten in a sea of gyrating bodies. There's nothing left to do, but run for the hills, or join. I choose join. Even Dara's mood lifts as our little group lets the music move us. Reminiscent of high school, small groups of girls dancing together—the only exceptions, we have a boy, and he and two of the girls never went to high school.

One song slides into another and I find myself face to face with Ric Brand. He slips his hands around my waist so smoothly, I barely notice until I feel the gentle pressure of him guiding my hips in time with the music.

It's one of those songs that's slow and yet up–tempo. Sensual, like my partner. All the lust I felt while cutting his hair comes flaring back. The feel of his chest under my hands. The music throbbing through me. Our bodies moving as one. Is this heaven? No, just The Meadows.

Eyes closed, I feel a finger lift my chin and his lips brush against mine. That finger moves along my jaw line until all his fingers slide behind my neck twining in my hair. There is a searing flash of light behind my eyelids and the heat of a ninety–degree day against my flesh, the smooth sweetness of honey on my lips. A path of warmth follows his lips as they trace along my jaw to my ear, gently grasping the lobe.

"My immaculate dream," he whispers, before sliding down my neck, pausing at the pulse point, his hand massaging the back of my neck. The other hand slides from my hip, resting on my lower back, pulling me against him.

Not that my body needs any help, or encouragement. What's not to like? He's a good dancer, sexy and knows the words to one of my favorite songs.

My blood throbs, pushing away all thought, leaving only sensation. His lips move back to mine, crushing, insistent, his tongue like candy invading my mouth. The hand at my neck slides upward, cradling the back of my head. His other hand moves lower, persuasively crushing me against him.

My hands rest on the sides of his face, my lips

devouring his. His hand and hips, guiding mine to the beat of the music. I so want to take this off the dance floor, right back to my place.

The fluttering in my stomach becomes a chunk of lead and the hair on my neck stands up with something other than desire. All the heat built up between us turns to ice as something sharp and pointy grazes my bottom lip. What in Hel's Realm? So much for wanting to take him home.

The music changes as fast as my mood, from slow and sensual to loud and chaotic. I give him a push. His confusion the last thing I see as I shove my way through the bump and grinders. Pressing palms against temples as his voice invades my brain, questioning, pleading. I hustle to the exit—not bothering to apologize as my elbows connect—lowering my hands only to open the door, stumbling into the warm stillness of the night.

Chapter 7

I know the secret he and Dara share. I should have figured it out long before the feeling of fangs on flesh. He's been mesmerizing me. The desire. The attraction. The need to touch him. Not just tonight, but also at the salon and even my dreams.

If my own heart hadn't been beating so damn hard I would have noticed the lack of his. I could have sworn I'd felt his beating as hard as mine. And speaking of hard. Sweat breaks out on my upper lip. I can still feel him pressed against me.

My body does a little shimmy as I recalled the trail of warmth left by his lips and hands. How is this possible? Another mind game? Dara's hands are always chilled unless she's fed recently. Maybe that's it. He had a snack before I had contact with him.

Probably the strangest is his ability to be out in the sun. Sure, he wore those dark glasses and kept his skin covered.

The thing that bothers me most is the how I felt. Not the kiss, but what broke that kiss. A swirling mix of pleasure and pain rides me as my tongue touches where his fang grazed my lip. I sway as a wave of dizziness hits me and I end up back against the wall concentrating on breathing. My tongue digs at the tiny nick as the pressure builds, throbbing between my thighs. Each movement torturous blend of pleasure and pain as cloth rubs against overly sensitive nerve endings. Pulling my lip between my teeth I bite down and end up on the ground huddled against the wall.

"Miss Fey, are you alright?"

A perfectly legitimate question, considering I'm sitting on the sidewalk panting like a dog in heat. I nod, even though it's clear I'm not.

Through a pre-orgasmic haze, I see a pair of black boots. Topping off those boots are jean clad legs, long legs. My eyes, of course, linger inappropriately on what tops them.

Swallowing, I continue the journey, wishing a few more buttons were undone, revealing the promise of rock hard abs. Skin as pale as mine—minus the slight greyish hue—peaks out above the open collar. Shaggy black hair frames a face lovely despite its ruggedness, and eyes that match the deep blue of his shirt. Brand's companion.

I can't really wrap myself around the why of it, but those eyes and the curl of his lips hold a hint of disdain. Maybe he senses what's wrong with me, or he's upset because I ran out on his friend. Either way it would be rude of me not to take the offered hand. That and I need some help standing.

There's a sharp intake of breath from both of us as a winter dry shock snaps when his hand wraps around mine. He pulls me up with enough force that I slam against his chest. Bracing electricity tingles through the thin fabric of my shirt and I see lust in those beautiful bedroom eyes as my nipples tighten.

Stern lips hover so close they draw me like a magnet and I brush mine against them. From flurries to blizzard, a low guttural growl deep in his throat as he sandwiches me between him and the wall. His hands braced on either side of my head, lips greedily consuming mine, icy cool, the first snowflakes of winter on the tongue.

One hand grips his hair pulling, his lips closer. The other meanders down a well-defined chest and around a firm waist, until it holds a muscular cheek in its grasp. That seems the invitation he needs to show me how much he likes it, like the battering ram against my stomach isn't enough indication.

He pushes off the wall, grasping my arms to keep me from ending up back on the ground. I realize the pounding in my ears isn't my pulse, but a techno beat, when the door swings shut and a group of partiers giggle as they pass us.

"Get a room," one tosses over his shoulder, followed by his girlfriend proclaiming him jealous.

"Perhaps I should escort you home."

A cruel chill wraps itself around me, no longer

the tantalizing thrill of winter's first touch, but the harsh reality of its dangers.

I nod, unable, or maybe unwilling to speak. Luckily, he keeps hold of my arm as I turn toward home. Knees of jelly do not good balance make.

"It's only a couple of blocks."

He nods. Maybe it's his turn to be unable, or unwilling to speak. Guilt? He has nothing to feel guilty about, I'm the sleaze kissing two complete strangers tonight. Two very hot—well, one was hot, the other icy cool—strangers. Talk about polar opposites.

It's a struggle, but I manage to keep from laughing when we come to the corner. School crossing guards come to mind as he bars me from crossing, looks both ways, then motions it's safe.

He finally releases the death grip on my arm at the door leading to my apartment. There's the slightest twist to his lips and that hint of aversion is back in his eyes as I fumble for my keys. He waits long enough for me to unlock the door and step inside, then turns and leaves. You'd think a girl whose throat you just stuck your tongue down would at least rate a goodbye.

The protective wards prickle across my skin as I flip the locks. The big bad world is still out there, even in small town Iowa. Twenty years ago, I might not have given the locks a second thought, but not in today's age. Why leave an open invitation?

Even if I did forget, the wards would let me know if anyone not on the list entered, with something more than that minor prickling. My private space is invitation only.

Shadows cast by streetlights shining through the tiny window lengthen and twist along the walls of the narrow staircase. Ankle high lights illuminate the treads adding an eerie glow to the already horror movie–esque feel.

This is my home, my safe haven. The heavy revolving lump in my stomach should not be there. My feet shouldn't be wavering between darting up the stairs, or back outside.

Gripping the handrail I pull myself onto the first step then another. My attempt at a calm, steady gait fleeting like the light the higher I go. I do a little hop, skip as the shadows reach further along the walls and steps. Feather light and slick, something briefly wraps around my bare arm. Shadows move. They're supposed to move when they are cast by moving objects, namely me. They don't reach out and touch you.

Deep breaths, meant to be calming become panting as I take the stairs two at a time, reaching my apartment in record time. Shaking fingers fumble the keys and my head smacks the door when I retrieve them. Finally, I manage to insert the key and turn both it and the knob. Stumbling inside I slam the door and lean against it shaking so hard it rattles against the frame. CC sits directly in front of me, eyes narrowed, ears back, tail twitching, staring.

"Yeah, I know," I say, between breaths, "I should have turned on the hall light."

I've never had to use it because of fear of the dark. I touch my forearm and the shaking intensifies. I'm not afraid of the dark, but what lurks in the dark is another story. Like shadows that reach out and touch you.

Chapter 8

There's nothing worse than the phone's shrill ring ripping you out of bed. Except, maybe, an idiot banging on the door.

"Hello." A little breathless after searching and finding the phone wedged under the chair cushion. Why is it you can never find it when you need to?

"Miss Fey?"

The hair on the back of my neck stands as I realized who it is.

"Yes." I try to sound casual, but it comes out all squeaky. Worse than a damn high school girl with a crush.

"This is Ric Brand."

Did I detect a note of amusement, or am I reading too much into it as always?

"If there is a problem with your cut you can call the salon tomorrow."

"No, no problem at all. I wanted to call and apologize for last night. I took liberties that were not mine to take. I would like to ask you to dinner. That is if you have not already dined."

I nearly drop the phone. Dinner? Was I going to be a main course, or an appetizer?

"Mr. Brand, your apology is accepted, but I have to decline. It's unprofessional to date clients."

"Do not think of it as a date, just two people who happen to be sharing a meal."

Maybe it's just my imagination and guilt, but I can feel the unspoken words. You didn't think it unprofessional to dance with one last night, or to kiss him.

"Miss Fey?"

"Yes?"

"Would you consider sharing the evening meal with me?"

"I've already eaten—would you consider a cup of coffee?"

He chuckles. "That sounds delightful. When and where?"

"Say in an hour at Midnite Expresso?"

"I shall see you then."

The line goes dead with a click, no turning back now. Great, I'm going to have a delightful cup of joe with a vampire elf.

⁂

The rich scent of my favorite caffeinated beverage sends trickles of pleasure across my skin as I step inside. Is there anything better than coffee? Chocolate maybe, and sex ranks very close, I suppose.

The interior of Midnite Expresso isn't your usual trendy coffee shop. No tiny tables with uncomfortable chairs, or those long bars with stools and computer jacks. Think of it more like your kitchen with mismatched dining sets, or your living room with chairs you can curl up in with a good book.

I wave to a few regulars and the staff before acknowledging my date, sitting at a table with his back to the corner.

"Miss Fey." He rises from his seat and pulls out a chair for me. "Thank you for joining me."

"Thank you for the invitation, Mr. Brand." Visions of Count Dracula surface with his formal tone and slight accent. What's with the ancient manners? Not that I'm complaining, I just assumed it a lost art. I force a giggle into a smile and sit down before it can escape.

"The pleasure is all mine," he says, sitting back down.

Two cups of steaming brew sit on the table, the one in front of me the perfect shade of caramel, the other black.

"I took the liberty of ordering for us. I guessed you liked cream."

Yet another liberty he's taken. I'm starting to get a picture of someone very used to getting exactly what he wants, and not above taking it if it isn't given, then apologizing after. It's a little—okay, a lot—unnerving, that he knew how I took my coffee. I wonder if he knows I prefer iced when the Iowa humidity starts to rise.

The smile gracing his face causes the blood in my temples to thud, far too intimate, like someone who knows your deepest darkest secrets. I'm reminded of the invading voice from last night. I have to work on those mental shields. The last thing I need is someone using my own thoughts against me, even if it is just how I take my coffee.

I gulp down a mouthful of my drink in hopes of rinsing away the foul taste of fear. It didn't work. My eyes water, accompanying the burn I just gave myself. Lovely, two more things I don't need right now, a lisp and runny mascara.

Out of the corner of my eye, I see Candy cleaning a nearby table. She flicks her head in his direction and nods, licking her lips. Okay, it's a little more than possible that she told him how I take my coffee.

My emotions are somewhere between fear and desire for the man across from me. I'm so wrapped up sorting out the two that I miss everything he's said. I see his lips moving, but haven't heard a word.

"I asked if you were alright. The coffee is extremely hot," he repeats.

Gods, I need to learn to pay attention, but something about this guy gets me thinking with the wrong part of my anatomy. All I can do is nod, my tongue still feeling like a bad case of road rash.

There's that smile again, accompanied by a gentle pat on the hand. Now I feel like a two-year-old. I don't know which is worse fear, toddler mode, or the tingling between my thighs that shows up when he smiles.

The pat turns into a caress as he pulls away. I fight like hel to suppress the shiver forcing its way up from the soles of my feet. I need to stay on track.

"So," I say, fighting the urge to wince when my tongue protests. "What brings you to The Meadows, Mr. Brand?" What I want to ask is why he hid his vampiric nature, but even I'll admit it's none of my beeswax.

"After last night you would think you would remember to call me Ric," his tone is teasing and those hypnotic eyes twinkle.

I so don't need a reminder of last night. Too late, warmth creeps up and through my body. Great, my face now matches the red of my tee-shirt. "Sorry. What brings you to The Meadows, Ric?"

His laughter causes greater havoc than his smile, a tremor starts in my lower extremities and radiates upward. Blood vessels constrict and parts that should stay hidden in polite company show themselves in all their glory. I can't tell if it's a natural reaction, or some kind of compulsion. Either way I need to learn some control. Luckily, he's either not interested in my perkiness, or polite enough to hide it.

"I came to visit a friend."

"I didn't realize you knew anyone here." Duh, as if I know anything about him, but I'm guessing this friend is the döckâlfar I saw him with last night.

"My friend does not live in The Meadows; he owns property outside the city limits."

"Do I know him? I mean, has he been to the salon, or could I have met him somewhere else in town?" Not like I can come out and ask 'Gee, are you the one I put the lip lock on, outside the club last night?' that would be rude.

"I doubt that. He prefers to keep to himself and lives primarily off the land."

"Interesting." I toy with my cup, remembering the feel of that wintery kiss so different from Ric's and yet not. Both filled with lust and a feeling of being devoured. But one fueled by flame and joint passion, the other by a chilling animalistic hunger. The memory of the dog standing at Ric's side outside my window flashes through my feeble little brain.

"Very, the man has quite the green thumb, grows tomatoes the size of softballs." He chuckles.

"That's impressive, but I hope they taste as good as they look." Iowa is a farm state, but that's not the kind of living off the land I imagined. If my suspicions of him being the 'dog' I saw are right, living off the land would entail hunting, and not of the orange vest variety.

"Oh, they do, trust me. They make a hel of a marinara sauce and with his venison meatballs it is like...let us just say every bite is a delight to the senses."

A nervous laugh escapes as little four–legged meatballs fuel my imagination. "So spaghetti and meatballs is what brought you to The Meadows."

"That among other things."

"Such as?"

"He also makes a great martini. Your coffee should be cool enough to drink now."

After taking a sip, I carefully set the cup down, wrapping my shaking hands around it. I feel him studying me, but fight the desire to look into those mesmerizing amber eyes.

"Let me ask you something," he says, finally lifting the heavy silence. "How well do you know Miss Kanika?"

What in Hel's Realm? Why the interest in Dara?

"She works in my salon and we're friends, have been for some time now. Why?"

His shrug is fluid, noncommittal. "Just curious, the two of you seem...close."

"I've known her since I started doing hair. She rents the basement from me."

Something in his expression says I'll kick myself later. Amazing how a pretty face can make you stupidly open your mouth and insert your whole leg.

The bells on the door jingle, saving me from having to say anything else.

"Is that not your receptionist?"

In walks Jenny, draped around her escort like the cheap tramp she borrowed the outfit from. If the skirt were any further north and the top any farther south, she would be wearing a belt. From the neck up, it's still plain little old Jenny, hiding behind a ton of makeup and porn star hair. I could excuse it if it was October, but it's June.

Her companion is another story, a suit clearly not off the rack, sleek, polished. I get the impression of an En, yet not, maybe his Talents are just weak. He looks like the type who would sneer at girls who look like Jenny did right now. There is clearly possessiveness about his stance, yet something tells me he'd toss her in front of a bus if it served his purpose.

My skin crawls. Do I not pay her enough? Has she caught the fever? Jenny hasn't noticed us, but he has and the way he watches us makes me want to run screaming from the room.

Chapter 9

I allow Ric to walk me home. It is just across the street, and he left me no choice. I draw the line at him coming up, leaving him at the side door. There is no telling what might happen if I let him inside my personal space. The shop I can handle, but not this. My hormones might take over.

Movement at one of the windows catches his attention and I follow his gaze. Just CC pawing at the curtains, but I have a feeling Dara was standing there a moment ago.

"Thank you for the coffee, but this is where I get off." Where I get off? Amazing how stupid I can be so many times in one night.

"And thank you for such an enjoyable evening." He leans ever so slightly toward me.

Is he going to kiss me? My heart flutters in anticipation as he leans closer. I do the whole head tilt thingy not even thinking about it and he reaches out and grasps my hand. What was that I said about being stupid?

"Goodnight, Miss Fey." He smiles, one of those I know what you were thinking smiles, and leaves me standing there wanting to beat my head against the building.

I do the only thing any self–respecting woman would do, I stomp my way up the stairs verbally abusing myself the whole way. Childish? Yes. Do I care? No.

"Hormonally challenged idiot, first you get upset when he does kiss you, then you get upset when he doesn't." Arguing with yourself is one of those no win situations, it doesn't matter which side wins, you still lose.

I reach the door still muttering, digging for keys I don't need. The door is already open, an irritated vampire leaning against the frame. She's seen my display on the street and probably heard everything I said on the way up.

She doesn't say a word, making things even more infuriating, just moves out of the way and lets me into my own apartment. Who does she think she is my mother? What is she doing here anyway?

A bottle of wine and pizza sit on the coffee table next to a couple of DVDs. Damn, I'd forgotten movie night.

Sighing, I reach for a glass and the bottle. She holds out the other glass as I pour.

"Hot date?"

I take a sip and shake my head. "Nope, just coffee, but that was hot. Sorry, I forgot movie night."

She shrugs, one corner of her mouth tilting upward. "With something that pretty dangling in front of me, I would forget movie night also."

Unfortunately, she chooses the moment I take a drink to crack a joke. I don't think snorting wine is the recommended way of assessing the bouquet.

"So was coffee informative?"

"Brand is here visiting a friend, I'm guessing the döckâlfar he was with last night. He has a place just outside the city limits. His buddy makes a hel of a marinara sauce and great martinis."

"Personally, I prefer Chianti with my red sauce, but to each his own."

"He is also interested in you." I swear I see a flutter of something cross her face. Fear? Anger? Interest of her own?

"What did he say?"

"Just wanted to know how well I know you."

"And?"

"I told him the truth, you work with me, we're friends and you live in the basement."

Her golden skin turns a sickly jaundice shade and her jaw tightens as she reaches for the bottle to refill her glass. "What else did you talk about?"

"Small talk mostly, then Jenny came in. Gods Dara, you should have seen her. Wrapped around some guy, dressed like, well, barely dressed." I take another sip and shake my head. "She looked like she was going to be interviewed for that documentary about hookers."

"Did you talk to her?"

"Nope, she didn't see us, but her date did. The guy was giving off some serious heebie-jeebie vibes. Made me wonder if I was paying her enough. I mean what if he's a client, or her pimp? I also wonder if working with so many Ens has given her the fever. He felt like an En, but a weak one."

"She is working and going to school, but I cannot see Jenny taking that up as a second career. As for her catching the fever, she seems too grounded."

"Yeah, but I'll review her salary tomorrow."

Chapter 10

I'm seriously considering closing up shop for the night. Shredding the Iowa Star without even finishing the article, I toss it in the trash. This time they are withholding the victim's name, a minor, and the cops are keeping the details to themselves. I rub my hands over my face, not caring if my makeup migrates. It's bad enough what that asshole is doing without going after kids.

"Can't they read the damn sign?" I mumble, hearing the jiggle of the door handle.

Lifting my head, I see Jenny relock the door. Not something I want to deal with at the moment. She looks normal enough, casual slacks and blouse, hair pulled back in a sleek ponytail, a hint of makeup. Not a trace of the super slut I saw the night before, but still not quite right.

What to do, what to do. Talk to her about what I saw last night? Mind my own business? Go hide under the covers? That third option sounds pretty tempting. I seem to be falling into the, if I ignore it, it will go away attitude.

"Oh, you startled me."

She raises a hand to her chest where an

interesting pendant distracts me. It's gorgeous, like nothing I've ever seen before, golden knot work studded with gemstones that shimmer like fire. Fire and power.

"Keely, are you alright?"

Reluctantly, I draw my attention from the stunning piece to her face. My focus is blurry, like looking through a window in the rain. Pinching the bridge of my nose between my fingers, I have to close my eyes. A headache must be coming.

"Keely?"

"I'm fine, just the beginnings of a headache." I open my eyes and everything is normal. As normal as life has been the past week.

Jenny steps behind the desk, looking at the appointment book.

"Your first client isn't due until eight, why don't you go up and take a nap. I'll call and wake you about 7:30."

Same sweet Jenny, I reach out to pat her hand and she pulls away.

"Sorry," she says, "I'm just not a touchy, feely person."

I nod, keeping my hands to myself. Jenny is always the first one to give a hug when needed, whether you want it, or not. Split personality? Last night she'd been walking on the wild side and today a reasonable facsimile of an executive's assistant, both a contradiction of the plain, submissive college student I thought I knew. I shouldn't leave her alone here after everything, but when Nyssa's car pulls around the corner, I figure what the hel. She won't be alone more than a few minutes.

"I think I'll take you up on that wake up call. Let the others know what's going on when they get here."

"No problem."

Jenny makes a shooing motion as she takes my spot behind the desk and smiles, but it never reaches her eyes.

⸎⸎⸎⸎⸎⸎

Sleep is out of the question—lack of time and fear of more strange dreams—so I just slouch on the sofa, CC draped across my lap. I feel as if I've been in this position forever, so when the phone rings I just assume it's my wake up call. The Captain yawns and tries to keep me planted as I reach for the handset.

"I'll be right down."

"That would be up, not down."

I laugh, not the voice I expected, but welcome more than she knows.

"Had a feeling I should call. Is something going on?"

Gods bless Annya and her feelings. She and I have been best friends since beauty school. Well, not at first. I hated her, she was so perfect, and come to find out she was scared of me. I was strange to say the least, still am, or so she reminds me.

"I saw The Sisters and they dropped a few none too subtle hints you might be up to your scrawny ass in trouble. Reinforcing the gooseflesh I get every time I think of you."

"Who you calling scrawny, ya Swedish Injun?"

"You, you albino twit." She laughs. "Now, out with it, what's going on?"

"Too much to even attempt to tell you in the amount of time I have." I look at the clock, nearly 7:30. "Here's the basics. Have the papers there reported on this scum bag they've dubbed The Collector?"

"Yeah, what's that got to do with you?"

"At least three of the victims were clients at the salon."

Her pause is deafening and her tone not very reassuring when she does finally say something.

"You want me to come down there?"

"Hel no! I don't want you anywhere near that kind of danger."

She clears her throat. "And what about you? I'm supposed to just sit here and worry?"

"No worries, I'll be fine." Even I hear the tremor of uncertainty in my voice.

"That answers it. I'll be down in the morning."

"No, seriously, I'll be fine."

"I'll let it slide for now, but if things get worse, I'm coming down there and dragging your skinny ass back to Sioux City."

"Yeah, yeah, yeah. I promise I'll call, or email soon to give you all the details, but I've gotta run. My appointment will be here soon."

"Well, be careful. I don't want to hear about some jackass running around making dead tissue grow unless it's you."

"I'll chat at ya laters, chicky."

"Back at ya."

It's funny how a simple phone call can ease the tension and give you a sense of security, even if it might be false.

Chapter 11

The usually peaceful drive to pick up stock at Witchy Weeds is disturbed by new questions brought up by my conversation with Annya. Is it possible The Collector isn't just punishing Ens by taking their Talents, but able to use them? If just a small amount of hair, or a nail clippings could give a caster control over someone what would the missing body parts do?

Pulling into the drive, I'm greeted by Mel's alarm system. Ranging in size from ankle–biter to knock–you–on–your–ass–and–keep–you–there–until–the–order–is–given–to–eat–or–release. I climb out of the 'Stang to a chorus of thumping tails and head–butts to the legs. I step over those flopping in my path demanding belly rubs. CC's not the only four legged critter intent on tripping me.

"Looks like you need something to help you relax," says Mel, already reaching for the appropriate remedies as I step inside Witchy Weeds.

Gods love her and her ability to know exactly what I need without asking. Peace and relaxation literally flow over me, possibly from spells carefully woven throughout the store, or the paraphernalia covering the shelves. More likely, the vibes Mel herself radiates.

All the credit for the products used and sold at Fey Creations goes to Mel. Her ingenious use of nature has produced a line that anyone can use, barring allergies, of course.

Most Ens have a real problem with commercial cosmetics, maybe it's the man-made substances, but an all–natural mix seems to work. When you look back at the history of cosmetics, things like berries for cheek and lip color, or crushed stone for eye shadows were used. Those ideas had to come from somewhere. Maybe they had been lost after many Ens stepped behind The Veil. Who knows? I'm not arguing with something that works.

"So what's got you so bunged up? Work? A man, or lack thereof?" A mischievous grin plays at the corners of her mouth as she begins pulling boxes of supplies for the salon.

Mel is the type of person who could brighten any situation. I don't even mind her teasing me about my lack of male companionship. Hippy chick through and through, from her tie–dyed apparel to her one–length nutmeg tresses, becoming more gunmetal by the year. Not my fault. She feels that to color what nature gave her would be a sin.

"None of the above." I grab some much–needed cooking herbs and spices and add them to my personal pile. "If anything is bothering me, it's all the strangeness going on lately."

She nods, slowly writing up the ticket. "The Collector."

"If you haven't already noticed three of the victims had their hair done at the salon. Not sure about the most recent, since they haven't released a name."

She nods again, sliding two bills in front of me.

"And one was a long–time client." I sigh, fishing the change out of the bottom of my coin purse for my purchases. "I guess I'm just wondering why."

Checking the total of the order, I fill out a check for the salon supplies.

"Why it was your client, or why the connection to Fey Creations?" she asks before helping me tote the boxes out to the car.

"Both," I reply, moving a brick over to keep the shop door open. I grab a box and follow her out, the questions from last night rearing their ugly heads.

"Mel, is it possible to use body parts, like the ones taken, in some sort of spell? Maybe to gain control of the Talent?"

"Why do you ask?" Her frown makes me feel like an under aged kid asking hypothetically how get a bottle of vodka, knowing you are probably going to try.

"No special reason." I scrape my toe against the dirt. "It's just something a friend said over the phone last night."

She stands with arms crossed waiting for me to finish what sounds like a bullshit story.

"She said she didn't want to hear about anyone making dead tissue grow unless it was me."

Mel rubs her hands over her face. "There are rumors of spells that can harness Talents allowing another to use them. Personally, I've never heard of anyone actually achieving it, but yes, I suppose it's possible. Is that what you think this Collector is doing?"

"I don't know what to think, but the possibility of it scares me."

"Me too, kid."

⟨⟨⟨⟨⟨≀⟩⟩⟩⟩⟩

Having put it off long enough, it's time for my least favorite task at the salon. Disposal of all the hair, nail clippings, or any other remains from services rendered. The smell of burning hair is often compared to burning chicken feathers. If this is true, then burning En hair is more like burning chicken droppings. The smell has to be removed with magical air fresheners. All the little green trees in the world won't cut it. My gorge rises at just the thought.

Oddly, light traces the edges of the backroom door and there's a faint rustling. Now I'm no superhero, just stupid and protective of what's mine. I debate between a broom and a pair of shears, deciding on the broom, more distance between me and whoever is invading my space.

I move toward the storage room and push the door the rest of the way open with the broom handle then pull back to swing. The slight form hunched over a pile of bags meant for disposal, turns squeaking like a trapped mouse, hands clutched over her head.

"Hel's Realm, Jenny, you nearly gave me a heart attack!"

"Sorry," she whispers, between gasps.

"No harm done, I probably scared you as much as you did me." Slightly embarrassed I lower the broom. "What are you doing here? Don't you have class?"

"Not until this afternoon, I thought I'd help out a little more, take these out to the dumpster for you." She points to the bags piled in the corner.

"I take care of those, you know that."

"I'm sorry. I was only trying to help." Jenny lowers her head, hiding behind a veil of hair.

Leaning my mighty weapon against the wall, I place an arm around her shoulders and gently ease her from the room. "In a way I'm glad you're here, I wanted to talk to you."

I position her in front of the dryer chairs and motion for her to sit as I take the next one over. She perches on the edge of the chair, hands clasped tightly in her lap, head bowed.

"Jenny, you've been with us over six months now and I've neglected to give you a review."

So far so good, only a slight tightening of her shoulders and she manages to look at me, even if her head is still bowed. What in hel is going on with this girl? Yesterday, self–assured professional, before that whore galore and now the submissive belle of a BDSM ball, I wonder how many personalities are stuck in that little body.

"You're doing fabulous, especially considering you hold down a full time job and go to school. Because of your performance, I've decided to give you a raise. An extra couple of bucks an hour will show up in your next check."

"That's all?" Moisture gathers in those big brown eyes.

Not exactly the response I expected and I'm sure it shows. "Were you expecting more?"

"No! No, that's not what I meant. That's all you wanted to talk to me about?"

Okay, she knows I saw her the other night and is waiting for me to say something. I'm not going to; it's none of my business. I know by giving her the raise I've kind of made it my business, but she doesn't need to know that.

"Yep, that's it. Why don't you take off, go study before you have to go to class."

"Thank you, thank you so much, Keely." She hugs me before practically running from the room.

I almost ask what happened to I'm not a touchy feely sort, but decide it's not worth it. Waiting until I hear the click of the deadbolt I take a deep breath and wonder just how stupid I am. What if it had been The Collector, or a thief? And why didn't I ask for help dragging in those boxes? With some reluctance, I turn back to why I'm here and shudder. Might as well get to it, it's not going to happen on its own.

A vacuum hose at each station leads to a canister located under the vanity. The stylist is responsible for vacuuming the remnants of every cut and placing them into individual color–coded bags. A different color bag for each stylist.

Some clients choose to take their clippings with them. This is fine with me. It absolves me of the responsibility of disposal. The individual bags not taken are placed in the storeroom.

Instead of simply dumping them, I incinerate them in a barrel specially prepared for holding witchfire that stands in the center of the room. Unlike plain fire, witchfire burns cold, leaving nothing behind. Not even ash.

I learned this lovely trick from The Sisters. My grandmother and her sisters are triplets and have always been referred to as The Sisters. They have a tendency to speak in unison, as if they are one entity. Some of my childhood friends found it difficult to be around them. It's disconcerting to have the same voice coming at you from three different directions. They are the only family I know. No one explained to me where my parents were. Most people just assumed they passed away. I stuck to the story, not wanting to admit I didn't know where they were, or why they left. Someday, maybe Eliza, Matilda and Nicolina will explain what happened.

Until then, it's back to burning hair. I can feel the bile rise in my throat and I try not to gag. I sort the bags by color, then carefully count and check the number with the services performed by the corresponding stylist. I count again, and then a third time.

There's one missing. One of mine.

Chapter 12

"And just what are you supposed to do, call the police and report a missing bag of hair?" Dara reclines, a dark blot of disheveled black and red, across a white couch. Even just pulled from slumber, she looks like she should be gracing the pages of some fashion rag. Now that I've awakened her I'm feeling a bit guilty and a lot nervous, but I didn't know what else to do.

"Hel's Realm, Dara, I don't know. All I know is one of the bags is gone."

Most people would think, *the world's not going to end over the loss of one bag of hair*, but I know better. Disposing of small pieces that seem like nothing to those who know zero about magic is probably the most important part of my job. Personal items can be used as tools, or weapons in magic. What can be more personal than hair, nails, skin and body fluids? Too many of our clients are powerful Ens, letting even the smallest bit of them fall into the wrong hands could be disastrous. Not just for business.

"Maybe it was moved out of sight. You said Jenny was in there when you came in, maybe she moved it, or it got tossed somewhere when you startled her. There is always the possibility that it was given to the client and you forgot to record it, it has happened to all of us at one time, or another."

I nod, then the floor tilts beneath me.

"Dara, what if it was Karen's?" The floor decides tilting isn't enough, it drops.

Here I am, head between my knees, a vampire hovering over me telling me to relax. Not exactly a relaxing situation, even if the vamp is a friend.

"What if Jenny took the bag?"

"Keely, you have read enough of those detective novels to realize the most likely suspect is usually never the right one."

"Yeah, but I live vicariously through those things, I don't want them bleeding into real life. I think I need some air."

Dara helps me to my feet.

"Yes, I believe you do. I did not think it possible for you to get any paler, but you look like the walking dead."

Uns have mistaken me for a walking corpse because of my skin tone, but to have a walking corpse tell me, I must look ghastly.

"You should go upstairs and lie down. Better yet, have a long soak in the tub, relax. I will handle your appointments."

I nod as she steers me toward the door. Luckily, tonight is a light appointment load and I have to admit I'm not up to dealing with the others, or clients. A long soak in the tub isn't going to fix the problem, but it sure sounds like a good idea.

❈❈❈❈❈❈

The scent of lavender lifts with the steam, a moist blanket of calm illuminated by the flickering glow of candlelight. Rich plum and cherry with undertones of chocolate and black pepper tantalize the taste buds.

My book rests on the edge of the tub all, but forgotten as I slide deeper into a cocoon of warmth, letting today's—hel, this week's—woes drown in water and wine.

Deep down I know there's a connection between the missing bag and The Collector. Call me naïve and possibly stupid, but I refuse to believe Jenny is that connection. The hooker wear of the other night aside, she's a good kid. She's good at her job and from my understanding does well in school.

Considering her background—having two Ens as parents and coming out an Un—maybe there's a little confusion about where she fits in, possibly a little resentment. But I still don't believe she's helping, or gods forbid, is The Collector.

That little voice of reason comes a tap, tap, tapping at the back of my brain. Two and two make four. Nope, not going to listen, not going to think about it.

Mel's admission of rumors alluding to the possibility of harnessing an En's Talent is more terrifying than the loss of a bag of hair. Unless that bag of hair is how they gained control of the En in question.

Oh, Hel's Realm, I need to stop thinking about this crap.

I take another sip of wine, letting it roll across my tongue. Stretching my neck and shoulders, I lean back, pulling in the spicy sweet smell of lavender, hold the breath and count to ten before slowly exhaling. Trading the glass for the book, forced relaxation and distraction, just what the doctor ordered.

Who am I kidding about trying to relax? There's no use forcing myself to concentrate. Right now my life is mirroring fiction, minus the hunky hero and the kick ass heroine. Instead, we have a couple of suspicious hunks and a timid receptionist— the stereotypical character everyone assumes just couldn't do it—who might be the big bad and me. There is no way I can hold a candle to any of these ladies. Not that I want to take on this big bad. I just want to go back to reading about things like this rather than living them. We all like to think we will do exactly what the heroes do, but until you're thrown into the story, you have no idea.

Enough. I trade the book for the glass and finish the contents. A little deep breathing and clearing of the mind. Starting with my toes and working my way up I force my body to unwind. By the time I reach my face, my lids already feel like ten pound weights and I let them drift down. My jaw descends, releasing a yawn before I knew it was building. A few more moments soaking and then off to bed.

Moisture laden air no longer carries the scent of lavender, but the sickly sweet tang of decay that toys with my gag reflex. Like a dead mouse the cat grew tired of and hid in some unknown region. Raising my arm, I bury my face in my elbow and breathe through my mouth.

Good gods, it stinks and it's dark. Too dark for me to make out the details of my surroundings. Extreme low light is not a problem, but anything less than moonlight is a challenge.

The ground makes a horrid sucking sound as I take a step and my stomach heaves. Slick and slimy it oozes between my toes with each squelching step. I keep moving, fearful it will pull me under if I stay in one place too long. The way it's crawling up my ankles, I'd swear it's alive.

Yep, this stinking shit is alive. It's making its way up my calves. Move faster? Yeah, there's a thought. The mind and body are willing, but wallowing through creeping crud makes it a challenge. A heart-pounding, high-stepping, stomach-retching, stinking-to-high-heaven challenge.

By now, I'm up to my waist in compost. Struggling to keep my head above the slime and ooze, remembering to breathe through my mouth seems like an extravagance. Even though my clawing at the thick air doesn't help—I'm not stupid, just panicked—I do it anyway.

Something about struggling in quicksand, making you sink faster tickles at the back of my brain. Reason and common sense get pushed out when in the middle of full blown panic. I start to wonder which is worse, drowning in muck, or my own vomit as I spit out a combination of the two.

Little Queen...

The gunk coating my ears muffles the voice, but I know it's Einen.

Wake up. I'm dreaming. I must have fallen asleep.

Nothing is distinguishable, a hazy kaleidoscope of light and color. Herb-infused water laced with Merlot instead of decayed sludge replaces oxygen. Leaden limbs thrash and claw at the oppressive bonds determined to pull me under. The vinyl curtain bunches in my grasp, leverage lost as the fabric gives way covering my writhing body. A blinding flash of pain erupting as my head connects with porcelain.

That crack to the noggin clears a path through the panic. I'm in the tub, not a swampy marsh, or even a river, lake, or ocean—not like there are any oceans near Iowa—I refuse to go down like this. Drowning in my own tub with a cheap vinyl curtain as a shroud.

My curtain–tangled hand slides along the side, elbow cracking the bottom, wedging my arm between the tub and my body as I roll. The curtain rolls with me, freeing the other arm. Flinging that arm forward I manage to hook it over the side and pull myself upward. Hoisting myself over the edge of my watery prison, I land in a painful heap on the less than forgiving tile. Choking and heaving as oxygen–starved lungs purge themselves.

Eventually I gather enough strength to pull myself out of the spreading puddle of pink–tinged bile mingling with the contents of the toppled bottle. The shower curtain dangles from the final two and a half hooks floating across rose stained water. The wine glass didn't stand a chance against my panicked thrashing. Various pieces of the bowl are scattered across the bottom. Still attached to the stem the base bobs at the foot of the tub. Evidently, wine isn't the only thing staining the water.

Like that two year old who only notices the pain of a scraped knee when pointed out, I now feel the sting of a multitude of tiny slashes compounded by as many bruises. My stomach does a flipity–flop as my brain registers the possibility of bits of glass embedded in those cuts.

All I wanted was some quiet alone time, you know, scented candles, warm bath, glass of wine. Instead, I get something out of a horror flick, minus the screeching music. Calgon, take me away now has a whole new meaning.

Chapter 13

The bathroom looking less like a battlefield, wounds tended to the best of my ability, I shift gears. A little something to help me forget my trip down the stinky marshland road, that nearly ended in a watery grave.

Ice cream—ice cream fixes every problem, right?—and a movie. I'll pass on action adventure, my life has enough of that, and romance is a no go on many levels. Maybe a comedy? I know someone, somewhere is laughing at me so if I can't laugh along I may as well laugh at something else.

CC ambles alongside me into the kitchen. "You need a snack too?" Stupid question, but I still feel the need to ask.

Grabbing a bag of kitty treats and the special gallon of ice cream—Mel so thoughtfully made for me—I head back to the living room. Who needs a bowl when you're the only one eating it?

It's June and warm, but I still snatch up the afghan my grandmother crocheted and tuck it around myself. One of those comforting things therapists would assume is a crutch and blame on something from my childhood. Like I care. I just need the reassurance right now of something normal.

CC stands territorially over the pile of treats, munching away while I fumble with the lid of my own treat and the remote. Creamy, chocolaty, coffee goodness. If Moocha Java doesn't make me feel better, I don't know what will.

Between bites, I flip on the TV, rotating through the channels. Nothing, nothing, oh gods, something I've been trying to avoid. The anchorwoman lays out the deeds of our favorite psychopath in vivid Technicolor. I force myself to touch the channel button and fail, hitting the volume instead.

"The collection count rises, cascading fear throughout the Des Moines area. They are withholding the name of the latest victim along with details of the trophy taken. Both local officials and the NTF are working around the clock to put a stop to this grisly compilation. Channel 8 sources report an object found at the scene could lead to a major breakthrough. Stay tuned for updates."

Gods, they're calling the body parts trophies now. I hit the channel up button and stab my spoon into the bucket. My treat tastes more like a trick. Even that's ruined.

There must be suspicions of both Un and En involvement for the police and the NTF to both work on the case. A soft breeze teases the sheers and I pull the afghan tighter, I need sleep, but I know the only thing found in my bed will be nightmares. Looks like I have a date with the T.V. Maybe someone will be showing 2001: A Space Odyssey. That movie never fails to put me to sleep.

※※※※

Jenny in her crazy hooker wear replaces the anchorwoman, Var Royd to her right, Alric Brand and his buddy to her left. Her laughter, the exaggerated, maniacal type lampooned in movies, is even more bizarre with her streetwalker appearance. The news desk covered in red cloth—no, blood, my blood—an altar to which my body is tied. Brand's fangs exposed, red drool running down his pretty face, his friend—looking like a cross between Hollywood's Wolfman and Anubis—sports some impressive blood-coated claws.

A star-like object, presumably torn from my ravaged torso, cradled in Jenny's hands held aloft, then outward, an offering to Royd. Somehow, I know this is the very essence of my Talents, rooted so deeply, my destruction is the only way to remove them.

The shadowy figure of my childhood friend haunts the edge of the scene. Instead of his usual watching, holds his pale hands out toward me.

A horrendous yowling drowns out the laughter

and stinging pain that shouldn't be there—I'm dead, right?—rips across my cheek. I can't breathe. Believable, considering my chest cavity lay open.

The ear splintering noise continues as the tingle of long unused limbs crawls along arms and legs. Something cold and wet presses against my lips, little puffs of air tickling then something akin to wet sandpaper rakes across my throbbing cheek leaving a damp trail.

I force sleep–crusted eyes open and meet golden green ones, the licking stops. A great ball of grey and white fur rumbles in satisfaction and I wrap my arms around him as I sit up. A dream, just a dream. I crush my savior until tiny pinpricks bite into me and he squirms free, the white fur on his head tinged pink. My cheek stings something awful as salty tears mingle with blood. I can't be mad. He did what he had to, but it doesn't stop it from hurting like hel. Thank the Gods CC needs me to feed him and clean his litter box.

He sits at the edge of the couch, watching me cry. I can't help a teary smile as he lays a paw on my leg, his little toes flexing. I stroke his back and he moves onto my lap, reaches up, and pats my unmarked cheek. My throat feels like I swallowed a pincushion as I choke out a thank you and cradle him against me.

Afraid to go to bed, I'd fallen asleep on the couch. The TV unbearably loud as some health nut rambles about the benefits of the exercise machine they're hawking. Fumbling for the remote, I flip it off. The Captain sits beside me watching for signs of instability.

"That was some nightmare, thanks." I gently touch my cheek.

His answer tangled up in a yawn, obviously satisfied I'm back to some sort of normality, stretches out closing his eyes. Lucky cat. There's no way I'll get back to sleep, might as well get a start on the day.

Coffee brewing, I check out the damage done to my cheek. Not deep, just enough to break the skin, bright blood against white skin. That dream was straight out of the Brothers Grimm. Unlike the modern day interpretations, there was no happy ending. CC deserves a special treat today, even if I will have to use a glamour to cover this up at work.

Wavering shades of grey gather around me, reflected in the mirror. Spinning around I find nothing, obviously leftover remnants of my dream. Turning I lean against the sink and stare at myself.

"It was just a dream, brought on by everything that's been happening. The shadow figure is my imaginary friend from childhood, my subconscious fleeing to a safe place."

Yeah, right, answers that little voice of reason as I open the cabinet, grabbing gauze and peroxide. The stinging pain as it touches the scratches is a small price to pay. That's twice he's brought me out of a nightmare. Maybe the little pig does care.

Peroxide splashes as my hand jerks. The burning itch of energy tumbles over my skin, signaling an attempted breach of the shields barring the entrance to my living quarters.

Chapter 14

I know I turned the deadbolt. Only two people have a key, Dara and I. Neither of us would have set off the alarms.

The blood pulses in my ears. What if whoever it is makes it upstairs past the tangle of wards and spells? Instinct says run and hide in the closet. The inherent need to defend my territory, says barge on down and kick some invader ass.

Whoever is on the other side of that door is possibly strong enough to push through all the safeguards placed on the building. Commonsense says nothing good will come of going down there.

I practically tiptoe into the living room, like that's going to make a difference. My not–so–friendly visitor probably already knows I'm home.

CC has his nose pressed against the crack below the door, rear end wiggling with the beginnings of a pounce. He turns toward me, eyes narrowed, letting out a horrendous yowl before charging, pushing me away from the door.

"Hey." I take a step back. "Contrary to your beliefs, I'm not stupid, but I do need to find out what's going on."

Sidestepping him, I head straight for the knife drawer in the kitchen. My Talents are far from defensive. Grabbing the largest blade, I take a deep breath and head to the door.

Bare feet have an advantage; they're quiet. Clinging to the wall, I make my way down the stairs, one at a time, trying to remember which treads squeak.

The closer I get to the door the stronger the warning pulsating across my flesh, until I'm virtually vibrating. Sounds on the other side grow more violent as the intruder attempts to bash their way through the door. They're probably counting on the daylight to stop Dara and figure I'm too big of a chicken to interfere.

I swallow back a wave of nausea. Someone has invaded my space. I don't care why—you would think I would—I just stand there shaking and sweating. Everything is fuzzy, muffled, I feel like I'm reliving the tub incident only this time I'm drowning in fear.

It has to be a thief. Why else would anyone want to break in? For all I know it could have been a disgruntled client, maybe one of those fairy fever-infected idiots wanting revenge for refusing their requests.

I shriek as a hand grips my shoulder and the violence on the other side of the door stops. Spinning around, I stand toe to toe with Dara.

Her hand grasps my wrist just before the tip of the blade touches her shoulder, the intruder's footsteps fading to nothing.

"The alarms woke me." She looks me up and down.

I'm probably a sight to behold, still in my pj's, hair standing on end, gash on my cheek, holding a rather large kitchen knife. Unlike Dara, in her silk robe and disheveled hair, looking like she stepped off the set of a photo shoot.

"Are you alright?"

"Yeah, a little shook up, but not hurt."

One of those ridiculously perfect brows rises.

"Seriously, I'm fine." I touch my fingers to the scrape on my cheek. "You can ask CC about this later, right now I think I should check the salon."

"I do not think that is such a good idea."

"Oh come on Dara, we scared off whoever it was. Why would they hang around?" I know the tremor in my voice isn't convincing her, or me that I'm past the fear of some shadowy figure lurking around the corner. Even if it is just the corner of my mind, gods know there are plenty of shadowy figures hanging out there lately.

"Can you wait until the sun goes down so that I can go with you?"

I shake my head, the look on her face admitting she already knew the answer. I have to keep telling myself it was just a botched robbery, not something foreshadowed by my dream. Going into the salon would help justify this little fantasy. Da Nile ain't just a river in Egypt.

❈❈❈

Dara refuses to let me go alone, even though she can't enter the salon, too much sunlight.

The frame around the door held, barely. Splinters of wood push outward and the door itself sits at an odd angle in the frame.

Dara grabs me. "Do not touch anything."

"Want to tell me how in hel I'm supposed to get in then?"

"You are not. You should wait until dark."

"That's not happening." I snag the spare key secured behind the small light outside the door. "Let's hope they didn't screw up the lock so badly this won't work, or I'll be going around to the street entrance."

The key slips in and with a little extra jiggling I finally hear the lock click.

"Are you still set on doing this right now?"

I nod, not really set, but not willing to flip on my back and let my yellow belly show. I step over the threshold. This is the point in the movie where everyone cringes at the sacrificial babe's stupidity and screams at the screen, 'Don't go in there!' Does she listen? Hel no, the big boobied blonde gets it, but not before she can pull the classic scream scene. Hands held in front of a teary face as she begs the monster not to ax her. If it all goes south, I hope I can live up to the image, minus the big boobs. That's something I'll never achieve.

Swallowing my fear, I take a step and then another until I'm standing in front of the open door between the break room and cutting floor. Another threshold crossed and I'm in the main salon. Even with the afternoon sun, it's still dim and shadowy. I'm feeling a little stupid for not flipping on the lights. Any other day it would have been the first thing I'd do.

Nothing looks out of place. One of my vanity drawers is ajar, but that could have been my bad. I highly doubt a thief would be interested in combs and brushes.

I head for the front door and give it a push. Sure enough the door is open. Letting it glide closed, my feet and brain argue, while something cold and ugly twirls in my stomach.

"Did you find anything?" calls Dara, clinging to the shadows of the break room.

Fanning a hand at the fire in my cheeks, hoping the tunnel vision will dissipate. "Yeah, the door is open, they used a key as far as I can tell."

That explains how they got past the wards guarding the salon. I flip the deadbolt and head to the desk.

No sign of tampering with the register. The appointment book is another story. Flipping through it, I find pages missing. What in Hel's Realm? If this was one of those dorky made–for–TV movies it would be my competition trying to steal clients, but that's just beyond stupid.

"Check the storeroom while you're back there, Dara."

"Done, someone has attempted to pry the new lock."

Grabbing the book, I head back. "Obviously it wasn't quick cash they were after. Whoever it was didn't bother with the register. The fact that someone tampered with the lock confirms my suspicions that someone stole that bag of hair."

I hand her the appointment book. "Along with the missing pages in this."

⁂

Having decided to keep the break–in to ourselves, it's business as usual. I don't want to think about any of my employees being capable of something like this, but I have to face facts. Our intruder used a key, there are only six in existence and two of them are mine.

I know I didn't do it and there is no way Dara could have made it outside, or across the salon in broad daylight to open the door. She's one of those vamps who can't tolerate sunlight, unlike my pretty stalker. That leaves three.

Nyssa, my bubbly little shampoo girl slash manicurist, Rey—who, if history is correct—is quite the trickster, both of whom have been with me at least six years. Then there's my multi–personalitied receptionist, Jenny. Who at the present appears to be completely clueless about the missing pages, along with the rest of us. If it's an act, it's a good one on all three counts.

Observations are set aside in the deluge of patrons. Busy doesn't begin to touch on a description of tonight. The place is packed. Maybe it has something to do with that article in the paper. I'm ecstatic because it means the salon is doing well. On the other hand, it keeps me from watching for clues.

The rap on the door of the facial room sets me off. When the door is closed, it stays closed. No disturbances short of a fire, or natural disaster allowed. I ignore it, continuing with the treatment, a firm believer that the client in your chair deserves your full attention. Besides, one small slip in manipulating the dead skin cells and the couple of zits she came in with could end up a case of full–blown acne.

I'm about ready to blow when Jenny pokes her head inside. "Sorry, Keely, I tried to tell them."

The magic in my fingertips fizzles and I shake

my hands, wincing in pain, when she's shoved aside. Talk about it not being my night. Nancy, face slathered in green goo, sits up, giving a little shriek as two men in black push their way into the room.

Yep, just like the movie and neither of them look as good as J in those suits and glasses. One, all brawn and no brain—obviously a berserker—barely fits in the doorframe. The scrawny one actually sniffs the air like a therian. Great, a tracker. Even if I wanted to run, I wouldn't be able to hide.

Never in my wildest nightmares imagined an NTF team visiting me. Any crimes involving Enchants are turned over to the Numinous Task Force, or NTF for short, a sort of magical police. The tracker says something about taking me downtown while the berserker grasps my arm. I instruct Jenny to get someone to take over Nancy's treatment and not to charge her. The others may not be able to finish what I started, but they can at least get the goo off her face.

A low buzz fills the salon as Frick and Frack escort me through the main floor. No cuffs, but that doesn't stop gawkers on the street, or those inside from assuming I'm under arrest. Even though they didn't say, you're under arrest, I make the assumption also.

Am I scared? No, more like terrified. Hel, I've never even had a traffic ticket, let alone been taken downtown. Guess I should have read my horoscope. It probably says get out of town. Fast.

Surprise, surprise, across the street stands Mr. Alric Brand, cell pressed to his ear, his companion in giant four-legged form. The dog seems a little more than agitated as Frack shoves me into the back of their car.

Chapter 15

The ride downtown is purgatory, on the way to my own personal hel. Frick and Frack speak too quietly for me to hear and all I can do is sit and shake, sweating like a pig despite the air conditioner.

My stomach feels like the time The Sisters let me eat practically a whole bottle of cucumber dressing on my salad then a box of root beer popsicles. Hey, I was five and learned my lesson by spending most of the night praying to the porcelain god. I only hope I don't have a repeat all over their fancy leather interior.

I'm having one of those, *what did I do to deserve this*, moments. Whose hair did I screw up to make them mad enough to sic the NTF on me? Did they have a bad reaction to one of my cosmetics? Not that any of those would rate a visit from NTF; it's more of an Iowa Department of Public Health issue.

We'd passed our last inspection with only a minor infraction of one stylist neglecting to sanitize his clippers between uses. As far as I know there haven't been any complaints filed against us. All of our licenses are up to date.

A bucket of sweat drenches me. Had they somehow put two and two together and get three victims who visited my salon? Do they think I'm involved with the attacks? That they could think I'm The Collector is enough to make me snort. Frack turns around and glares at me, an educated guess, considering I can't read his expression through the dark glasses, not that it matters. We've arrived.

※※※

All the mystery surrounding NTF headquarters is greatly diminished by their decorating choices. It's like walking into a concrete bunker. No windows, no magazines on the small table in reception, not even annoying elevator music. The only attempt at warmth, a small plant on the front desk. Wilted and brown, but at least it's a color besides grey. You literally feel your mood hit cloudy–day–depression mixed with a touch of claustrophobia.

I have the urge to raise my hand and shout, jawohl as the beefy receptionist scowls at me from behind mannishly–thick–framed glasses. Give me credit, I don't, but I have to bite my lip to keep from giggling. I gently stroke the leaves of the wilted plant as I pass, bringing a look of horror to the receptionist's face. Geez, it's not like I could do any more harm to the poor thing.

One of my escorts opens the only door, besides

the one I want to use, revealing what looks like an endless corridor. As I pass through the door, I give that poor browned plant one last look and stumble forward as Frack slams into me.

I'm sure my expression mirrors the front desk Nazi's shocked face. The plant isn't brown any more. The leaves are green and tiny buds are appearing, but before I can bother questioning what happened Frack pushes me down the hall.

Guess what? More grey, this time cinderblock highlighted by flickering fluorescent tubes overhead. Every so often, we pass a steel door, of course, no windows to allow a peek. That claustrophobia thing presses in as my captors make a Keely sandwich coming to a stop in front of one of those nasty doors. Frick slips his passkey through the slot and a buzzer sounds as the door opens.

My stomach is twirling, my heart beating so loudly I'm sure they can hear it. This is it. It's all over. I'll go in that room and never come out. I try to take a step back. Frack gives me a little push and I stumble over the threshold.

The furnishings are even sparser than the entrance of the building. One chair on either side of a table, just like in the movies, but no swinging bare bulb, just the unflattering fluorescent lights. One of the boys grasps my arm, moves me to the chair farthest from the door and none too gently suggests I sit.

Okay, I can handle that. What I can't handle are the manacles built into the tabletop. A numbing tingle races up the back of my calf as I bump the leg of the chair, discovering another set. God's, I hope they aren't going to use them.

The first real show of emotion from either of my guards is the grin on Frack's face when he sees me eyeing them.

"I don't think we will have to use those, Miss Fey," says Frick, taking the chair across from me.

I nod in agreement, swallowing hard enough to make my throat hurt. I feel the spells, something to make a prisoner behave wrapped around another to drain, or contain any Talents.

Frick smiles and rests his forearms on the table, a feeble attempt at friendliness. Frack stands blocking the door, feet slightly apart, arms crossed. I do a bad job of preventing a shudder and his lips curl upward making me shiver even more. Maybe it's my imagination working overtime, but I get the distinct feeling he'd love it if I tried to escape.

Frick's questions all come out like the teacher in the Charlie Brown cartoons, wah wah wahwah wah. My biggest distraction is those stinking glasses! We're inside, take the damn things off. I mean, rude, right? What are they trying to hide with them, or is it just another attempt at intimidation?

"Miss Fey?"

I give myself a mental shake as Frick leans in

and says, "Have you heard a word I've said?"

Biting my lower lip, I shake my head.

He sighs, removing the glasses and I'm wishing he'd left them on. I've been told the pale silver of my eyes is disconcerting, but they're nothing like this. White eyes stare at me, not the milky, or cloudy look of cataracts, or the blind. I mean totally white, no iris, no pupil, just white. I've never been this close to a tracker before, never wanted to be. Those eyes just amp up the desire to be as far away from him as possible.

"Then let's try this again. Do you know Eric Sampson?"

Again, I shake my head, looking at the tabletop, the far wall, even Frack, anything to keep from looking into those spooky eyes.

"The name doesn't ring a bell, but that doesn't mean he hasn't been in the salon. We see a lot of people."

"Maybe this will jog your memory." He slides a photo across the table.

Wincing, I pull it closer. "It's pretty hard to tell with all the bruises, but like I said he could have come into the salon."

"So you're saying you know the boy."

"No, at the risk of repeating myself, I said it was possible. Again, we see a lot of people in the salon."

"Like these people?"

He slides more photos toward me, rambling off their names, but he doesn't have to. I know all three of them.

"They were in your salon too, weren't they?"

I nod, sniffling and wiping my eyes. Something a little more substantial than pictures clunks down on the table.

"What about these, do they look familiar? They were found at the scene of the last attack," he says, one finger sliding it toward me.

I can see what they are, even through the plastic baggie. My name visible under the gore coating the blades.

My head reels as I picture myself in an orange jumpsuit, one of those formless ones that do nothing for the figure not to mention how unflattering it'd be with my coloring.

This could completely destroy my life, even if they get it through their thick skulls I have nothing to do with it. Look at the wrongly accused from the past, forever tainted by accusations of crimes never committed. Their lives and reputations are worth less than gum stuck to your shoe.

The picture of the boy shoved under my watery gaze, a finger punctuating every word against the table.

"Those scissors—"

"Shears, they're called shears." Stupid I know, but it comes out all the same.

"Those shears were used to snip off this child's Talent."

No. My mind says it and my lips form it, but it doesn't come out. "What was his Talent?" I finally manage to whisper.

"He was an incubus, or would have been when his Talents came into their full power."

The word snip is totally inappropriate considering how dull those shears are. I know from experience. It hurt like hel when I snipped my own fingers, while cutting with them. You don't feel the pain of a cut with sharp shears. It takes seeing the blood, or possibly hanging skin to know you've cut yourself. That's why they'd been retired.

That boy's Talent was hacked off, an excruciatingly painful way to remove it. If you haven't already guessed where an incubus's Talent lies, use your imagination.

The poor thing hadn't even reached puberty. Why someone would attack the child before his Talents had fully manifested I have no idea. It just goes to show you how perverse and twisted this asshole is, unless my fears are correct. If he's collecting and using Talents this boy would have done him no good. That would make this a copycat. Doesn't really matter if it's The Collector, or a cheap imitation. They think it's me.

We all look at the door as a buzzer sounds.

Chapter 16

The door opens, revealing a slick–looking dude arguing with other MIBs in lawyerese about my release.

Frack in linebacker stance, is obviously spoiling for a fight and the others don't seem too keen on letting me just walk out.

"Is Miss Fey charged with a crime?" Lawyer man moves past the guard at the door.

Who in hel sent a lawyer, especially one with a suit that costs more than a year's profits?

Frick, slips his glasses back on, barely able to contain his distaste. Wonder if it's lawyers in general, or this one specifically. "There is evidence that leads us to believe she knows something about The Collector. At least three of the victims were clients of her salon."

Bonus points, I guess. He didn't say they think I am The Collector, just that I know something. The keep–your–mouth–shut look the lawyer gives me isn't necessary. The baggie laying there in front of me is motivation enough. If it wasn't, then what the contents were used for sure is.

"Circumstantial," he says, waving at their

evidence. "Just because the victims came to her business establishment does not mean she knows their attacker."

Frick picks up the baggy like it's filled with doggy droppings. "And these?"

"Again, circumstantial, anyone could have purchased a pair of shears and engraved her name on them."

"They are covered with her fingerprints."

He shrugs. "Isn't it possible they were taken from her workstation?"

"Hey, are you saying we took them?" asks Frack, so obviously the brawn and not the brains of the duo. That's what happens to many of the berserkers hired by the NTF. They are forced to induce the rage so often their ability to reason is wiped out, similar to the side effects of steroids.

Frick sighs. I'm betting he's wishing his partner would disappear, or at least keep his mouth shut as a slow smile creeps across lawyer man's face.

"You have two choices, charge her, or let her go. Clearly, the shears and recent visits to her salon are not enough, or you would have her in those." He motions to the manacles and I bite the inside of my cheek.

Lawyer man dismisses Frick and Frack, coming to my side of the table. He helps me up, gently wrapping his arm around my shoulders, leads me to the door. "You've been traumatized enough today, Miss Fey, let's get you home."

Home, yeah, that sounds good. I hunch my shoulders, feeling every eye on us as we walk through the door. A part of me waits for, *don't leave town*, but it doesn't come.

The bright sunlight is nowhere near as blinding as the cameras that flash the moment I step out of NTF headquarters.

The man with the expensive suit steps in front, a shield between the crowd of reporters and me, then two others join us. These two are similar in build to Frack, probably berserkers also. They make good bodyguards and excellent bulldozers as we mow our way through the crowd.

Someone pushes my head down and hustles me into the waiting limo. Yes, limo. For a moment, I feel like a celebrity, and then reality slaps me. These people think I'm a criminal. Not just any criminal, but The Collector. I can just imagine the headlines now, *Local Stylist Center of Collector Controversy.*

The nightly newscast will be even more humiliating when it reaches out beyond the greater Des Moines area and my family and Annya get to watch my *celebrity*. I can hear the disappointment in The Sisters' voices already. *We didn't bring you up that way.* Annya will try and make light of the situation. *Couldn't you find a better way to get on TV?*

Giggles build to hysterical laughter complete with tears streaming down my face. I bury my face in my hands; laughter mixed with sobbing wracks my body. There's a reassuring pat on my shoulder. My new lawyer, I'm guessing. It only makes me laugh harder.

"I don't know about you, but I need a drink."

My sobbing laughter turns to hiccups and I nod as he opens the bar and pours two glasses of amber liquid. Instead of sipping what I assume is whiskey, I down it in one gulp, letting the strong liquid burn its way down my throat.

"Smooth," I gasp with a giggle. "Thanks, I needed that."

Taking the glass from me, he smiles, a little more than confused by my attempt at humor. "No problem," he says, handing it back refilled.

Being a lawyer certainly has its high points, like limos stocked with *very* expensive whiskey.

"I suppose I should introduce myself," he says after taking a sip of his own drink.

"Yeah, that would be nice, along with an explanation of why you came to my rescue back there."

"Mark Jacobs, Miss Fey. Mr. Royd sent me."

If this car weren't so damn smooth, my stomach would swear we just hit the biggest pothole in Des Moines.

"What the..."

He smiles and takes another sip, predatorily, like the sharks lawyers are accused of being. I down the drink and close my eyes, hoping to slow the dizziness that threatens. When I open them, there are three fingers of whiskey in the glass.

"Are you trying to get me drunk, Mr. Jacobs?"

He laughs. It's actually a nice laugh, not at all sinister. Not really sure what I expected. Maniacal super villain laughter?

"No, Miss Fey. I would gain nothing if you were to become intoxicated."

I nod and lean back in the seat. Plush leather envelops me, butter soft under the fingers and extremely rich to the nose.

"Don't suppose you'd be willing to tell me why Mr. Royd sent you to help me?"

"I protect Mr. Royd's interests."

"Huh? What do you mean, interests? I don't even know the guy."

"No, but he knows you."

"That still doesn't explain why I would be considered one of his *interests*."

"If you wish me to be blunt..." he pauses and I nod. "He owns the loan on your salon. If you go down, the salon closes and he loses money. My job is to keep you out of jail and defend you, if the need arises."

Talk about too much information. Finding out that Var Royd literally owns my ass is the last thing I need to hear.

By the time we pull up outside my building,

I'm all warm and tingly. What can I say? I'm a little buzzed. Okay, a lot buzzed. I drank three glasses. In some ways, it's probably a good thing. In others, not so much.

Reporters and gawkers have already surrounded the building. As the car door swings open I see Nyssa forcibly removing some of them from the salon.

"If you're not here to get your hair done—some of you really need it—then get out!" I hear her yell.

Gods, that's going to play well on the news, my shampoo girl insulting reporters.

Following Jacobs out of the car, flanked by what I assume are Royd's private guards, the press converges. I feel like a piece of sticky candy discarded on the sidewalk, with ants rushing in for a bite.

I'm not claustrophobic, at least not in the conventional sense. Small spaces don't bother me, it's people crowding into my personal space, jostling, shoving, most of all touching me. Yeah, I know I work in an industry dealing with people and there's a lot of touching. That's one-on-one, not a crowd and they aren't touching, or in this case trying to grab me. I do the touching.

"Relax," says Jacobs, flashing me a camera-ready smile. "I'll take care of them. The boys will get you inside, virtually unscathed."

I recognize the attempt at humor, even

without the wink, but the word *unscathed* isn't very reassuring. Especially, when all I see is a flood of bodies pressing forward, expressions ranging from glazed excitement to rage. Breathing becomes short, quick gulps, and that bass line thumping through my body must be my heart.

How had my life gotten so out of hand?

The boys each take hold of my arms, just above the elbow and we force our way through the crowd. Their sheer bulk shields me from most of the throng, but there's always that one idiot. This idiot decides it's wise to thrust a mini recorder practically up my nose. Before I can even think about reacting, two impressively large backs block my view of what becomes of the overzealous reporter. I bolt for the door, slamming it behind me. The boys stay outside flanking the door. The recorder lies in bits and pieces, the owner's ass planted firmly on the concrete next to it, a nasty little warning to those who would try to pass them.

It takes a minute, but I soon figure out the reason for the silence. The only bodies in the salon are staff. Not a single customer. On the desk, nothing, but eraser shavings coat the remaining pages of the appointment book. Everyone has canceled and not just my clients. I want to cry until I notice Friday night. Lorelei is still down at seven. Then I do cry, even though it comes out more of a strangled laugh.

Everything I've worked for, down the tube. With the scandal of me being hauled in by the NTF all the rave reviews in the world aren't going to keep old customers, or generate new ones. Guess it might bring in a few rubberneckers, but that's the last thing I want.

All I wanted growing up was to be normal. Then I came to terms with who and what I am. Okay, that last part I'm not totally sure about. Not knowing your parentage doesn't help and there's no discussing a topic with The Sisters that they don't wish to discuss.

When I decided on being a stylist, I had a goal and worked like hel to achieve what I have. Now in a matter of days that rug has been yanked from under me and I feel like that lost teenager again. I don't want to be the freak everyone stares at, not again!

At least Lorelei hasn't deserted me. She couldn't possibly be planning on calling later to cancel, or worse, being a no-show. Could she? Slumping down in the chair, I cradle my head in my hands. Can it get any worse?

Sure it can. I've got a staff whose clients have canceled because of me. My alleged guilt just cut off their livelihood. The best thing for them would be to distance themselves from me. What about Jenny? Will this turn her to a life of ho-dome? .

Wait a minute, where is Jenny?

Chapter 17

I don't remember seeing her when I came in, but that doesn't mean she's not here. Then again, maybe she left after all the excitement. She does have classes to attend. Jerked out of my pity party I glance at the room, then around the partition between reception and the cutting floor.

"Where's Jenny?" I ask the huddled mass of my esteemed lawyer and colleagues.

They look like rabbits caught in the garden—if I don't move, you can't see me—before they finally look at me.

"She must have left after they took you," says Nyssa.

"Did she say where she was going, or if she'd be back?"

"Nope, and I didn't ask. Guess I was just too busy with customers leaving, the phone ringing off the hook, and a pissed–off vamp to notice."

I nod, imagining the phone frenzy as clients spread the word of what they'd see through the digital airwaves. At the front desk, I bring up the contact list in the computer and dial Jenny's home number. No answer. I try her cell, it goes straight to voicemail, could be turned off, or she's in another call. Maybe she saw the number and decided not to answer.

None of this matters when a brick flies through the front window. Particles of glass in various sizes spread across the floor and furnishings, magazines scatter where the brick pushed them after bouncing off a table. Echoes of bitch, murderer, and other choice phrases follow. The sound of shattering glass and my involuntary scream brings the others to the front with some astounding speed.

Seeing the mess, the destruction of my property, my heart stops fluttering and the tears that threaten dry up. I now know what they mean by seeing red.

"Come back here and say that to my face, you assholes!"

I know it's stupid and childish, but I can't help myself. I've had enough of being accused and abused for one day. Thankfully, no one tells me how stupid and useless my little outburst was Matter of fact they pretty much pretend nothing happened.

Nyssa and Rey are hard at it with the broom and dustpan. Jacobs is on the phone with the police and the boys are outside scaring—no, it looks like talking to some of the bystanders. In their case, it could be one and the same.

I flop down in the chair and stare at the window, smashed, just like my life. I bite my lower lip to keep it from quivering. In a matter of hours, I've lost everything I worked so hard to achieve. The curious have gathered as a police car pulls up and Jacobs walks to the curb. I should be out there dealing with this, but my limbs are like jelly and my brain fuzzy with anger, self–pity and fear.

I can't afford a lawyer, especially one like Jacobs and I'm not about to take Var Royd's charity. How in Hel's Realm am I going to afford to pay him? The pencil smudges on the pages of the appointment book have already proven I have no income. Sure, I have a little in savings, but I doubt it's enough to keep him in limos and pricey whiskey. There's probably enough to pay my bills for the next couple of months, but what about the others?

Rey and Dara make commission, but no appointments on the books means fifty percent of nothing. Nyssa gets a commission on her nail services, but I pay her an hourly rate for shampooing. So much for that raise I promised Jenny.

Things must not be going very well outside. I can't see Jacob's face, but his posture has stiffened and the boys look none too happy. The cop's smug expression clinches it as he scribbles something in his notepad before getting back in his car. My esteemed lawyer comes back in, expressionless, but tension rolling off him like the stench of perm fumes. Can things get any better?

The grit of eraser under my arms reminds me,

I have something to do. No matter how selfish I want to be, I have to do the right thing. They need to distance themselves from me, and I know they won't do it on their own. That also means talking to Dara when she wakes up and telling her. She should also probably find a new place to live.

With Jacobs on the phone again, I gather my courage and stand up.

"Guys, I need you to come here a moment, I have something to tell you."

They glance at one another as they walk over. Nyssa's perfect little brow furrows and Rey shrugs.

Taking a deep breath I spit it out, "You're fired."

"Excuse me?" Nyssa suddenly goes ghetto on me, head bob and all.

Rey's laughter just makes me want to I yell, psych, then join in.

"Okay, that went well."

"You can't fire us." Nyssa pushes her four-foot-something frame up into my face. I fight the urge to take a step back.

"The name of the place is Fey Creations and I'm Fey...so um...yeah, I can."

"Well, I'm not going." Rey continues to chuckle as he moves off to his station and lounges in the chair. "You can say whatever you want, but I don't think any of us will leave. We've got it too good here."

"Good?" I try to keep my voice at a normal level, but fail. "You have no appointments on the books. I barely have enough in savings to pay my bills; I can't afford to pay Nys, or Jenny. Do you want to tell me how you plan on supporting yourselves?"

Climbing into my chair, I bury my face in my hands. Argument I expected, but not flat out refusal, or laughter.

"Darlin', this is the best salon I've ever worked in and we all connect like...well, like family. I'm not leaving and you can bet the others feel the same."

"Rey, if you guys don't distance yourselves from me and this cluster fuck I've got going on you'll be finished. I don't want to sound like a mob boss, but you'll never work in this town again."

More laughter, this time softer, like a big brother indulging his baby sister. "Those old biddies chasing youth and the groupies will be back before you know it. Trust me, I've been in worse situations and this will blow over quicker than you think."

"I don't know." I shake my head.

Nyssa stands between us clutching the framed review. "I'm with him, I'm not leaving either. You need us."

"I could take your keys."

"Try it," they both say.

"I could change the locks."

"You can't afford it," says Rey with a giant grin.

Nyssa giggles as she hugs me. "We're not going, so get used to it."

"Okay, okay, I give."

Chapter 18

Jacobs sits at the break room table, leaning heavily on his arms, the bridge of his nose pinched between his fingers. The earpiece from his cell phone lays abandoned to one side of the table and the phone teeters on the edge of the other. One small jostle of the table and it will crash to the floor. This can't be good.

"Miss Fey, Keely. May I call you Keely?"

"Sure." I take the seat across from him, reminiscent of my earlier experience, without the fear of torture.

"Here is the essence of our situation. We have a serious problem. Even though you weren't charged, the press and others are under the impression you either are, or are in league with, The Collector. After the earlier display, I anticipate more retaliation. The local authorities have all, but outright denied my request for protection and the NTF is unresponsive."

The set of his jaw and frustration in his eyes is a clear indication he doesn't trust them and I probably shouldn't either. Nor did I trust the local authorities.

Sheriff Bogner, or as he prefers—major emphasis on prefers—Sheriff Frank, conjures up childhood memories of Porky's and The Dukes of Hazzard.

What we have here is a 6'7" troll, tiny by troll reasoning; whose parents cruelly named him Frances. Maybe the unlit cigar continuously clenched between his teeth is some sort of compensation. It's released to fingers the size of ring bologna when he's about to make a point. The unlucky recipient of that point is subjected to a couple of inches of masticated, soggy goodness waved in their face. Just thinking about being on the receiving end of one of those conversations makes my stomach curdle.

There is nothing for that cigar–chomping good ol' boy to gain by securing my safety. So, I can safely say putting my fate in his hands would not be the wisest course of action.

The Meadows isn't wholly an En community, so it's only natural we have a few Uns on the force as well. There is a steady stream of trainees trying out their authority before moving on.

Two of these newbies—guess I can't call them that anymore, they've been here almost as long as I have—decided to stay. A bumbling second–in–command and the naïve follower always begging for approval. Neither inspires more—probably less—confidence about my safety than their self–

serving boss. Face it, when it comes to police protection, I'm screwed.

"But it was the NTF who brought me in, just because of the victims that were clients and those stupid shears. They didn't know about the bag of missing hair."

"Missing bag of hair?"

I explain how we bag and tag the remnants of all services performed in the salon and how I dispose of them. A glance at Nyssa and Rey reminds me, I didn't tell them. From the shock and anger on their faces it occurs to me, they can be taken off the suspect list.

"And the shears?"

"They're mine, the pair I received in beauty school. I don't use them anymore. They're too dull to cut with. I just keep them for sentimental value."

"Did you tell the detectives they are yours?"

"No!"

"Any idea how they came to be in their possession?"

"They had to have been taken before the break-in."

A chorus of 'Break-in?' fills the room.

"Someone broke in yesterday. Change that, they let themselves into the salon with a key."

"Did you report this to the authorities?"

I shake my head. "No, all they took were pages from the appointment book."

"And, very possibly, your shears." Jacobs scribbles in his notebook.

I shake my head. "They had to be taken before that to coincide with the last victim."

The increasing lines around Jacobs's eyes and the hard downward turn of his mouth a sure signal of displeasure. The urge to stand with chin tucked, hands clasped behind my back, scuffing my toes across the ground while punctuating every one-word sentence with 'sir' makes me squirm. I never noticed how hard the break room chairs are.

"Is there anything else you need to tell me? I can't help you if you don't tell me everything you know."

Self-preservation trickles into my weary little brain and lights a fire under that part of me worried about saving my own skin. Last thing I want is to cast the light of suspicion on Jenny, but considering the evidence I don't see how I can get around it.

Rey and Nyssa seemed genuinely surprised at both the missing hair and the break–in. There's no way Dara could have done the B&E, not in the daylight. That leaves Jenny as the only other person with a key, not to mention I found her rummaging around in the bags. That she's not here and can't be reached doesn't help the situation.

Fear mingled with shame dots my skin. Taking a deep breath, I spill how I'd gone to the salon after picking up supplies, intending to stock the shelves while the remnants burned. How I'd found Jenny in the storage room and after she left I counted and recounted the bags. From the look in his eyes, I don't have to explain the importance of the missing hair. I then move on to the break–in and how I'd found the pages from the appointment book missing and Dara had found the door to the storeroom tampered with.

There I'd done it. I'd tossed my friend and co–worker under the proverbial bus. Not a good feeling at all, matter of fact, it sucks. Made worse by the fact that she's not here to defend herself.

"Your luck may have turned, Miss Fey. If nothing else you've given me a plausible defense."

"You can't be serious? Jenny wouldn't be involved in something so... Vile." Nyssa searches each of our faces.

My cohorts continue to debate Jenny's innocence and what each feels is the best course of action. While I debate whether to continue my little pity party, or to put on my big girl panties and take charge of my totally f'd up life. The party sounds like a lot less work. I know what I should do, but did I mention the totally f'd up part?

I'm not feeling real confident about digging my way out of this. Being grounded for climbing out of the window—just to see if I could—was nowhere near the life sentence this mess will be. We're talking time in the poky, or gods forbid, death. Grounding sounds really, really good right now, so does being fifteen again. I'd settle for six months ago, before my life became tangled up in all this crap. On top of it, I'd just played the childish game of *she did it, not me,* possibly condemning someone along with me.

"It's settled then," says Rey, disturbing my little party.

"What's settled?" I'm just about to the point of crawling under the covers and crying for mommy.

"We close up shop until further notice. Dara stays here and keeps an eye on things and you, my sweet, move in with Nys." The mischievous twinkle in Rey's eyes is unmistakable. "Unless you prefer my place?"

"Oh, hels no!"

Suddenly those big girl panties become Wonder Woman's tights, I realize I'm not ready to relinquish control. That's the thing about pity parties, they are strictly for one. When someone else joins, it's over. No matter what they say, or do, it's never what you want. Probably because most of the time you just want to wallow.

Protests to my outburst come to a halt as the phone's shrill ring echoes through the salon. Maybe I'm getting a reprieve from the Governor. Or maybe it's the missing Jenny with a few answers.

Chapter 19

"Anybody going to get that?" I ask, still reeling from my mood swing. I must be PMSing out, practically begging someone to take over and make this mess go away and when they do, I jump their shit.

"What the hel am I paying you for?"

I can't tell if Nyssa is sizing me up for a cold shower, or ready to withdraw her offer of room and board as she backs around the corner to silence the ringing. Highly doubt I'll be asking her for a shampoo any time soon, unless I want a shower. That hose can easily slip, even in practiced hands.

I watch the others while pacing the room, weighing my options. I'm torn between snarling at them for treating me like a child—which I deserve—and begging forgiveness—which I don't.

"Right back at you!" I hear her say followed by "Assholes," and the angry clicking of heels before she rounds the corner.

"Crank call?" asks Rey.

She nods, sitting down.

Jacobs sighs. "It's only going to get worse."

"Then what do I do? Sit here and wait for the

next idiot with borderline intelligence and a brick, or better yet, a can of kerosene and a match?"

Nyssa snorts and Rey flat out laughs. I know they're thinking about Frankie who's a few Tarot cards short and thinks he's a fire god. After the tornado of '05 he gathered lawn debris and other various items, doused it with a few gallons of kerosene and tossed a match. After everyone's ears stopped ringing, they figured out it wasn't another disaster, just Frankie. The fire department put out the mile high blaze as he was taken to the emergency room. During the ambulance ride, he explained how the storm had gifted him with the power to control fire. A lack of all facial hair and the wispy smoking strands left on his head told a different story. It does no good to remind him he's an Un, you'll just get an imaginary fireball tossed at you.

"I suggest you either stay with your friends, or you could take Mr. Royd up on his generous offer."

"Huh?"

"Mr. Royd, along with retaining my services, is willing to put you up in his building. It has the finest of security; you would be more than safe there. I've been instructed to deliver you, if you so choose."

The last thing I want is to be under Royd's protection, but the desire to see inside those fancy digs of his, that's something to consider. Come on, give me a break, who wouldn't want to see inside one of the richest dwellings in the greater Des Moines area?

A month's rent on one of those places could open a chain of salons. The kind of salons where I can stand back and be as pretentious as those morons in the reality shows who think they can do hair. I mean, please, you know one cut—taught to every stylist and you don't even improve, or change the style—and you get your own show? Hel's Realm, I remember in junior high when the look was fresh, now it's just 70's retread.

"I don't know. I can't leave CC here by himself and what about Dara? What if someone firebombs the place while she's asleep?"

Rey clears his throat, Nyssa standing beside him.

"You guys should high tail it as far away from me as possible. I couldn't live with myself if you guys got hurt."

"The majority rules, darlin'," Rey grins, "and we win. Not going anywhere. Matter of fact; think I'll just plant myself right here in this building until this blows over. Like you said, Fangs downstairs needs someone to watch during the day."

Nyssa does that little *mm hmm, girlfriend* thing, that I detest. No one should swivel their head and call each other girlfriend, especially white people. You just look ridiculous. If she does that snap thingy I'm just going to have to unload on her. I suppose I should cut her some slack for the years I spent saying *choice*, or *like totally*.

Nah, ain't happening.

"It seems you've made your decision." Jacobs hands me his business card. "Should you need me, don't hesitate to call."

I watch him leave taking the pretty, shiny car and the protection of the Brawny Twins with him. On the flip side of the card, I find Var Royd and a number scrawled in magnificent script. Somehow, I know this isn't the lawyer's writing.

Chapter 20

"They actually think *you* are The Collector?"

If it weren't so ridiculous, or disgusting, I'd take Dara's comment and laughter as an insult.

"Or that I know something about him," quickly adding, "or her."

It has nothing to do with being P.C., or feminist. I know how lethal females can be. Sitting across from me, behind a beautiful veneer, is death by fang. Next to her sits a voluptuous package that could easily drown more than your sorrows. Dara and Nys are more than proof that men don't hold the title of most dangerous.

"What a crock." Rey is unable to hide his disbelief.

"Yeah, you couldn't hurt a fly," says Nyssa.

"Hey." Truly offended now, considering my quest to put the smack down on one of the pesky buggers. A few snuck in around the hastily patched window and proceeded to dive bomb us.

"Okay, strike that," she giggles, "your aim just sucks."

"Ha, ha, very funny. Die you little bastard," I say, focusing on the swing. The fly bounces off the swatter, hits the floor where it buzzes and flops before Rey steps on it.

"See? She can hurt a fly."

"Yeah, but you killed it," says Nyssa.

"Now that we have established the fox has a rapport with insects, other than fleas, shall we move on to more important details?" asks Dara.

Rey sneers at her while scratching behind his ear.

"Yeah, like what are we going to do about this?" I wave my hand toward the empty salon. "And what about Jenny? I don't know about you guys, but I'm a little worried. Tried her home and cell, but no answer."

Rey and Nyssa nod, Dara just sits there.

"You think she did it." Nyssa swings her chair around to face Dara.

"I said no such thing."

"You didn't have to; your lack of response says it all."

Dara shrugs. "I am simply looking at the evidence. The most logical explanation is that she knows something."

I hold up my hands trying to ward off a catfight. "Enough. Face it, none of us knows anything for sure," I look at Dara, "right?"

A single bob of her head is the best I'm going to get.

I've been awake for over twenty-four hours,

accused of being The Collector—veiled as the accusations might have been—and found out Var Royd owns my business. In its present state, he could call in the loan and I'd have less than nothing. Top that off with the crowd of gawkers and reporters outside. The last thing I need is my support team fighting.

"I know you guys mean well, but this is getting us nowhere, not that there's much we can do anyway. Especially me, I'm too damn tired to even think let alone do anything."

With the weight of everything, I sag back in the chair, letting my exhaustion take over, then rethink it. Slithering forward until I reach the edge, I toss what little energy I have into pushing myself to stand up.

"I'm sorry. I need to get some rest."

Dragging myself up the stairs, I give a fleeting thought to Nys and Rey. They're big kids and I hope smart enough to get some rest. If not, too bad. I'm not going to let that keep me from a hot shower and soft bed.

I half expect to see a pair of judgmental, golden–green eyes and an angrily twitching tail when I open the door. Instead, I find the hairball stretched out across the bed, fangs exposed in a gaping yawn when I cross the threshold of the bedroom.

"Nice to see you, too." I plop down on the edge

of the bed and kick off my shoes. "Life sucks, kitty."

He gives a halfhearted meow as I curl up next to him and play with his ears. I'm starting to sound like the whiny heroines I despise, always complaining and never doing anything to fix their lives. Just sitting back, letting everything happen to them. Maybe it's time I take charge instead of waiting for someone else to fix my life. Continuing to stroke his fur, I begin to relax and my eyelids droop. So much for that shower.

❈❈❈❈❈

Cooling moisture clings to my skin, sucking away the warmth. A slow, swirling mass of misty air obscures my legs and the ground. I'm almost afraid to move, but I can't stand here shivering forever. If I trip, I trip. My heart flutters, thinking of falling below the dampness, drowning in it.

Get a grip. It's just a dream. You didn't fall asleep in the tub again. You're safe in bed. But the fear doesn't want to give in to common sense.

Closing my eyes, I take a deep breath, then slowly let it out before opening them. Nope, still stuck in dreamland. Only one thing to do. Wake up.

"Ouch!" Okay, so pinching doesn't work. My sight wavers in the combination of tears and mist, but something, or someone stands in the distance.

Vereinen. It has to be. As usual, just out of focus, hovering around the boundaries of my dreams.

"Hey," I yell, waving my arms. It's about time he gives me a heads up on why he's back in my life after all these years.

No acknowledgment, no movement at all. Asshole.

"Hey." I start toward him, fears forgotten, intent on my destination. "Einen."

Slogging through the fog, my limbs are heavy. Breathing labored, my lungs feel like they are filling with the suspended moisture. Clothing is now a waterlogged weight. Soggy strands of hair cling to my face and neck. Trickles of water send shivers down my spine and blur my vision even more. No matter how far I walk, I never get any closer. It's like being on the treadmill of the damned. Like being on any treadmill is good.

"You've been hanging out in my dreams and I want to know why," I shout at the distant figure. "Why are you back and why won't you show yourself?"

Slowly he raises his hands and lowers the hood. I stand frozen, mouth gaping. What I see scares the crap out of me. Pale skin with a greyish hue and hair the color of white gold. It's like looking in a mirror.

Fear thrusts me forward and I find myself sitting upright in bed, clutching at a tangle of damp sheets. Breathing as if I'd run a marathon. Pulse thumping in my ears. I can literally feel the big veins in my neck and temples throb. Yep, I just had the shit scared out of me.

Slowly, I pull myself to the edge of the bed. Resting elbows on thighs, pressing palms against eyes. After thirty–some–years, I find out my imaginary friend looks like me. Creepy and a little annoying considering I've thought of myself as a one–of–a–kind for so long. That and he's prettier. It must be some sort of subconscious association my addled brain is making.

Too creeped out to go back to bed, I grab my robe and slip it on. Wait a minute. A wave of nausea hits my gut like a prizefighter. There's a lovely bruise blooming on the inside of my upper arm. On the other hand, maybe I'm going nuts.

Chapter 21

A strange little sound emanates from the direction of the couch as I enter the living room. Up pops Nyssa, ten tons of hair spray, severely dented, leaving her big 'do at an odd angle. She yawns, blinking matted lashes.

"You're up."

"Why didn't you use the guestroom?"

"Wanted to be near the door," she says through a yawn, or that's what I think she said.

"Okay. Where's Rey?"

She points to the door and flops back, pulling the blanket over her head.

I open the door and a body falls in. At least it's breathing. Dead would be more consistent with my life lately. Looks like Rey spent what was left of last night and this morning propped up outside my apartment.

He crawls inside, grips the end of the couch and pulls himself up; bopping Nyssa's blanket covered 'do in the process.

"Mind starting the coffee and feeding the cat while I take a shower?"

"Think I can handle that." He stretches to his

full six foot height after several cracks and pops.

I almost feel sorry for him, but I do have a guestroom. There was no need to sleep in the hall, or play watchman at my door.

Closing the bedroom door behind me, I pick up the card Jacobs left me and stare at the number on the back. It's now, or never. Grabbing the phone I head into the bathroom and start the water, hoping it will keep Rey and his super–sensitive ears from overhearing.

Taking a deep breath, shaky fingers dial the number. It begins ringing and my thumb hesitates over the button to hang up.

"Hello," says a honey–smooth voice on the other end.

Sweat breaks out on my upper lip as my thumb hovers.

"Hello?" repeats the voice, "Miss Fey, is that you?"

Too late to hang up now. He must have caller ID. I raise the receiver to my ear.

"I know it's you, Schattenkind." The slightest edge of irritation taints the seductive cadence.

"Huh?" I say without thinking. "I mean, yes, it's me."

"What can I do for you, mien Schattenkind?"

"I'm just curious—wait a minute, what's a shatten kind?"

His laughter reverberates through the phone

and across my body. I grasp the edge of the sink as everything becomes fuzzy. Black and white and grey all over. Like my whole world is nothing, but shadows.

"Is that why you called me? You are curious about a word?"

I shiver, the kind of shiver you get when someone grazes their fingers seductively across your skin. Imagine what phone sex would be like with this guy. On second thought, don't. I need all my wits, what little are left, around me.

"No," I say slowly.

Robbed of not only color and definition, everything sounds like it's coming from the bottom of a well, my own voice included. I shake my head, color and sound pop in and out.

"Then what is it you are curious about?"

I bite my lower lip, knees turning to jelly as heat flashes through my lower, suddenly not–so–private, parts.

"Well, let's start with Jacobs and then why you wanted me to have your number."

"Perhaps we should discuss this in person. I will send a car."

I lean against the wall and slide down, knees too weak to hold me up. Not exactly what I expected and before I can decline, the line is dead. The bastard hung up on me. Laying the phone on the floor I decide the steaming bath I ran is a bad idea.

A cold shower would be far more appropriate.

❊❊❊

The girl in the mirror looks confident. She wants answers and is going to get them, even if it means finding a way to sneak out and meet with Var Royd. I just hope that thought seeps in and settles the wiggles in her stomach before she chews off all her lip-gloss.

"You've made your decision, for better, or worse, now all you need to do is figure out how to get past the Wonder Twins."

Sure, I could ask them to go with me, but something tells me Royd won't tell me shit if he has an audience. This has to be one-on-one. I need to know why he financed the loan on my shop than. A hair salon is hardly the type of investment someone like Var Royd would be making. And why me? Then there's the German phrase, what's that mean? If I knew how to spell it, I could plug it into an online translator, but that ain't happening.

Taking a deep breath I open the door and the scent of fresh, brewed coffee teases and tantalizes, pulling the willing straight to the source. He-who-will-not-be-ignored glares at the three measly pieces of kitty kibble in his bowl.

"I thought you were going to feed the cat."

"The container's empty."

"I..." Strangely, the little part of my brain that keeps me from saying something stupid kicks in. "Damn, that's right. I forgot to get another bag."

Sitting at the table, Nyssa cradles her dented head in her hands and Rey clings to a mug for dear life. Inhaling the scent of my caffeinated addiction, I fill a cup and lean against the counter.

"So, whose bright idea was it for Rey to spend the night in the hall?"

Nyssa glares at me, but it's difficult to take a bed-head raccoon seriously.

Rey slurps the last of his coffee, then holds his cup out, grunting something to the effect of, "Who do you think?" His own appearance less distressed, probably due to spending part of the time as a fox, patrolling the building.

"Dara's orders?"

"Of course," pouts Nyssa, lifting her smeared face.

Wish I had a camera so I could show people why you don't sleep in makeup, as if the damage to your skin isn't enough. I fill Rey's cup and top off Nyssa's, feeling guilty they had to put up with Dara. Only slightly, considering what I'm planning. Now all I have to do is ditch my houseguests. From the looks of them, it shouldn't be too difficult.

Chapter 22

My second limo ride in as many days, too bad it's because I'm infamous instead of famous. Sitting in the back of Royd's limo, I feel the slightest twinge for slipping out. I never once promised to stay put while Nyssa showered, nor did Rey need to know that 'forgotten' bag of cat food I sent him after is actually in a higher cupboard. Can't keep the bags where CC can reach them; he'll just tear them open and feast until he bursts. It kind of amazed me Rey couldn't smell it. Oh well, just makes things easier for me.

The car is waiting outside and so far, everything has gone smoothly. I left a note on the table to give the others a clue as to where I am, in case things go south. Pulling a Lorelei, I'm able to slip out without revealing my features. The press and gawkers can only speculate it was me they saw.

My rush to the car nearly halted by the sight of Brand and that giant dog standing across the street.

Damn, I figured stalker boy would have lost interest after the NTF hauled me away. He gives me a slight nod as I climb into the backseat. The intensity of his gaze sears me like a flat iron set on high, squeezing the air from my lungs.

I can't help turning to watch him shrink and disappear as we head out of town. What is he still doing hanging around? The haircut wasn't that good. Maybe it was the free regenerative service I performed and he wants longer hair.

Fever flashes across my cheeks and spreads. Could it be the kiss? Yeah, it was pretty hot for me, but I bet he's had better. Speaking of comparisons, one kiss leads to another. Wonder if he and his buddy have compared notes? I don't know which bothers me more, them laughing at, or fighting over me. The fighting is a much better ego boost, so I guess laughing wins.

Hold the hormones, babe. What if he's The Collector and I'm on the collectibles list? My tummy takes a tumble that no amount of the pink stuff will help. How could I be so stupid?

"Shake it off," I whisper, "you have more important things to think about."

Like what comes next. Being so proud of myself for deciding to take charge and pulling off my slick getaway, I realize I haven't thought this through. Confronting Royd was the plan, but how? I'm going to be on his turf.

Doubt creeps its way along my spine as I stare at the window separating me from the driver. Have I planted my foot in a big old pile of shit? Is this really Royd's driver? What if he's The Collector?

What if Royd is The Collector? I rest my hand on the door latch, breakfast wanting to make a repeat appearance. Coffee going down, good. Coffee coming back up, not so much.

"Are you alright, Miss Fey?" an overly professional voice comes over the intercom.

Either the glass between us isn't one way, or touching the handle triggered something.

"Just a little car sick, not used to riding in limos."

"There is bottled water in the mini fridge, or the bar may contain something that might settle your nerves."

Yeah, something to relax my nerves, I reach toward the bar, remembering Jacobs's whiskey. My hand snaps away. What am I thinking? The last thing I need is to be <u>that</u> relaxed. Nervous and sober, Royd's delicious voice played havoc with my hormones. Imagine what they would do relaxed and a little tipsy.

I swear the driver's shoulders shake with laughter.

❦❦❦

Talk about a taste of the Big Time. First, the driver helps me from the car. Now a doorman swings one of the double glass doors open, tipping his hat as I pass. I restrict myself to a quick smile and thank you, instead of the regal looking–down–the–nose nod my smart-ass side wants so desperately.

Wards shimmy across my skin—not unpleasant, but a little too intimate for my liking—as I step across the threshold. I wish I knew what kind of wards just took liberties not offered on a first date. I find it difficult to imagine Royd using magic with the rumors about his anti–En beliefs. It's even harder to wrap my head around the abundance of En employees.

"Miss Fey." A china doll blonde comes around the desk to greet me. I take the offered hand gingerly, fearing breaking the porcelain limb. No worries, she has the grip of someone who could probably bench–press me without breaking a sweat. "Mr. Royd is expecting you in the penthouse."

It's a little more than difficult to refrain from snorting and rolling my eyes. The penthouse, of course. All the better to view his domain.

She escorts me to the elevator manned by yet another livery–clothed hunk o' burning love. I wonder if there is a screening process to eliminate the unattractive, or even average.

"This is what Dorothy must have felt like."

"Miss Fey?" asks the tempting elevator attendant.

I feel my cheeks grow hot. Did I just say that out loud? Damn. I shake my head. "Nothing, just talking to myself."

The pretty, pretty nods and gives me an even prettier smile. "If you'd like to have a seat, we'll arrive at your destination momentarily." He waves his hand to a settee along the wall.

Seating in an elevator? What next, a fridge in the bathroom? Gods, the man just has too much money. I decline and stand gripping the rail so hard my fingers start to throb and knuckles turn translucent. The combination of the waiting room feel, harp music and the chimes at each floor, I wonder if there will be pearly gates at the end of my journey.

When those chimes sound for the last time, the flipity–flop in my stomach, that the pretty sparklies distracted me from, returns. A creepy little kid's voice sounds in the back of my mind, we're here. The doors open and I realize the only escape is this elevator. I swallow back a nervous giggle when the elevator boy takes a step back, motioning me forward. My feet become magnets as I shuffle ahead, the desire for information barely outweighing that of flight.

Chapter 23

After the elevator, I expected something more ostentatious, 24k gilding everywhere, chandeliers, maybe Louis XVI furnishings. Not to say the place isn't posh, just more along the lines of minimalist. Soft blues and white, giving the effect of floating in midair, nothing that hints to the owner's personality, or maybe the room does give a hint. Cold. Impersonal.

"Miss Fey, welcome to my home."

That smooth–as–silk voice sends my pulse racing. I berate myself for my lack of focus, letting him sneak up on me. Others have pointed out that I'm easily distracted and this proves their point.

He motions to the rounded seating area surrounding a fire pit. It dawns on me that he's waiting for me to sit first. Raising my chin I take the three steps down into the living space. He follows close enough I feel the brush of warmth along my neck and want to scream, 'Back Off.' I doubt yelling at my host will get me very far so I bite my tongue and perch on the edge of the sofa.

His knee brushes my thigh as he sits and my hands ball into fists. It's obvious he delights in pushing the boundaries of personal space. The raised brow and curl of his lips challenge me to say, or do something. I fight the urge to slide over, or better yet move to the opposite side.

"Has any of your curiosity been sated, Schattenkind?" The corners of his lushly-kissable lips curl.

I shake my head. Foolishly staring into his eyes, a summer sky swirl of blues and gold. Hel no, it hasn't and the list just keeps getting longer.

What's up with being turned on by virtually every male who crosses my path? With the exception of a few—I repress a shudder picturing Frick and Frack. I've had my share of indiscretions. In gentle terms, I'm not hanging on to a wilting flower waiting for Mr. Right, but I also don't get it on with every Mr. Right Now. I don't like my hormones running in overdrive. It doesn't make a bad situation any easier.

He tips his head forward, his gaze somewhere between seductive and menacing. Licking my lips, I look down, trying to focus on why I'm here and not asking for a tour of his bedroom.

What this guy does to my baser instincts is beyond comprehension. I mean he's smoking hot—Johnny Depp, with golden blue eyes and sandy hair, hot—still, no one's ever had the effect he does on me. Multiply the lust radiated by the elves by a thousand and add the desire to bow down and worship at his feet. *Shake it off, get down to business.*

"Why did you buy the note on my business, Mr. Royd? Why did you put Mr. Jacobs on retainer for me? How about the offer of a place to stay? Oh yeah, what does that German stuff you keep calling me mean?" Like a waterfall, it all tumbles out, but man it feels good. I can breathe again, the weight lifted from my chest. Relief doesn't last. He actually has the nerve to laugh at me.

"Shall we start with, you calling me Var? Mr. Royd is so formal, far too formal for friends. And I do hope we will become friends, Keely."

My name comes across like a caress and I shake it off. "Call me cautious, but I think I'll stick with Mr. Royd."

"As you wish." He stands, deliberately brushing against my arm as he unfolds himself. "I am a terrible host, forgive me. Would you care for some refreshment? I think something stronger than tea is called for with the questions you pose."

Without waiting for my answer, he moves to the bar, grabbing two glasses and a fancy crystal decanter. I'm betting the amber liquid inside costs as much as the bottle, if not more.

I'm getting the feeling he's never going to answer me as he pours two fingers worth into each glass, handing me one. Nice hands, long fingers, nicely shaped nails. Good grief, of all the stupid things to be distracted by, what am I thinking?

Wondering who does his manicure should be the last thing on my mind.

"Now, where were we?" He makes a point of brushing against me yet again as he sits back down.

My skin feels tighter than one of Nyssa's dresses and as hot as a curling iron. If he's using touch to distract me, it's working, but I can't let him know that.

"Oh, yes, your questions. I placed Mr. Jacobs in charge of your legal defense to protect my investment."

"That's what he said."

"My offer of a place to stay was also a way of protecting my investment, both actions stemming from my purchase of your note. I still feel my offer would be far more protection than what your friends and the First Arrow can give."

"But why did you buy it? Wait—First Arrow? Who, or what is that?"

He swirls the liquid—I discover its scotch by sniffing while pretending to drink—in his glass. I wait for him to elaborate, but I'm starting to think Hel's Realm would thaw before I get an explanation, or the other hell will freeze over. Doesn't matter which you believe in. The likelihood of either isn't going to happen in my lifetime. Not that I have the inside scoop, but I doubt either possibility.

"It was a good investment," he pauses, taking

a sip. "The First Arrow is a person and you know her quite well. I believe she resides with you."

"You mean Dara?"

He nods.

"What's with you and the weird nicknames?"

"Perhaps you should ask her."

He's not about to tell me and from his almost shit–eating–grin my asking her will probably cause havoc. Havoc, I get the feeling he would enjoy a little too much.

"Will do, but back to you owning me...I mean, my business." More laughter at my expense, but I deserve it for the slip up. "Supposedly, you hate Ens, why would you finance one?"

"Quite to the contrary, mein Schattenkind, I love Ens."

The moment the words leave his lips, I *know* he loves Ens. Warmth wraps itself around me. He loves me. If I could remember my parents holding me, *this* is what it would've been like. I want nothing more than to bask in the moment, to tell him anything he wants to know and probably things he doesn't. Looking down I see my arms wrapped around myself and I can imagine the idiotic grin as my facial muscles pull tight. What in Hel's Realm is he? Definitely not Un, but not En either.

"What are you?" I whisper, peeling my arms from around myself.

There's a musical tone to his laughter and a pull to join in, but I fight against it.

"A man, Keely, just a man."

The way he says my name sends shivers of desire deeper than skin and I see my hand reach toward him. I yank it back, digging my nails into my palm, holding it close at my side. Physical appearance aside, he is definitely not a man in the true sense of the word.

"As for the name, perhaps you should ask your guardians what it means." He toys with his glass.

"My guardians?"

"Yes. I believe you call them The Sisters."

"So you know my grandmother and aunts? What do they have to do with this and why should they *explain* this word to me?"

"I know them." There is a slight tightening around his eyes and jaw line. Displeasure? Anger? "Not as well as I thought. This meeting between us should have happened many years ago."

"Okay."

"Do you know what Ørlög is Keely?"

"Yeah, it's another word for wyrd."

He shakes his head. "No, they are very different. Ørlög is the collective, Wyrd is the individual."

"You mean like the world versus one person?"

"Exactly." He stands and moves to the window. "Ørlög cannot be changed, no matter how we deviate from the path of our wyrd. We may extend the time before an event happens, or how it happens," he looks over his shoulder, "but it will happen."

A chill slinks over me and the room fades to a foggy gloom as he speaks. When he turns, quietly delivering that last line, he goes all Vincent Price on me. Ominous shadows cling to his face, a deviant sparkle in his eyes. All I can do is sit there, mouth gaping, until instinct kicks in and I slide a little closer to the edge of the couch, eyeing the door.

His laughter pulls my attention back, his face its normal beauty. The room lightens and I feel the warmth of summer. No matter how warm and comforting it appears, I can't contain the shiver riding along my spine.

"Forgive me, I did not mean to alarm you."

Scrubbing my palms against my jeans, I clear my throat.

"This ørlög has what to do with me?"

"Your guardians should have better prepared you for what is to come in your future."

What can The Sisters tell me about my future? Sure, they have *visions*, but always told me they are never that simple, or clear, just flashes really. He's making it sound like they know all. As a kid, I thought they did when they caught me doing something I wasn't supposed to, but found out later most parents have that ability. One mother told us it was called, *been there, done that*. Not that

I ever wanted to picture any adult—especially my grandmother and great aunts—doing some of the things we did.

"I can see you do not believe me."

"Sorry, but I think they prepared me pretty damn well for the future, considering my parents just dumped me on them. They fed and clothed me, sent me to school and taught me right from wrong. They are good women, who devoted themselves to protecting and supporting me." I'm on my feet, invading his personal space, just a fraction away from sticking my finger in his face.

Perfect features turn to ice and stone. Summer sky eyes cloud over becoming winter grey. "I think it's time for you to go."

My skin feels two sizes too small, hot and itchy. Like a tight, wool sweater. How dare he get all pissy with me after insulting my family? "What?"

He doesn't acknowledge my question, simply turns and leaves the room. On cue, the elevator door opens, revealing a sad smile on the pretty face of its keeper. Having been dismissed like a disobedient child, the last thing I want is pity from an ornament.

Chapter 24

With a little smooth talking—something I'm rarely known for—I convince the driver to leave me just outside of town. We both agree that the limo showing up at the salon again would just fuel the imagination of the paparazzi and gawkers, blowing my cover.

I trade my slipping out disguise for an old baseball cap and hooded sweatshirt, pushing the scarf and coat into my duffle bag before slinging it across my back.

I wonder if this is how Lorelei felt in the hay days of old Hollywood, switching one disguise for another, always hiding from the press and her fans.

Tucking my hair under the cap, I flip the hood over the top. Yeah, I know it's June, but a girl's gotta do, what a girl's gotta do. The warmth won't bother me, I've always run a little colder than what's considered normal.

With any luck, no one will give me a second glance; just assume I'm one of those so-called rebellious teens. The pink—not a color I would choose for myself, it was a gift from my grandmother—jacket and lavender ball cap could raise questions, but I'm hoping they just figure I'm a poser.

Bag slung across my back, hands shoved in my pockets, I make the trek back into town, imitating the defiant walk seen in every mall in America.

The plan is to slip into Midnite Expresso, wait until full dark, then circle the block and climb the fire escape to my apartment. That is, if the morons aren't completely surrounding the building by now. I highly doubt ol' Sheriff Frank will chase them off my property. Once inside an angry mob will be the least of my worries. I'll have to put up with a pissy water sprite and therian. Then there's the vamp, who makes a mob with pitchforks look like a basket of kittens. Wow, makes you want to jump in the car and skip town instead.

With a covert look, over–the–glasses, under–the–hat brim, I see the vultures still milling around outside my building.

The steps to Midnite Expresso stop me in my tracks, but not my forward motion. I end up on my knees, sprawled across the two steps, the brim of my hat resting precariously against the door. One false move could mean disaster for my little charade. I push the glasses back up onto my nose, then slide fingers under the hood and hat making sure my distinctive silvery hair stays undercover.

I take another peek at my fan club, wiping my hands along the thighs of my jeans. My disguise seems to be working; they haven't even given me a second glance. I turn just in time to get out of the way of a man, cell phone attached to his ear, barreling through the door. Another reporter if the bits of conversation I catch is any indicator. Keeping my head down, I slip around him and into the shop.

Intoxicating scents wrap themselves around me and I feel the beginnings of a smile. This is a safe, familiar place. Nothing bad can happen here, right? Wrong. The place is full of cameras, laptops and people chattering away on cell phones. Reporters. Caffeine. Duh, should have known better.

A momentary glance when I came in is the only attention I've warranted. Hands thrust in my pockets, head dipped low, I make my way over to the counter. Standing in line, I contemplate hiding in the bathroom.

"Next," shouts Candy, her temperament tonight nowhere near as sweet as her name suggests. "What can I get for you?" She eyes me warily, somewhere between disdain and distrust.

"White chocolate mocha," I say, feeling the need for something indulgent.

"Whip cream on that?" She checks off the order on the side of the cup before handing it to the pixie hovering over her shoulder.

"Yeah." I slide a five across the counter as she rings it up.

Reaching for the money, she stops, staring at my hand. Damn, is it possible the simple act of resting a very pale hand against a very dark counter could blow my cover?

Candy looks up, eyes narrowed, then nervously glances over my shoulder before whispering, "Keely?"

"Yeah," I say tipping my glasses forward, letting her see my eyes.

"What the hell are you thinking?"

"Obviously about getting my caffeine and sugar rush on." I give her a weak smile to match the weak joke.

Her attention darts to the press-room behind me. "You need to get out of here."

"Actually, I was hoping to hang here until full dark, so I could sneak around the block and into my building."

She shakes her head. "If you haven't noticed they've turned this place into press central."

I nod. "'Spose it's because there's a direct sight line to my place. That, and you've got coffee." I grin and grab the drink, the pale greyish tinge of my complexion accented by the pure white of the cup.

"Leave it to you to worry about your next caffeine fix when the rest of the populace is conducting a witch hunt and you're the target."

"You don't think..." I can't even finish the question, my throat tightening up.

She shakes her head, wiping the counter. "No, now do yourself a favor and move away from the counter, you're drawing attention."

I set the cup on the counter. If Candy was able to tell it was me by the color of my hands someone else might also, but it doesn't mean I'm going to waste a white chocolate mocha! I'll just improvise.

Pulling the sleeve over my hand before picking up the cup, I sneak a peek around the room. The horde is busy with their mobile devices. Glancing back at Candy, a sad little smile twists at her lips, but her eyes say *get out*.

I weave my way out of the shop, avoiding most of the bodies, until I'm at the door. I end up face to face with a reporter. Judging by his girth, more accustomed to sitting behind a desk than being on the scene.

A sloppily done tie, too short and too wide, lies awkwardly across the expanse of his already stained shirt now dotted with the same hot, sticky goodness decorating my sleeve.

The throbbing in my chest warns me to keep my head down as I try to slide past him, mumbling sorry in answer to his outrage. The guy grabs my arm, sloshing more coffee across my already soaked hand.

"Hey, let the kid go," shouts Candy. "I put up with you guys setting up shop here, but I'll be damned if I'll allow you to harass our customers."

The guy growls and gives my arm another tweak.

"I said let him go."

I nearly blow it when she calls me *him*—pink jacket and all—but manage to keep my mouth shut. He releases his grip with a little push and I skitter out the door.

The relief of making it outside is short lived, more jackasses with notepads, cameras and recording devices line the sidewalks, interspersed with people ranging from the curious to fanatics carrying signs. Some with very disturbing depictions of what they would like to do to me.

Feeling a twinge of guilt for the other businesses along Main Street, I take a slug of my drink wishing it held something stronger than coffee. That twinge is short lived as I think of the profits rolling in for the Midnite Expresso from all the coffee–swilling morons wanting a chunk of me. Basement Brews didn't seem to be hurting either, judging from the line leading to the door. At least something good has come of my little mess, hopefully the other businesses not within walking distance benefit too. Maybe Lorelei will have them wrapped around the building waiting to get in tonight.

Pushing my luck, I weave my way through the crowd, ears perked at any mention of my name. Speculation over my involvement is the topic of choice, most not caring one way, or the other just there for the story. An overwhelming portion convinced—without a doubt—of my guilt and a teensy group is defending me to the point of raised fists.

Truthfully, I'm a bit surprised with all the Ens and other magic users in the mass of people, none have used their Talents to sniff me out. Relieved, but still surprised. Maybe there's too strong of a signature from my building for them to pinpoint my location.

Kira/Tiffany is with a group of kids, chanting something about me being 'wrongly accused' in a less than polite vernacular. It feels good to have someone on your side, but I still have the urge to tell her to scat before she and her friends get hurt.

The crowd parts enough that I see a familiar car parked in its usual spot. Whoa, it's after seven and Lorelei didn't cancel. She isn't going to like that I'm late. It's okay if you have to wait on her, but she hates having to wait for you. The door swings open proving the point as she steps out. There's a moment—the quiet before the storm—of silence before a tornado of questions and cameras strikes.

She's talking, but I can't make out what she says, until she smiles and silence once again descends. That smile always leaves me a little uneasy. I've said it before and I'll say it again, I don't swing that way. When she begins speaking again everyone, myself included, takes a step toward her. I try and shake it off, forcing my feet to stay planted. Her voice weaves itself through the people, gathering them closer to her. Just like her cousins, the sirens, her voice holds the amazing power of suggestion. No wonder they flock from miles around to hear her sing at Moonlight Lake.

From what I can see the people seem to be in a state of rapture, probably similar to what sailors felt when the Rhein maidens detoured them from the gold. Most of them wear silly grins. Many of the men—scratch that—many of the men and a few women have longing, or lust in their eyes.

Even with wet hair and no makeup, she inspires desire with just a word. Holding her arms out wide, something comparable to Royd's power glides over the crowd. A wondrous feeling of being loved and wanted, as if she's embracing each of us individually. I bite the inside of my cheek trying to shield myself. Yes, pain seems to help, on the flip side, it sometimes intensifies the feeling. Slowly the crowd slides to either side of me and Nyssa steps out beside Lorelei.

"Hurry up and get in here, Keely. She can't hold them forever."

I look around stupidly, like there's another Keely standing out here.

"Kick it in gear, woman," says Rey, from behind them. "Don't make the vamp come out and get you." He chuckles and then yelps.

Picturing Dara throwing something at him from the safety of the shadows, I sprint across the street and up the stairs. Once I'm through the door, Nyssa close on my heels, I turn and watch Lorelei let her arms down. There's a lot of head scratching going on, a few angry faces and even more disappointed ones.

"Remember to drop by Moonlight tonight around eleven, boys," says Lorelei, that breathy little girl voice somehow carrying above the rumbles of the crowd. She blows them a kiss before backing into the salon and turning to me.

"You're late." With a flip of her hair, she stalks off to my station. "No need to thank me with words, just do your magic," she says, sitting down in my chair.

Well, this is easier than I thought. Stripping off the stained jacket, hat and glasses, I follow. The prickle along my back and shoulders causes me to turn and face a group of three very pissed off co-workers. Maybe I spoke too soon.

Chapter 25

Nyssa is the first to break silence, rushing over to hug me then slap my shoulder. "What were you thinking, running off like that?"

"Ow!" I rub my shoulder, for such a tiny thing she sure packs a wallop.

"Hey, don't damage her before she fixes my hair."

"I just wanted some answers." I step behind the chair, comb in hand.

"Did you get any?" asks Rey, lounging across his chair, a dangling foot tapping to heavy drum beat of the music.

"Interesting choice of music for business hours. Not really."

Rey laughs. "We let Dara pick, and the only client in the place is the one who saved your ass, if you haven't noticed."

I feel my shoulders droop at the reminder that their livelihood teetered on my finding a way out of this mess.

"Hey, no worries, darlin'." He gives me one of those casual smiles that curls the toes of other women. While it doesn't have *quite* the same effect on me, considering I *know* him, it lessens the guilt.

"Do we dare ask where you went for these answers?"

Sweat breaks out across my upper lip when I see the nasty look on Dara's face reflected in my mirror. "I think you already know."

"Pay up, water munchkin." Nyssa sighs and slaps a wad of bills into Rey's outstretched hand.

Smoothing the last roller into place, I move Lorelei to the dryer. There's absolutely no way to avoid Dara now, but I try anyway, slipping into the break room for a soda. I don't need a seer to tell me she's following. The clickety–clack of heels and casual slide of loafers announce the other two are trailing after. Maybe they think they can soften the blow, but I'll put my money on them just wanting to see what happens.

Getting a soda out of the fridge, I lean against the counter as I open it, waiting for all hel to break loose.

She enters and calmly takes a seat at the table. *Hmm, Dara calm. Bad sign?* Clasping her hands in front of her, she stares at me. Like a parent waiting for a disobedient child to explain why they did what they did and what they learned from it. I've got news for her, two can play this game. She's not my mother. Hel, we aren't even related. I hoist myself up onto the counter and take a deep drink of my soda. Just what the Dr. ordered. My palms are a little moist and not from the condensation on the can.

Rey clears his throat and moves to the fridge, grabbing three beers. I don't condone drinking during open hours any more than I do playing heavy metal music, but considering the circumstances, I don't bother saying anything. Rey passes them out and they all turn, joining in the staring match.

"Not fair, three against one," I say, trying to lighten the mood. No luck. I'm met with three sets of eyes, one glaring, one amused and the third almost sympathetic. "Okay guys, what do you want to know?"

"Let's start with why," says Dara. "You knew the danger of leaving the building on your own. You also know that Royd is dangerous."

"I'm sorry. I know it means next to nothing at the moment, but I am. I just needed to take matters into my own hands, I saw a way to get some of the answers I needed and took it. I won't apologize for that, but will for tricking Nys and Rey and causing all of you to worry."

"Accepted." Rey raises his bottle tipping it toward me. Nyssa nods in agreement, the worry gone from her eyes, replaced with their usual sparkle.

"Keely, you have no idea the trouble you are in," says Dara, the bottle dangling from her fingers.

"Sure I do. I've been unofficially accused of

butchering Ens. Whoever actually committed the crimes has used my salon to acquire the means to do so, making me an unwitting accomplice. One of the most influential men in Des Moines owns my ass. I don't know what in hel he is, or what he wants and the people who can tell me more than likely won't do it in a manner I can decipher. My salon is in the toilet; my employees are destitute because of me, and one may have taken up prostitution. Don't tell me I have no idea what kind of trouble I'm in. I know full well what kind of trouble. Has anyone heard from Jenny?"

They say silence is golden and right at this moment, I agree. That little spew sure felt good. Maybe I should let things out more often. The look of shock on their faces is enough to sustain me for a week, but no one answers my question about Jenny.

"Well? Has she called?"

They share a look that makes me more than nervous.

"No one knows and the police are looking for her."

An invisible weight crushes down. "Because of what I said?"

"Actually, when we had not heard from her we began to worry and tried to track her down. When that failed, we filed a missing person's report. Unfortunately, that put an even greater shadow of suspicion on you. So, no, we do not know where she is and no, you did not know the entire scope of the trouble you are in." Dara sets her beer down none too gently. A frothy trail erupts, making its way down the bottle and across the table.

"Oh, crap."

"The *crap* is going to hit the fan, if you don't get your skinny buns out here and finish doing my hair. I have to get to work." The forgotten Lorelei stands in the doorway, patting her rollers.

I grimace, sliding off the counter and follow her.

"Sorry about that," I say, my fingers moving over her head as fast as they can. Nyssa joins us, taking on the other side. "The last thing I want is to make my one and only client late, especially one who saved my butt earlier."

She grins. "Do you know how hard it is to find a good hairstylist?"

I grin back. "Nope, but I still appreciate you not jumping ship on me." I work my hands through her now freed tresses and grab the spray. Both of us hold our breath as I put the finishing touches on her now glamorous mane. "Want me to do your make up and save you some time?"

"No, I'll be fine. They can't start the show without me." She winks, tossing a tip onto the vanity before sauntering off to the front desk.

Tossing my cape onto the chair, I put my comb

into the sanitizer before looking at the tip. Holy crap. I was used to a ten, sometimes a twenty when I'd done something more than the usual. I think she missed a zero tonight, in my favor. Grabbing the hundred, I scurried up front, but she'd already driven away.

Nyssa giggled from behind the desk. "She wondered how long it would take you to notice."

"She told you about this?" I ask, waving the bill in the air.

Nyssa nods, still laughing.

"Looks like supper is on Lorelei tonight."

"I'll call in an order and pick it up if you find out what the others want. Unless you want to surprise them with pizzas," she says, already looking up the number for Basement Brews.

"Sounds good to me. I'll get Rey to help you."

※※※

Over pizza and beer, I try to explain what happened with Royd. His cryptic words confuse the others as much as they did me. Except for Dara. Somehow I get the feeling she knows more than she's sharing. It's probably going to take divine intervention to get her to spill.

I decide to save the First Arrow stuff for a more private conversation. By the end of our meal, everyone is in agreement that first thing tomorrow I call The Sisters and attempt to get them to explain. It's also agreed that they probably won't give a straight answer. Such is my life as of late.

Chapter 26

"Knew this day would come. Inevitable. Hid you as long as possible. Protect you, we cannot."

Three voices in unison. The Sisters must be using the speakerphone I got them. If the surround sound effect isn't bad enough, they're stuck in fantasy land mode and I fear at any moment I'll be called *my precious.*

No matter what Royd thinks, I'll never get a clear answer from the triplets. Knowingly, or not, they've mastered the art of confusion. I didn't even have to say anything when they picked up, they just started talking. They probably knew I was going to call before I did.

"Protect me from what?" Futile I know, but got to try.

"Destiny."

"And what might that destiny be?"

"You will know when the time is right. Many choices you will have to make. Choose carefully."

"So you can't, or won't tell me?"

"To tell would do no good, only harm. You must discover alone. Help you, we cannot."

"But I need your help. He said I was supposed

to ask you." And against my better judgement, I picked up the phone.

"*Of whom do you speak?*"

"Var Royd. He said you should answer my questions."

The hissing I hear is obviously not from the phone as it fades to whispers I can't decipher. I think I hear words like dangerous, destruction, and death, three d's I don't want to hear. Especially together.

"*How do you know that name? Stay away from him.*"

"Trust me, it's not like I'm purposely trying to make friends with him. He seems to be taking a rather personal interest in me lately." I'm not about to tell them he owns the note on my business, that would probably send them over the edge. "He calls me mein Schattenkind. What does it mean?"

"*A mistake was made in the past, but the sun burned away the shadows. Law was ignored in the present and history threatens to repeat. Protections placed are waning and the Shadow King presses against The Veil. Future's outcome is unknown.*"

Crapnar. Sun beats shadows, yeah. Mistakes in the past, laws broken, history repeats and the future is unknown. That tells me so much. How the hel does this apply to me?

"*Stay away from the Sun King. His Shield will protect and his Sword will cut, yet loyalty wavers.*"

Sun King? Shield? Sword? Great, more stupid clues to nowhere. "What does Schattenkind mean?"

"Shadow child."

Sun burned away shadow. My stomach begins to do loop–de–loops and a nasty, burning flavor hits the back of my throat. If he's the sun, I must be the shadow. Schattenkind. Wait, Shadow King? Einen? If I'm the mistake of the present, is he the mistake of the past?

"Keely, dearest, I'm glad you called. We've been so worried about you with all this Collector business." Master Yoda times three disappears as my grandmother Matilda's voice takes the lead, yanking me from thought.

It'll do no good to question her about our conversation. I don't know if they truly don't remember what happens when they go into prophecy mode, or if it's just an act. They claim ignorance and I've never been able to prove otherwise.

Nervous pacing ends as I reach the living room, lowing myself onto the couch next to Nyssa.

"She knows we worry about her, you don't have to tell her," says Eliza. "And don't coddle her, she's a grown woman."

"She's not coddling her," chimes in Nicolina.

"Hi, Aunt Liza, Aunt Lina. I'm fine Grandma. Everything is fine, nothing to worry about."

"Why did you call?" asks Eliza, the blunt one.

"She called to chat. Didn't you, dearest?" says my grandmother, Matilda.

"Of course she did, she loves her grandmother and great aunts." I can almost hear the smile on Nicolina's face.

"Yes, I love you all and miss you, but I did call to ask you something." Here goes nothing. Maybe they will stay with me long enough to give me some sort of clue as to what their earlier words meant. "Do you know a Var Royd?"

Silence, deafening silence. If I'd heard three thumps, I'd at least know I gave them heart attacks. The silence stretches on. Either they know something, or they're flipping back to prophecy mode.

Eliza finally breaks the stillness. "Stay away from that man. Do you hear me, Keelina Monday Fey?"

Matilda and Nicolina echo her sentiment and I wince as Eliza practically yells my full name.

"Yes, Aunt Liza, I hear you."

My entourage snickers. This is why I didn't want an audience. Amped up animal hearing sucks. Luckily, I'd been out of the room for the important stuff. I hope Eliza doesn't start using embarrassing childhood stories as life lessons with them listening.

"That man is nothing, but trouble."

"Yes, Aunt Liza. I wouldn't worry about it. He probably just wants to sell me insurance." I roll my eyes. Talking to The Sisters can reduce me to a petulant teen in a matter of moments.

"This call doesn't have anything to do with that Collector business, does it?"

"No, I just called to check on you three and now that I know you're all fine I better get going. I have some cleaning to do."

There is no way I'm going to mention getting hauled in by NTF, my wicked bad dreams, or the incident with the plant. I didn't tell the others and I don't think I will, at least not yet. In person, I would never get away with lying, but over the phone I stand a chance.

"Take care, dearest," all three say in unison.

"Goodbye Grandma, Aunt Liza, Aunt Lina. Love you all. Take care." I hang up before they can add, or question anything else.

Flopping back against the couch, I look at the others. "Well, that was fun."

"So your middle name is Monday?" Rey laughs. His knee–length braid, dangling over the edge of the chair, sweeping back and forth across the floor in front of CC "Monday's child is—"

"Fair of face, yada, yada, yada. Yes, I was born on a Monday. I know, not very original."

"I'd take Monday over Wednesday any day. Who would want to be cursed with woe?"

"Better be careful. If he catches that, it's going to hurt," I say, nodding at CC, hoping to change the subject. The last thing I want to discuss is my middle name, supposedly given by my parents. I don't resent them leaving, not much anyway. I'd just like to know why.

"No worse than Nys pulling while she braided it." He sways his head, making the cat skitter across the floor. A pleasant, harmless distraction to watch after everything else that's happened.

"So, what did the German mean?" asks Nyssa, joining in the hair versus cat game by wiggling the braid in front of his nose then holding it just out of reach. CC sits up on his haunches, batting at it. He loves the challenge almost as much as the attention.

"My shadow child."

"Huh, wonder why Royd keeps calling you that." Rey shifts in the chair when Nyssa pulls a little harder than intended, or maybe it wasn't an accident. Her smile reminds me of the little sister of an old high school friend when she used to torment us.

"Good question." If they didn't hear it, I'm not about to repeat the little sun destroys shadow bit.

"Maybe it has something to do with your coloring," he says. "You are kinda grey. Not that that's bad, just unusual."

"Yeah, I know, usually reserved for the dead."

"That's not what I meant. Not everyone can pull it off—it looks good on you."

I can't help grinning as he flusters along. Laying my head back against the couch, I sigh and close my eyes. "I'm not any closer to answers than I was before. The only people who can fill me in aren't willing to do so."

"Could be they aren't able to." He shifts again as Nyssa and CC begin a game of tug of war. "I know The Sisters have that whole fortune cookie Talent, but sometimes with destiny and prophecy stuff those in the know are restricted from saying anything that might change it. Not much consolation, but that's the way it works."

"Well, it sucks when you're in the middle of it." I lean forward, resting my elbows on my knees and twirl my thumbs. "You guys ever wonder about the stuff Dara doesn't tell us?"

"Like the vamp stuff?" asks Nyssa, dropping Rey's braid when CC grows tired of the game and wanders off.

"No, I mean her personally."

"We all have our secret pasts we don't like to talk about. Doesn't mean it has anything to do with what's going on with you." She sits down next to me.

"Royd purposely mentioned her having ulterior motives in our friendship."

"I still say he's not to be trusted," says Rey and with that, the subject is dropped like a hot potato. He swings around sitting upright in the chair.

"So girls, what's on the agenda for tonight? Probably not a good idea to go to the club, unless we want to be clubbed."

"Ha, ha, ha, very funny. You're the one they would probably club, that is after they have a royal hunt." Nyssa giggles.

He makes a noise of disgust and rolls his eyes. "They don't *club* the fox, they shoot it."

"Either way it ends bad for you." She tosses one of the pillows from the couch at him.

He tosses the pillow back. "What do you suggest we do, my little water lily?"

"How about chick flick night?"

We both groan, neither a fan of the genre.

"Hey, at least they have happy endings and no one dies."

"Beg to differ," Rey says and holds up his hand, ticking off movies where someone ends up with a horrible disease and dies, or sacrifices themselves to save another. Nyssa's pouty lip growing with each down-turned finger.

"It's decided, no chick flicks."

"Hey, what about Dara's vote?"

"Like she would ever voluntarily watch a chick flick. Jenny would be a better bet."

"That reminds me, any news about Jenny?" I ask, reeled back into the conversation.

They shake their heads.

"I'm worried about that girl."

"Maybe she went back to Nebraska." Nyssa hugs the pillow Rey tossed at her, during their little chick flick discussion.

"It's not like she has any magical Talents The Collector would be interested in."

"No, but there are plenty of other predators out there," I say, reminded of the guy I'd seen her with.

The warm June day suddenly feels like January, their conversation churning up all kinds of images. Including, but not limited to, the night I saw her in the coffee shop. I haven't told them about that little scene, bad enough they know about me seeing her before I discovered the missing bag.

"So what's it going to be horror, or action? We could go sci–fi if anyone is feeling a little spacey." He tosses another pillow at Nyssa.

Thank the gods for Rey and his ability to flip the subject, and Nyssa's short attention span. My own attention still focused on my absent receptionist. Something tells me she's a missing piece in the puzzle encompassing my life. A puzzle made up of mistakes, broken laws, kings and repeating history.

If Einen is the shadow of the past, will I be the shadow burned away in the present?

Chapter 27

Surprise, surprise, I'm left behind as the other two go pick out our entertainment for the night. When I offer to buy pizza again Rey stoically tells me to fix nachos, he's tired of pizza. Before I can protest, they scoot out the door. I can still hear their laughter as they practically run down the hall.

Nachos, how in hel am I supposed to pull that off? Guess making nachos out of nothing will keep my mind off shadows and sunlight. A shiver runs down my spine and my tummy does that nice flipity–flop again. Enough, I need to stop thinking about it at least for the moment.

Opening the fridge for a soda, I find it practically overflowing. The first cupboard I can reach is full and so are the others. My keepers have been busy. This place doesn't resemble my kitchen and by that, I mean it has food. Besides things like cereal, instant potatoes and frozen stuff to pop in the oven, or microwave, my kitchen is usually pretty bare. This is like a...well, a normal kitchen.

Humming the Twilight Zone theme, I gather hamburger, veggies and cheese. "They want nachos, they get nachos."

Several layers of meat and cheese later, my nachos resemble more of a casserole than your typical munchies. Bowls of chopped lettuce and homemade pico de gallo wait on the counter. I'd even gone all out and filled little dishes with salsa and sour cream. This was going to be one fancy movie night at casa de Fey.

The cat, so thoughtfully winding himself around my ankles, takes off with a stream of indecipherable screeching for the door. Either Dara has decided to join us, or my grocery fairies are back. Obviously Dara, when the door opens and I'm not overwhelmed with chattering. Shoving the *nachos* in the oven I head to the living room, finding CC curled up on her lap as she lounges in Rey's vacated chair.

"What did The Sisters reveal?"

"Nada, as usual." I sit down, her raised eyebrow a hint that I'm supposed to elaborate. "A bunch of mangled crap about my destiny and that they hid me as long as possible."

"Any hint as to what this *destiny* is?"

I shake my head, pinching the bridge of my nose between my fingers. "Nope, can't tell me because it will do more harm than good. I'll find out when the time is right and I'll have choices to make. Like I said, mangled thoughts, no answers, not even a hint."

No, I'm not about to divulge everything. She

hasn't been totally forthcoming with me either. Not that I'm placing my trust in Var Royd, but I know she knows something she's not telling.

"What about the part about protecting you?"

"Couldn't tell me that either. I did find out mein Schattenkind means *my shadow child*."

She doesn't look surprised—not that calm, collected Dara ever looks surprised—but one eye twitches ever so slightly. If I hadn't been studying her, I would have missed it. A small crack in her usual cool armor.

"Hey, I've been meaning to ask you, does the title First Arrow mean anything to you?"

Wow! Could that be shock I see passing over her face before her expression becomes even more blank than usual? Voices echo in the hall and the door swings open, saving her. Rey and Nyssa enter laughing and shoving, a bag of videos and case of beer in hand. Damn, yet another unanswered question.

"You'll be happy to know, we compromised. Nyssa gets her romance, albeit a little sick and twisted in the beginning of the series, and the rest of us get some laser action."

"Can we skip the part where she plays dumb blond and you try to drag the title out of her? Perhaps moving right to the viewing?" Dara asks.

Nyssa nods enthusiastically. "Han Solo, yum."

"Just pop the movie in while I get the munchies,

don't forget the surround and curtains." I had to throw in that last dig, but my sarcasm is lost. Rey is a fanatic about atmosphere and usually harps about the tiniest details.

The teasing and petty bickering makes it feel almost like a normal night. Everyone settles in for a night of Mexican food and intergalactic war, except me. I can't get my mind off the words *shadow child*.

Chapter 28

Stumbling, crawling, pulling themselves across the ground, they gather around me. Slack–jawed vacancy replaced by adoration. Hands ranging from skeletal to the newly–deceased reach out, attempting to grasp my cloak, but pass through the insubstantial fabric. No, not fabric, but living entities, wavering shadows wrapped around my body, caressing, stroking.

These things that huddle around me, I know what they were, what they are. There will be no excuses, no questioning, all I need to do is ask, no not ask, command. They are mine to do with what I will, just like the shadowy forms that surround me. Anything I desire. Mine. Just say it and it shall be.

Something on the fringe of the crowd catches their attention. With more grace and precision than I expected, they part, leaving a path. The bowing and scraping is now directed at another. I know without asking who the shadow–cloaked figure is. Jealousy flashes as their devotion turns and I can feel their confusion as I picture them destroying this intruder.

"Control. You must learn control," says the

voice I used to call friend. "If you do not embrace it, do not *take* the power, it will destroy you."

I feel it more than hear it ripping through the rage that encompasses me, but something clicks. Making me painfully aware of my surroundings and the flood of emotions I'm riding. He lowers his head and fades into the darkness. Leaving me lost, confused, and a little more than scared as the crowd turns its attention back to me.

⁂

I wake drenched, clutching at the tangle of sheets binding me to the bed. This has to stop. Surprisingly enough my heart hasn't propelled through my ribcage. This had to be the most disturbing of the dreams yet, even beating out my own death. I'd had no control in that one. In this one, I was the one in control and I liked it. Strike that, I loved it. All that power.

Rolling from the bed, stumbling into the bathroom, sheet and all, my stomach takes a dive. I heave until every last chip and its toppings are gone, then rest my head against cool porcelain.

Remnants of the dream hang behind my eyelids like some warped silent film. Dead things, beginning with the plant at NTF headquarters, working up the food chain until they are of the two–legged variety. They reach toward me. They chant my name, even that stupid plant. "Plants can't talk."

"I know plants can't talk. Did someone have a little too much last night?"

I scream as blinding brightness fills the room and throw my arms over my face in a feeble attempt to block my eyes. With a resounding click blessed darkness returns.

"Keely? Are you okay?"

Rey is leaning over me. I can see him, but it just isn't registering. So cold. So very, very cold. My teeth are chattering and I'm shaking so hard every bone in my body aches.

"Keely? Nys! Get in here, there's something wrong with her, and it's not a hangover! Geez, Keely, let go that hurts."

He places his hands over mine where I've grabbed his shoulders and removes them. He winces as he touches one shoulder, then the other, drawing back blood-coated fingers. "Gods, girl that was quite the death grip you had there."

I want to apologize, but with the word death, my shaking intensifies and I can barely see, let alone speak.

"What's wrong with her?"

"Don't know. At first I thought she was hung over. Hasn't said a word, just sits there all glassy-eyed, shaking like a damn vibrator. Nearly shredded my shoulders when I tried to calm her down."

Someone is touching my face and I try to swat the hands away.

"Hey, it's me. Nyssa. She's all clammy. Looks like she threw up. Food poisoning?"

"No, we all ate the same thing."

Their voices are garbled and faces all streaky and fuzzy. The pain. I've never felt such pain. Passing out is a definite possibility, but that would mean sleeping, sort of, and I don't want to go back to that nightmare world. Somewhere in the depths of my addled brain I feel wet sandpaper sliding against my face.

"Back off, CC, she's sick," says Rey.

Hissing, growling, and a shout of pain before the rough wetness is back. CC My cat, not a new form of nightmarish torture.

"Should we call 911, or a doctor?"

You'd think when you're lying on the bathroom floor shaking like an epileptic the words doctor and 911 should be of some comfort. Hel and no. Doctors equal needles. I've always had a fear of needles and those words cut through my convulsed mind bringing the pain of thousands of them stabbing me in every place imaginable.

"No," I forced through chattering teeth. There's another fear for you, dentists. The slamming of my jaws probably caused some serious damage.

"But Keely, you're sick," says Nyssa, hovering over me.

"No. Doctors." Forcing the words out hurts almost as much as the tremors ripping through my body. I want it to stop, but not at the expense of being poked and prodded.

"Get her back into bed," says Nyssa. "I'll make some hot tea, maybe we can warm her up."

I moan when he lifts me, followed by a series of whimpers as we move across the room.

"Sorry darlin'," he whispers, the warmth of his breath against my ear a strong contrast to my icy skin.

I nearly bite through my lip wanting to scream as he lays me on the bed. He pulls up the covers, then slips in beside me.

"Now I know you're sick," he chuckles against my neck. "Any other time if I'd crawled into bed naked with you, you'd have tossed me across the room."

I hear the words, but they don't mean shit. I struggle to get closer to him, wanting to crawl into the intense heat of his body.

"Damn, it's like hugging a block of ice. What the hell is wrong with you, or would that be hel? I've heard her realm is pretty damn cold." He slides an arm and leg under me, wrapping his whole body around mine. "Don't cry, sweetheart, we'll get you warmed up."

I hadn't realized I was until his fingers brush my cheeks.

"Rey, what in Hel's Realm are you doing?"

"Warming her up. Do you know a better way than body heat? Wouldn't hurt if you crawled in here too, and it would definitely help me having two girls in bed."

The scratch of Nyssa's lacey pajamas is like razor blades after the smoothness of Rey's bare skin, but she is warm.

"Gods, she's a frickin' iceberg."

"I know." His grip tightens around me. "I'm afraid she's going to hurt herself with all this shaking. Fuck."

My ears are buzzing so loud, I feel more than hear Rey whisper against my neck and shoulder. I snuggle in closer to his animal heat. Pain, so cold it burns fills me, shoves its way to the surface. The tingling stretch of my skin feels like a unitard ten sizes too small as it tries to contain whatever it is that wants out.

The power. Take it.

"Einen."

"Who the hell is Einen?"

The tiny bit of my brain still conscious tries to explain, but my lips don't cooperate.

Take the power. Control it, or it will destroy you.

"It's okay, Keely, just try and relax." Rey wraps his arms tighter and tosses a leg over mine, encompassing me in warmth.

Come to me. I will help.

"Can't. Don't know how."

The shushing noise, intended to be calming, rings like a freight train in my ears. In the dark, I can feel their movement. An undulating curtain of shadow drapes across the room, lowering itself over me.

Chapter 29

Moonlight leaches color, leaving everything in shades of grey. Shadows, cast by undetectable objects, slither across the landscape. Disembodied whispers, things that should terrify me, are now commonplace, almost comforting.

Alarm bells sound at that feeling of security. I ignore them, relishing not having to deal with life. The pain I couldn't escape in the waking world now almost nonexistent.

I know he's here before his arms wrap around my waist, pulling me against him. I also know what he's thinking. No, not some magical link, just his baser needs pressed hard against my tailbone. My own thoughts move in the same direction as his hands slide the length of me. Fingers snag the tie holding my robe as they move down my waist, briefly cradling my hips before continuing.

The loop fastening the robe gives away and those hands find bare flesh. Frustratingly slow, they move back up until they cup my breasts, thumbs gently circling my already stiff nipples. I moan as his lips find the sweet spot at the base of my neck and shoulder. The one that makes me melt back against him.

"Smaller than I like, but they will do," he says, his breath tantalizingly hot against my neck.

Smaller than he likes? This brings back painful memories of how I fell for breast *enhancement* cream. Hey, I was sixteen and still wearing a training bra. Not like it worked, and age didn't help either, no matter how much The Sisters promised it would. I'm scarcely out of an A cup.

Spinning around, I find myself faced with the mocking grin of my imaginary friend and he's beautiful. And an asshole. Beautiful, but still an asshole. Giving him a push, I pull my robe closed and cinch the tie.

"Come now, it is not as if you do not know you are far from," his eyes linger on my chest, "well-endowed."

He reaches out, fingers brushing against my collarbone. "If it is any consolation, they are nearly perfect in form."

Standing there like a fish, mouth gaping, I can't even come up with a decent comeback. Instead, I stupidly say, "Really?"

"Yes, really." He pulls me back against him.

I try to push him away again, but fail, caught in the circle of his arms.

"If you do not wish this kind of attention, you should not appear unannounced in someone's home wearing practically nothing."

"What in hel? All this time you've been hanging

out in my dreams, you finally decide to talk to me and it's to insult my boobs?"

"Shh." He places a finger against my lips. "Invoking, or provoking a goddess, especially that one, can be dangerous. And I did not insult," he focuses on my chest again, "as you so eloquently put it, *your boobs*."

I bat the finger away and scowl, earning me laughter.

"Look you're the one who's in my dream, not the other way around."

This earns me even more laughter.

"You think this a dream?"

I nod.

"My dear, this is no dream."

I shake my head. "Nope, this is a dream, just like the other times I've seen you."

"No, *this* is not a dream, but you are correct in part. The other times I came to you, you were dreaming. Although, not always did your consciousness stay within the bounds of what you perceive as reality. There were brief moments you crossed boundaries."

He sweeps me back into his arms, holding me against him so tightly I can barely breathe.

"But this time, you crossed even farther," he says, before his lips molest mine.

Okay, molest isn't the right word. You can't molest the willing and boy, am I willing. A release

I didn't know I was searching for is right around the corner. I can feel it. Crushed against my thigh.

His fingers tangle in my hair, pulling my head back as his lips trace a line from my lips across my jaw and downward. I tense for a moment as he lingers on my neck. Another elven vamp? No, or at least no fangs, but there are teeth I find out as they graze my nipple, extracting a moan.

"Wait. Stop." I manage to reluctantly, detach his lips from my body. "I need some answers, Einen, and have a feeling you know what they are. Some of them, at least." Reminiscent tremors of pain echo along my skin.

Our eyes meet and tears push their way to the surface. I want so much to hate him for leaving a scared, confused child, but I can't. He's here now, filling a part of me that had been missing. "You said you'd help me."

Those beautiful, full lips, that so recently sent shivers of desire through me, constrict to a downward line. Eyes of pale silver darken to storm grey.

He'd also said he'd always be there for me, but that had been a lie. What makes me think he's willing, or capable of helping now?

Einen reaches out running a finger through the wetness of my tears. I feel myself leaning into his caress as his hand cups the side of my face. There's none of the *spark* I felt from touching Alric, or his icy counterpart, but something else. Something that frightens me. A longing, a need, a rightness to his touch. Like finding the missing piece of a puzzle, or a part of yourself you never knew was missing. A slow smile curls his lips as he drops his hand and I blink my way back to reality.

"They speak untruths."

"Who does?"

"Those you surround yourself with. Some want your power for themselves, others wish to destroy you. Some, in an act of what they perceived as protection, love even," his scowl deepens, "have made it possible for you to destroy yourself."

"What are you rambling about? Who would possibly want the power to grow hair?" Another hairstylist sure, but what would that gain someone else? I shiver at the thought of Dara, or Rey wanting what I've got. No way, they're my friends. Right?

"So are you talking about The Collector?" The imagination runs wild wondering if one of my friends is that monster.

He shakes his head. "They do not need to wield it, only use you as a conduit. Have you not been called Schattenkind?"

I nod, waiting for a better explanation of what that is exactly.

"You have the power to do more than just make hair grow. The *dream* that brought you here, that is a taste of what awaits when your Talents are no longer held in check."

Laughter bubbles up and spills over. "I've had my Talents since I was a teen. Yeah, I was a little late in getting them, but still."

He sighs and looks away, shaking his head. His lower lip caught between his teeth shouldn't be so damn enticing, but it is and it stops my laughter cold. A vision of that lip between my teeth sends a flood of heat to my cheeks.

"Perhaps we should continue this conversation at another time."

"Wait, I want to talk about this now," I yell, but it's too late. He's faded into nothingness.

Chapter 30

Warm and comfortable, I detest whatever brought me to the state between dreamy sleep and fully awake. I fight against it, wiggling down in the bed, begging sleep to take me back. Something stirs against my back and I freeze. Opening my eyes, I find an arm slung over me. A man's arm. I lift my head slightly and identify the tickle across my waist—my very naked waist—to be a rope of red hair. Oh gods, what have I done? I don't remember having *that* much to drink. What happened last night that I ended up in bed with not only a man, but an employee and friend? I squeeze my eyes closed. Movies, nachos, a couple of beers with Nyssa, Rey and Dara, that I remember. It's afterward that's the problem.

I went to bed, bad dreams. Waking up, tossing my cookies, or in this case, nachos. It's hard to remember the cold, considering I'm so warm now, but I was freezing. Voices surrounding me, Rey, Nys and I think CC was there too. Shaking, pain, being put in bed again. I don't want to remember the dreams, but I know they are behind what happened. Something chased them away. Einen.

Einen was back in my dreams, or as he claims, I paid him a visit.

None of that matters. What matters is figuring out how I'm going to deal with the warm body wrapped around me. His arm loosens and I wiggle out from under, sliding to the edge of the bed. Turning to grab the sheet is a big mistake, my hand freezes mid–way as I take in my living, breathing blanket. Damn, Rey is even more beautiful naked.

"Like what you see, ma chéri?" His chuckle turns to a full out belly laugh as I wrench the sheet, flipping him onto his back.

The door swings open and I hold the sheet in front of me in a poor attempt to cover what everyone has seen by now.

Nyssa stands there holding her hands over her eyes, peeking through spread fingers, a big grin stretching from ear to ear. "Now there's a scene for the record books."

With a snort, Rey grabs for the other half of my sheet. Yanking it away, I push the blanket toward him. "Like you weren't in here with us just moments ago."

She shrugs, moving into the room, followed by Dara, who leans against the frame, arms crossed.

"Somebody mind telling me how I ended up in bed with Rey? And Nys? Naked?"

"Moi fell prey to your seductive charms," says Rey, with a wink as he pulls his pants on.

It's my turn to snort. "Yeah, right."

The playfulness is gone, his expression so serious I barely recognize him.

"You were sick, this morning. So sick, we thought we'd have to call 911."

I nod, remembering arguing with them, and Rey joking about being naked in bed with me. The cold, the pain. What I can't remember is what brought it all on. He sits beside me, draping an arm around me.

"I found you on the bathroom floor shaking, your teeth chattering so loud I could hear them before I came in. You couldn't say anything, just stared at me all glassy–eyed. We were scared and you were so cold. That's how you ended up in bed with us. We were trying to raise your body temp."

I nod.

"Can you tell us what caused you to freak out like that?"

Looking at Dara, tingling cold begins at the base of my spine, spreading frosty pain across my skin. "Dead things."

❊❊❊❊❊

I sit enfolded in Rey's arms shaking, barely hanging on to sanity while visions of outstretched arms— dead arms, attached to dead bodies—reach toward me.

He pulls me back on the bed, wrapping himself and the blankets around me. "I think you better skedaddle, Dara."

Through the haze of fear and death, I see Nys pushing Dara out of the room.

His voice rumbles in my ear, the words unimportant, only the sound of his voice, soothing my shattered nerves. Keeping the imagined dead at a distance. Maybe he knows this and continues to talk, mostly idle chatter.

I'm the one in control, I tell myself. It's just my imagination. His arms tighten as a violent tremor rips through me.

A distant ringing and raised voices. The phone. I try to concentrate on what's being said, anything to take my mind off the horrific images floating in my brain. It doesn't matter. Those calling me metaphysically don't give a shit who's on the phone.

"Raise your shields, Keely." I hear Rey mumble against my ear.

The wall. Brick by brick I picture it blocking the groaning, grabbing things. Dead things. A giggle escapes as his grasp tightens—a death grip—turning to sobs with my own ironic joke.

A brick falls, icy pain erupts and another brick falls then another. The vice of his arms and legs unyielding, holding me taut against hot, living flesh.

Control. You must learn control. If you do not

embrace it, do not take the power, it will destroy you. The words ring in my head as I slam a brick into place. I don't want this power, or the euphoric greed I felt in my dreams. Another brick in place.

A grey and grizzled hand pries it away and grabs my wrist. I scream. Every muscle seizes. Never had they actually touched me, this is a completely new version of hel. All the bricks begin to tumble and I scramble back, joyous cries filling my head as the dead slink forward. In my thrashing fit, my head connects with someone, or something and blackness descends in a pain–filled rush.

Chapter 31

Someone stands beside me picking up the bricks, putting them in my hands. Forcing my hands to the tumbled mess, showing me how to place them correctly. The hands are long and elegant, not meant for a bricklayer. When they touch mine, I see a similarity in coloring and a jolt runs through me. Attraction? Recognition? Static electricity? I know this person, this man. My safety net from childhood, the one I told my deepest secrets, the one I ran to when things didn't go my way. No matter how much I want to, I can't make out his features, a shadowy blur. I squint, trying to see past it, reach toward him, but he steps back into obscurity.

"She's slept for almost twenty-four hours."

"Should we try to wake her?"

"Do you want to see a repeat of what happened last time she woke up?"

"Not really. Wait, I think she's coming around."

The whispers cease and I feel their stares. This time I remember what happened and damn, does my head hurt.

"Who cracked me in the head?" My voice

scratchy, strained, probably from all the screaming. Thank the heavens, I don't have other tenants, or neighbors.

"How are you feeling?" asks Nyssa, her voice shaky.

"Like I've been hit with a truck. Sorry I scared you guys."

"Hey, it's not like you planned it." Rey grasps my hand, gently rubbing the back of it.

"Not in this, or any other lifetime." I give his hand a weak squeeze, gasping with each strained movement as I attempt to push myself into a sitting position.

"Want me to get you some water?"

I shake my head, wincing. "Coffee and some aspirin."

"I don't think that's such a good idea considering—"

"Look Nys, I appreciate everything you guys have done, but I need a jolt of caffeine and something to take the edge off this headache."

I can see her disapproval in the dim light as she looks at Rey and he nods.

"One small breakdown and you guys think you need to mother me." I try to make my tone light, but with the amount of pain I'm in it comes out more like a complaint.

Nyssa lowers her head and turns to leave. "Be right back."

"Nys, I didn't mean it like it sounded."

"She'll get over it, she's...we've all been worried about you."

"Where's Dara?"

"Probably hiding in the basement. Think she's a little pissed I kicked her out earlier."

I nod seeing the faint line of light rimming the curtains. "About that, why'd you kick her out?"

His face twists in confusion. "You don't remember?"

"I remember visions."

He circles his hand in the air, urging me on, but I fear saying it out loud will cause it to happen again.

"Let's leave it at they weren't of sugar plum fairies."

"That's why I sent her out. She's no sugar plum fairy. I thought maybe she was making things harder for you."

Closing my eyes, I take a deep breath and slowly exhale.

"You okay?"

"Yeah, head just hurts."

"If it's any consolation, so does my jaw."

"Oh Rey, I'm sorry." I should have seen it right away, the swollen, angry red and purple flesh is pretty hard to miss even in the dim lighting. Tells you how much these *attacks* have rattled me.

"Not a problem, after all I got to cuddle you

again," punctuated with a lurid eyebrow wiggle.

"Yeah, about that... Don't suppose you, or anyone else has a clue what's happening?" I have Einen's words and the strange garble from The Sisters along with some very mixed signals from and about Var Royd. Then there's Dara, or *The First Arrow*, gods know what that means, or how it affects me. I need to know who I can trust in my own little circle. Part of me wants to hightail it to Sioux City and Annya's apartment, but the NTF would probably frown on that.

"Rey?"

His Adam's apple rises and drops. I clutch his hand as he tries to pull away. He knows something.

"Are you afraid of me?"

He shakes his head and then turns toward me. "More like afraid for you."

Slowly I let his hand drop from mine. Waves of fear sweep through the room, not all of it his.

A diminutive form at the door clears her throat before bringing me my drugs of choice. I toss the little white pills into my mouth before wrapping my hands around the steaming cup. The hot liquid jarring, tears spring up as it sears the roof of my mouth, washing the pills down an already ragged throat. Lowering the cup to my lap, I lean back and close my eyes.

No matter how much I'd love to ignore what happened, I can't, but I'm sure not going to face it naked. Not as if everyone hasn't seen what little I have to offer. Laughter turns to a moan as it shakes my abused body. I hold up a hand when they move toward me. There's nothing they can do anyway.

"Are you okay?" asks Nyssa.

I nod; even though it's evident, I'm not. On many levels.

"I need to get in the shower."

Nyssa takes the cup from me and Rey leans in to help me from the bed. Gently, I rebuff his hands.

"Sorry, I know it seems silly after everything that's happened." For a second time I'm glad they've neglected the lights. My face is probably somewhere between strawberry blonde and fire red.

He takes off for another room, leaving Nyssa to tend to my delicate sensibilities. Leaving me relieved that any typical filthy comments are kept to himself, yet empty over his fear of me.

Using the sprite as a crutch, I make it to the bathroom and into the shower, praising the inventor of the little stool inside. There's no way I can stand and taking a bath would take too long. I'd probably drown due to lack of muscle control.

The water feels delightful, rinsing away the scent of my bed partners and my own stench. Loosening the aches and pains of muscles I never knew I had. I don't want it to stop, but hiding under a stream of slowly chilling water isn't an option. Getting out is a little easier, but my skin is still overly sensitive to the fabrics of the fluffy towel and clothing Nyssa gathered.

Nyssa leads me to the couch and CC immediately wanders over. He tentatively paws at the couch until I pat the cushion beside me and he jumps up.

My stomach growls as Nyssa returns with a plate of scrambled eggs and toast. "Thought you might be hungry."

Food hadn't registered on the scale of importance until the sight and scent hit me. Everything else is forgotten. I shovel fluffy, buttery goodness into my mouth, not caring how unladylike it looks.

CC watches intently. I offer him a bit of toast. He sniffs it then goes back to watching. Instead of an official taste tester, I have an official food sniffer. If he'd made that little scrunchy face, I'd know not to eat it, so it must be okay for me, just not enticing enough for him. The plate licked clean, Nyssa replaces it with a cup and I lift it to my nose reveling in the intoxicating aroma.

The light pounding on the door can only be Dara. *Since when does she knock?* Fear wriggles it's ugly little self inside me as I remember how just the sight of her triggered my little mishap. The doorknob jiggles and I look at Royd his brow wrinkling as he studies me.

"You can't keep her out forever," says Rey. "Eventually she'll grow impatient and just come in. She didn't mean to cause any harm, but she's worried about you."

I nod, rubbing my hands up and down my arms.

"Cold again?" he asks, moving to the edge of his chair.

I shake my head and drop my hands.

"Cat got your tongue?" A half–assed smile on his face as he wags a finger at CC "Give it back."

"No, just nervous." A poor attempt at a reassuring smile, but I try just the same.

He nods and Nyssa opens the door.

"Come join the party, Dara."

A less than perfect Dara steps in. Ouch, did I do that to her? Nyssa and Rey looked tired and a little bedraggled, but Dara looks like she's been run through the wringer.

"How are you feeling?" she asks, standing next to the door, fingers just inches from the knob.

Damn, if I answer wrong, she's going to bolt. "I'm fine, but you look like shit." I wrinkle my nose, and then punctuate it with a grin.

"Long night, day and night again." Her smile strained as she stares at me, as if she can assess my health, mental, or otherwise with just a look.

"Don't just stand there, you're making me nervous." I nod in Rey's direction. "Like he said, come join the party."

Her shoulders drop to a normal level and her

smile widens, then fades as she perches on the arm of the couch.

"Well, now that the whole family is here, let's get down to business," says Rey, doing his best impression of Brando. Trust me. It sucks. He sounds more like one of the Muppets, the old geezers in the theater box, to be exact.

Nyssa rocks with laughter on the arm of his chair, planting a tiny fist against his shoulder.

"Ow," he says, rubbing the offended spot, then pretends to glare at us. "Hey, she hits pretty hard for a teeny, tiny thing."

Things are looking normal for the moment. Normal is exactly what I need right now, or as normal as this group can be. True to form, our little breather is blown all to hel when the downstairs buzzer sounds.

Chapter 32

Dara punches the intercom button, "Yes?"

"Hello First Arrow, is Miss Fey available?" With that greeting, the owner of the voice can belong to only one person. Var Royd.

Nyssa frowns and Rey leans toward me. "What the hell did that mean?"

"You got me, but one of these days I'm going to find out."

"You've heard it before? From *him* I take it?"

I nod, watching Dara's barely controlled anger as she presses the button again.

"What do you want, *Sun King*?"

Whoa, that's what The Sisters had called him. Obviously, Dara knows much more than she's let on. Maybe Einen was right.

"I assume it is evident I wish to speak with Miss Fey."

Now Rey jumps up and as Dara presses the button he says, "You know what they say about assuming things. It makes an ass out of you and me."

It earns him a grin from Dara.

"Okay, enough with the taunting. Let's see

what he has to say." I get up and move to the intercom. "What do you want, Mr. Royd?"

"It would be wiser to invite me in, Miss Fey."

"Fine." Ignoring the protests of my companions, I buzz him in and return to the couch.

He doesn't even bother to knock, motioning for someone to wait in the hall as he steps into the room.

"It seems there was another attack last evening." Royd's eye contact and the unspoken message it holds is a little too much for me to handle right now.

"Let me guess." I lay my head against the back of the couch, closing my eyes. "I'm the prime suspect."

There's no need to open them. I can feel my companions' unspoken responses—tension and fear infused with outrage.

"But Keely was here all night, we know that."

"Yes, my little nixie, but the NTF is not inclined to believe her friends."

"You can verify it," says Dara, something in her voice hints at things she knows, but has not shared.

Something to do with this whole *Sun King*, *First Arrow* bullshit, would be my guess. Which I'm going to figure out, it would just be easier if she shared.

"I only just arrived."

"Yet your dogs have kept watch, reported to

you." Dara's tone dangerously soft, something I recognize, but I'm not sure Royd will.

I open my eyes and wish I'd kept them closed. Dara's freakishly catlike eyes narrow as she stares him down. The tiny slit of their pupils quickly expand nearly blotting golden irises, very much like CC before he pounces on unsuspecting prey. I swear that if she had a tail, it'd be twitching.

Royd either doesn't notice, or chooses not to. His tone laced with cruel coyness. "There are also reporters and others watching, First Arrow."

Her hands ball into white knuckled fists and lips twist, baring her fangs in all their pointy glory.

Doesn't he know how dangerous it is to provoke a vamp? Geez, does all that money make him think he's impervious, or is he just stupid?

"Enough." I jump between them, a hand held out in either direction. "I'm not in the mood for a pissing match."

Something between a hiss and growl emanates from Dara's direction and Royd's grin widens.

"I said enough!"

Everyone pulls back as I look at them. Fear and confusion bitch slap me and my vision darkens. Dara slowly backs away from me. Rey and Nyssa slink in behind her, eyeing the door. I know I don't get mad very often, but I don't think it's that terrifying.

Royd's expression is neutral, almost blasé, and

kind of insultiting considering how the others are reacting. "Reign in your anger, Schattenkind."

His tone only adds to my frustration. My skin becomes a unitard several sizes too small, squeezing painfully. With the lack of circulation comes an incessant itch, like a bad case of psoriasis that you want to scratch. To hel with scratch. You want to shred the offending virus from your skin.

"Schattenkind." His tone is soft, but the grasp on my wrists, not so much.

He hides it well, but I can see agitation through the cracks in his calm veneer. I can also see the bloody trails my nails left along my arms, but they still itch and I fight his hold.

"Control them."

"Who?"

"The shadows, Schattenkind."

All the heat drains from my body and my teeth begin to chatter as I look around the room. Shadows stretch from every corner, sliding across the floor and walls converging on the huddled group of my friends.

"How? I'm not doing this."

"Yes, you are. Now disperse them."

I hear the door open, unable to see it behind the curtain of darkness. A blinding spot of light appears in the shadowy cage containing the others.

"Milord," yells Brand.

The shadowy film that coats everything writhes

with a life of its own, deepening to near pitch black. Licking my lips I take a jagged breath and squeeze my eyes shut, wishing the shadows away. No such luck, the once blinding light, now no brighter than a child's nightlight, the only sign they are still there.

"I can't. I don't know how."

Royd drops my hands pushing me toward a chair as he turns. "Cover your eyes," he says over his shoulder.

I drop my chin to my chest and squeeze my eyes shut, bringing my hands up to cover them. The weight of yet another failure pushes me further into the chair.

The warmth of a roaring fire in winter. The heat of a summer day. The melting force of a blowtorch. The pain of, this is what it must feel like in the center of the sun. Light builds behind my covered eyes matching the intensity of the heat, until spots dance across the lids. Huddling in on myself, I want to scream, or stop, drop and roll, maybe both. Coherent thought is not exactly high on the list of priorities. Neither is following directions. I open my eyes and my jaw drops.

White–hot light fills the room, the receding shadows nearly dispersed. A floating sword bathed in a golden glow. Light and shadows refract against a body kneeling in front of the group. My ears ring with the fearful cry of a fox. A Nyssa–sized bubble of undulating water. Most shocking of all, there's nothing to mark the place where Dara stood, except a few stray scraps of flaming cloth. Dara. She can't take this kind of light. Oh gods, I've killed her!

Ears ringing, I can't hear myself think let alone scream, but Royd looks back at me. His eyes two radiant orbs, mini suns set in a blazingly beautiful face. "I told you to cover your eyes!"

"Dara!" I point to what's left.

I just sit there, mouth hanging open as he turns away.

The shadows have receded back into the corners of the room, smoking wisps of darkness. The light dims back to a normal 60-watt level, and Royd is shaking me until my brains rattle.

"I told you to cover your eyes, you little fool." The concern on his face more than his harsh words brings me out of my stupor.

"Sorry," I mutter, lame, but I can't come up with anything better. He pulls me into his embrace. I shiver as his breath blows the hair away from my ear.

"Do you not know it is dangerous to look into the sun?"

I pull back a little—okay, a lot—confused. He laughs, hugging me once more before turning to the others.

"What was that?" Nyssa stands in a puddle of

water. I swear the fox is laughing as he looks at it, if Rey were in human form potty jokes would abound. I hope she has the forethought to come up with some rebounds about the stench of burning fur.

The walking shield turns out to be that cool taste of winter I'd sampled outside Atramentous. His animosity toward me downright chilling.

Brand has sheathed his sword, something I'm personally grateful for, considering the intensity of the anger I feel directed at me.

His Shield will protect and his Sword will cut. A shiver rides along my spine.

"I see everyone survived virtually unscathed."

As the words leave his lips, my tears escape. "Not everyone," I manage between hiccuping sobs. Slowly everyone turns toward the smoldering remains of cloth and ashes where Dara stood.

Royd's laughter is a slap in the face of my grief and I return it, my palm connecting with the side of his face.

Brand and his friend step toward me, but he waves them away. The menace in his eyes and grasp on my wrist contradict the smile gracing those lush lips.

"First Arrow, would you reveal yourself and put Miss Fey's fear to rest?"

Dara enters from the hall leading to the other rooms. Most of her clothing still intact, but any exposed flesh sports a painful looking sunburn.

The instinct to rush over and hug her is flattened by the rigidness of her frame. Her fingers clench, unfurl and clench again as blank eyes stare at me from under scorched bangs.

"As you can see, your vampire is virtually unscathed, Miss Fey."

Dara takes a step toward him and stops as Brand and his friend move between them.

"In answer to your question, my little Nixie; what you felt was a taste of what Miss Fey is capable of."

Nyssa shivers as she stares at me.

Great. Just when I thought my friends couldn't be any more afraid of me, Royd tosses another log on the fire.

"I. Didn't. Do. Anything."

"Control your anger, Schattenkind, or we will have a repeat."

I flop back in the chair in a fit of not–so–righteous anger.

"What about the light and heat?" asks Nyssa.

I'd like to know that too, but Royd just smiles. Looking at Dara, I can practically see the wheels spinning as she studies him. Going to have to pump her for info later, that is, if she even wants to be around me after Royd nearly roasted her.

Royd and his posse huddle together. I want to approach Dara, but I can tell she's trying to listen in and I'm a little afraid of what kind of reaction

I'll receive. Nyssa keeps watching me from the corner of her eye. Rey cocks his head to one side and wags his tail when I look at him, but doesn't come within reach.

Maybe it's best I just sit here and let them come to me. After all, we just found out I can summon shadows. Shadows that can kill. Guess it explains why Royd keeps calling me Shadow Child. It kind of tops the freaky scale. Couple that with my magnetic attraction with dead things and it completely blows the scale. Can life suck anymore? You bet it can.

Chapter 33

The crowd outside my building has intensified with the discovery of another victim. Royd's, I mean my lawyer, stands on the steps in all his dramatic brilliance. Explaining how I couldn't possibly have perpetrated the crime. I had been at home and had witnesses, including the crowd themselves, but it doesn't seem to soothe the savage beasts.

Curled up on the couch, my grandmother's afghan wrapped around me, I've always felt calm with the blanket near and even calmer with it draped around me. Maybe she wove some sort of spell into it. Don't care. I'm just plain worn out. I don't even care what the others are chattering away about I just want to sleep.

Bits of the conversation float my way along with glares from Teiran Rand. Snickering brings an even nastier look, but I can't help it. Come on, it's funny—Rand, Brand—and I'm too tired to care. What's not funny is how beautiful he is, even when he's sneering at me.

Even though I'm tired, I appreciate the candy store in my living room, maybe a little too much. Alric, sticky sweet honey that you want to drizzle on everything. Teiran, white chocolate and peppermint, smooth and cool on the tongue. Rey, a sweet candy shell with an even sweeter surprise inside. And Var Royd, one of those mystery gumballs where you don't know if you're going to get sweet, or sour.

I'm not tired anymore, but hungry and not for food. Every male in the room whets that appetite and the burning need between my legs blinds me to the fact that none of them are on the menu.

I try to pick just one. *What about a combo platter? Oh, hel, just take them all.* I need to leave the room and quickly.

Flinging the afghan aside, I bolt for the bathroom, slam the door behind me and click the locks into place. Sitting on the edge of the tub, I rest my head in my hands, pictures of naked me and naked them floating behind my lids. Every nerve is on alert and the slightest movement causes an intoxicating sensation of pain mingled with pleasure across my skin.

"What's happening to me?" I whisper, tears of pain and frustration to spilling. As if this whole shadow, dead thing isn't enough, I have to morph into super slut.

I flip on the water and strip down, tossing my wet panties against the wall. Step under the icy stream and stand there willing the water to wash away the thoughts, pull the heat of desire away.

The forceful spray stings my skin and I turn my back, shielding already taut nipples, now painfully rock hard. Whoever said cold showers were the answer should be shot. It's only making it worse. Shutting off the water, I huddle in the tub. Shivering, fighting the desire to call to any, or all males present. A moan is ripped from me picturing taking each of them, or better yet all of them at once. Four sets of hands, lips, tongues... *Gods, stop it!*

Even my own hands rebel. I pull them away from my breasts, lacing my fingers into my hair, clutching my head. Flesh throbs similar to my calling the shadows, but without the itch, this time with an erotic caress. So tired. If I could just fall asleep.

Dragging myself from the tub, I grab my robe. As the fabric drags over sensitive skin, I bite my lower lip until the metallic saltiness of blood touches my tongue. Forcing my feet across the floor, I make it to the bedroom, waving off the questions that follow me.

Door closed, locks engaged, I fall into bed. Tears flow freely as I give in, letting the sensations ravage my body. Screams minimized to whimpers, buried in my pillow. All I want is release. Darkness hovers, creeping across the room. I'm not sure if they are conjured shadows, or if I'm near passing out. I vote for passing out and let the darkness consume me.

♴♴♴♴

"Allow me to heal what ails you." I feel the warmth of Einen's breath as it sends shivers of pleasure through me. His hips grind against me, promising even more delights.

"Yes. Please."

He takes a nipple between his lips again. The veracity of his sucking power promises a huge hickey later, but do I care? Nope. With how good it feels he can suck all he wants as long as he—oh yeah, shares with the other one. My fingers tangle in hair the color of white gold, pulling that magnificent mouth closer. That overly skilled mouth moves between my breasts and down, fingers releasing my sloppily-tied belt.

"Gods," I whisper as he kneels before me, tongue teasing my belly button.

His explorations move across my stomach, lips and teeth nibbling at my hip bone. My knees buckle and gently he helps lower me to the ground until we are face-to-face, or as face-to-face as we can be. The top of my head rests just under his chin, and I'm not a short girl, standing five ten barefoot. My line of sight hits approximately at his Adam's apple, which raises and lowers as I press myself against him.

Liking the response, I slide my hands down

his chest until they rest on his hips pulling them tightly against me. If the hard bulge I'm feeling against my stomach is any indication, I'd have to say he likes it as much as I do.

Shaky fingers—not sure, if it's need, or nervousness—pluck his shirt from his waistband. He generously assists me by removing it himself and I stare in awe at a smooth, luminous bare skin. Hesitantly, I brush the cool satin planes of his chest, feeling the rumble of a growl beneath my fingers.

Grasping my arms, he yanks me toward him, lowering his face until I'm looking directly into his eyes. Those pale silvery eyes are black, not just an expansion of the pupil, but the entire eye.

Chapter 34

Deep meditative breaths slow the pulse, relax the muscles. Slowly my fingers unfurl, releasing the sheets. The thumping in my chest goes from car stereo base to boom box and finally handheld radio. That was some ridiculous dream. It had to have been brought on by my overactive hormones. Hormones so out of whack that I'm having sex—okay, foreplay—with an imaginary childhood friend. Who, as it turns out, isn't so imaginary.

The Sisters have never been entirely truthful with me about my past, or my future for that matter. I've always just assumed things. Like my parents' disappearance, my heritage in general, or that they really are my family in the traditional sense. I don't resemble any of them. Yeah, the fact that I have at least some elven blood makes a world of difference, but still. Recent incidents have brought a lot of this into question.

I don't have time for a face-to-face confrontation and the thought of the three of them on speakerphone makes my head ache. I'll never get a straight answer anyway.

Then there's Royd. Everything he's said and

done. Sure, he saved my butt on a couple of occasions, but I have to ask, what's in it for him? It's creepy that he shows up when I'm in trouble, or sends his lawyer. Not to mention the pull he has over me, to go from hating—or perceived hate brought on by hearsay and the media—to wanting to have sex with him.

That brings up a whole new subject. My behavior. I can't go on forever blaming everything on my new Talents, no matter how much as I'd like to. It also brings up the question of why they decided to manifest now. Why not earlier in life? Like childhood, when I could have been taught how to control them. Replaying the conversation with The Sisters I start to wonder. Is it possible I've been deceived yet again?

"Keely, Lorelei will be here soon."

"Oh crap," I mutter, looking at the clock. I've got about ten minutes before Lorelei is banging at the door instead of Rey. "Be there in a minute."

Flinging aside the sheets, the cat howls in protest as he tumbles across the bed.

"Sorry, bud." I hustle my ass to the bathroom for a quick makeover.

Feeling semi–functional, I head to the kitchen, wiggle my fingers at my houseguests—thankfully, the tantalizing trio are gone, Royd and his entourage are the last thing I wanted to see—grab a cup of caffeine and head to the salon.

"So, you're still alive," says Lorelei as I open the door enough for her to get in then slam the lock home before anyone pushes in behind her.

"If you can call it that."

She drops her purse at my station and follows me to the shampoo bowls.

"What no Nyssa tonight? Am I the happy recipient of a Keely's Magical Fingers Shampoo?"

I laugh piling her hair into the basin and wetting it down. "Yep, complete with scalp massage."

"Damn, a girl could get used to this." She practically purrs. "Maybe you should get in trouble everyday so I can have you all to myself."

"Funny." I dangle the hose dangerously close to her hairline. She giggles as a fine spray of water coats her face.

"You know what I mean." She relaxes back and closes her eyes as I begin scrubbing.

I've always stood by the idea that a good shampoo is the base for a return clientele. Some people forget this business is all about the client. A good shampoo and scalp massage is the first step to putting them at ease. If you don't have that basic skill down you don't have any business picking up the tools. I may be talented with the shears, but my shampoos kept them coming back in the beginning of my career.

"Over already? Can't you just do that a little longer?"

"Not unless you either want to be late for work, or go with wet hair."

Her bottom lip juts out as I lift her head wrapping a towel around her hair.

"Fine, be that way."

I laugh, stepping behind the chair as she slouches down so I can roll the top of her head.

"You ever going to let me cut any more than just the ends off this stuff, Godiva?"

"Funny you bring that up, I was thinking about asking you to bob it to my chin after the party."

"Wow, that's pretty drastic. Sure you're ready for that?"

"Why not? It's not like you can't put it back if I hate it that much."

"True."

It's now, or never, might as well ask her.

"About the party..."

The chair swings around, nearly pulling the roller from the half–wound section. "Oh hel no, you are *not* canceling on me."

"I wasn't going to cancel." I swing the chair back. "I just wasn't sure you still want me there."

"Of course I want you there. Why wouldn't I?"

"What about your other guests, won't they...um...be upset the supposed Collector is there?"

"Who cares what they say and if they don't like it they can leave. I just hope they can swim. You haven't heard from your receptionist, have you?"

I shake my head. In all the excitement, I'd forgotten the missing Jenny. Makes me a great friend, huh?

The last roller tucked into place, I move her under the dryer and grab the manicure table.

"I repeat my earlier surprise and appreciation," she says with a grin as she points to her favorite polish. Like I needed a clue. She leans back and closes her eyes as I slowly work through the steps.

It's nice to be back in the salon, surrounded by familiar smells and sights, even if the place is empty. Even nicer is the leisurely pace I'm allowed to take, giving my one and only client my full attention.

I suppose I should be bitter about this whole mess, but some small part of me isn't. The experience has made me appreciate everything and everybody I have in my life. I know it sounds like a cheesy, Hallmark moment, but it's true. Not that I'll ever admit it out loud.

Now if I could only sort out my new rebellious and unwanted Talents and the secrets that lie behind the scenes. All of which seem to be tied to me in some way, from Royd's interest to Dara and The Sister's omissions. I can almost bet Rey and Nys are also keeping things from me. Oh well, not much I can do about it and we've already proven bad things can happen when I get upset. That thought just leads to my dream buddy and

Vereinen's world is not one I want to experience right now, let alone drag Lorelei along for the ride. If that's even possible, but why chance it?

Finishing the last nail with topcoat, I tighten the lid and stand to check her hair. Not quite done. She turns down the offer of a beverage, or magazine and closes her eyes as I replace the hood. I take the time to straighten up my station, then peek around the corner to reception. Outside the reporters hover around the door like the vultures they are, maybe I should sneak her out through Dara's basement entrance. Not that she'll let me. Lorelei loves to flaunt what she's got.

That voice can influence anyone, or anything with the potential to hear. It's been said she's influenced plants to grow. Now *that* is what I call a useful Talent, unlike the ability to call life–sucking shadows to life. Well, at least I can make hair and nails grow, very useful in my line of work. On that cheerful note, I wander back and grab a soda.

Interestingly enough, I'm not the only one in the break room.

Chapter 35

A scrawny figure in dirty hooker wear is scavenging through the fridge. When I flip on the light, she bangs her head and turns a frightened, tear–stained face toward me.

"Jenny? Oh my gods, I've been so worried." I move toward her and she backs away shaking her head.

"Don't come near me. I shouldn't have come here."

"Of course you should have. Are you in trouble? What can I do to help?"

"I'm sorry, Keely, so sorry."

She backs around the table and I stupidly follow her. Shaking her head, hands held out in front of her she makes it all the way around to the door and darts out. Talk about not all brain cells firing, I should have stayed at the door. Chasing her out and down the hall, she disappears down Dara's stairs. I hear her tumble down them, grunting with pain as she gets back up and struggles to the outside door. The apartment door opens just in time for me to run smack into Dara, and Jenny slips outside.

"Damn."

"What's going on?"

"Jenny," I say, between pants, definitely time to get my butt back on the treadmill.

"She was here?"

"In the break room. Gone." I point to the door.

She looks at the door. If looks could kill it would be deader than its knob. It's still light outside so there's no way she can make chase. "Damn."

"Already said that."

"At least we know she is still alive."

I nod. "Gotta get back to Lorelei." So not looking forward to taking those steps again.

"I will let the others know."

"Okay," I say, already headed back up the stairs. "Thanks."

Lorelei's already sitting in my chair fingering the rollers. "I get it; you did all the extras and expect me to take out these." Her grin flips as she studies my face. "What happened?"

I take a deep breath, then slowly let it out, rolling my head from side to side before taking out the curlers. "I found Jenny in the break room."

"Really?"

"Yeah, she ran like a rabbit and I stupidly thought I could catch her."

"I wonder why she was skulking around."

I don't bother answering, shielding her eyes as I mist her hair with spray.

"No clue. I just wish she would let us help her."
I set the can down.

Giving her hair a final fluff, she looks at me in the mirror. "Some people don't want to be helped."

I nod.

"And it's not your job to help everyone. As soon as you realize that, you'll sleep better." She winks, flipping a wad of money on the vanity before heading to the door.

I close and lock it behind her, catching a glimpse of the enamored crowd outside before turning away. She's right, of course, but I still feel responsible for Jenny.

❁❁❁❁❁

Back upstairs, my apartment is in turmoil. The three of them shouting about what should be done about Jenny, each with varying opinions. Dara's all for waiting until full dark and tracking her down. Rey agrees, but not with the same vengeance. I have no idea why Dara is so upset about this, unless it's the violation of her personal space. I can relate, but as Nys points out, it's Jenny and she obviously needs our help. My getting involved with the discussion won't help anyone, but the more they yell, the more agitated I get.

"Stop," I say softly. Too softly, because they keep on going, or maybe they are ignoring me as usual, so I repeat it a little louder. Still nothing. My skin feels too tight. There's a rustling in my ears and an irritating itch slowly progresses along my flesh.

"Stop!"

And they do. Amazing. But the looks on their faces isn't one I want to inspire. Fear. Even Dara's typical composure laced with it.

"Her eyes," whispers Nyssa.

I stare at her and she looks away. "What's wrong with my eyes?"

"N–nothing."

"They've changed Keely, they're black," says Rey quietly.

"What, like my pupils are dilated?" No one owns snippy like I do right now.

"No," he shakes his head and nods to the mirror. "Like everything. Nothing, but black."

I turn to the mirror. No wonder they're scared, I am too. A startlingly white face stares back at me, fingers brush against luminous skin. It glows, not with the sun—like light Royd projects, but softer, more like moonlight. My eyes are black, no white, no iris, or pupil, just blackness. Like Vereinen's. The reflection becomes hazy and I fall into that blackness.

Chapter 36

Who put glitter on my ceiling? When did I get shag carpet and why is it damp? My fingers dig in and I feel something push up under my nails. Eww, someone spilled something disgusting. Somehow, I've fallen into the 70's complete with shag carpet and disco–effect ceiling. To make an already weird situation weirder, everything is in black and white.

The sounds of every cricket, owl and other night dweller are louder, more distinct. Like someone flipped the switch on the city, removing all its familiar white noise.

It finally dawns on me the shimmering orb above isn't a ceiling lamp, but the moon. That means this nasty carpet is grass and the gunk under my nails is dirt. I'm outside which explains the disco ceiling. Stars. What a relief, but how did I end up outside?

Slowly I push myself into a sitting position, my body aching with each movement. Head throbbing until I can almost swear the stars are coming from behind my eyelids.

Trees dot the landscape and I smell a hint of roses. Maybe a garden nearby? But definitely not the city. A park? Someone's backyard? Oh hel. Pinching the bridge of my nose, I take a deep breath and slowly let it out. Maybe if I click my heels three times and wish really, really hard I'll get to go back home.

Gentle hands brush against my shoulders, pulling me back against a firm body and for a moment, I relax as arms wrap around me. Must be Rey. I'm having one of my episodes.

I remember them yelling and me wanting them to stop. My skin felt too tight, it couldn't contain my body, wanted to burst. Then fear when they finally looked at me. There was a stranger in the mirror with luminous skin, kind of like that moon overhead, and blacked out eyes. Pitch black then nothing until the simulated shag under my fingers.

"I see you have taken the time to visit." Warm breath rides across the back of my neck, lips brushing with each word.

Um...okay, not Rey. I look down at the pale hands on my arms, nearly a match. Vereinen. Damn, that means I'm in dreamland again.

"It wasn't by choice, so don't let it go to your head."

His laughter echoes all the way down my spine in a very disturbing way. Not unpleasant, which makes it even more disturbing.

"Dumb question, but where am I?"

He laughs again, the tingling effect on my body

doubles. "My gardens, would you like to see them?"

"Sure." Anything to keep him from touching me, knowing all too well where that would lead.

He helps me up, wrapping my hand around the crook of his arm. So much for that idea. We walk at a leisurely pace. I get the feeling it's less because of my infirmity and more because that's just how he does things. Slow and precise.

"Are you chilled?" A sly smile plays at his lips.

I shake my head, not cold, just imagining what else he might do at a leisurely pace. No way am I putting that into words. I've got enough problems.

A heady sweetness floats around me as we walk the path through his garden. I can distinguish roses and lily of the valley, but the others are lost on me. The flowers turned shades of silver grey and black by the moon, a photographer's dream. When we come to a bench, he motions for me to sit and lowers himself beside me.

"So what brings you to my realm?"

I explain the yelling, my anger and the changes to my appearance.

He nods thoughtfully, intent on my every word.

"The angrier I got, the more my skin itched and tightened, like it would explode any second. The fear on their faces only made me angrier until I looked in the mirror. My eyes..." I shake my head, unable to describe what I saw without shivering.

He drapes an arm around me, pulling me

closer. "Your Talents were attempting to break free," he whispers against the top of my head.

I sigh, leaning into him, knowing he's right.

"Had those that bound your Talent let it develop as nature decreed there would not be such violence to your body now."

I pull away and look at him. "You're saying someone put some sort of block on me?"

He nods. "Possibly out of what they considered love, but more likely out of fear. Foolish, to say the least, but whoever did it must have been very powerful to contain it this long."

My thoughts go to The Sisters. Are they powerful enough to pull off something like this? Did they have help? Royd maybe? Well-meaning, or not, it opens a whole can of worms.

"But what about my ability to grow hair and nails? Why wasn't that blocked?"

He shrugs. "It is possible that small portion of your Talent leaked around the block."

"Or maybe they didn't want to leave me Talentless?"

"It is a possibility, but my thoughts would be that they were only interested in containing the destructive nature of your Talent and protecting you. By allowing that small portion to remain unfettered, it left an opening, a drain. Think of it as a river feeding a stream, block that stream and the river would overflow, leading to destruction."

Shivers race along my skin, leaving a hot, cold trail of gooseflesh.

"If you do not learn some control, it will eventually destroy you, tearing you apart from the inside."

"I don't want it, never did. I just want them to go back to what they were. Can you put it back? The block?"

"No, I fear it would do far more damage. There is no turning back."

I can't help the disappointment and know it shows when he gives my shoulders a brief squeeze.

"I could help you."

"Help me? How?"

"Teach you how to control your Talent, how to use it."

Okay, call me crazy for even considering—I just might be in the near future if this keeps up—but it makes sense. Who else would know how to control and use these Talents? Duh, the only other shadow elf.

Since he's in an answering mood, I decide to go no holds barred. The man has had his hands, as well as other things, on me so why be embarrassed? "Don't suppose my...uh...increased libido has anything to do with this rising Talent."

To his credit, he doesn't laugh. His lips twitch, but he doesn't laugh. "Your body is going through changes you should have encountered years ago. I suppose this increase, as you call it, is a side effect."

Freakin' great! I'm going through puberty again. Just what I need right now, my body thinking I'm a boy–crazed teen.

"Is it all males, or of certain heritages?"

"I find *most* men attractive, but I'm most drawn to döck and liosâlfar." A bit of an exaggeration considering I've only met one of each and I don't know what the hel Royd is. "I assumed it had something to do with my half–breed heritage."

He laughs. "There is nothing half–breed about you, Little Queen. You are full blooded âlfar, born of one döckâlfar and one liosâlfar."

You've got to be kidding me, I'm a freakin' full–blooded elf. That would mean The Sisters aren't only lying to me, but also not my *real* family. "Go on," I say, not wanting to deal with those thoughts right now.

"Like calls to like. Dark and light are the two halves that make you what you are—each deliciously enticing in its own right, but never enough. Tell me you do not feel the veil of power and need that hangs between us?"

I look away, staring at my hands in my lap.

"I will take that as merely a feminine refusal to answer. We both know you are not chaste. You, yourself have admitted as much. If you wish answers, then give me the respect of not hiding behind pretenses."

My jaw tightens and I lift my head a little higher.

"There is no need to get angry, I did not intend insult."

I look away, knowing he's right—especially after our last encounter—but being called a whore still stings, no matter how it was intended. I nod my head and he places his fingers under my chin, lifting it until we are eye to eye.

"There is also no need for embarrassment. This is something neither of us can fight. Trust me, I have tried." He grabs my hands, pulling me to my feet. "Do all women in your world wear such decadent garments? They leave very little to the imagination."

I stand silently as he circles me, stopping behind, his breath hot against my skin. Lips stroking that sweet spot where neck meets shoulder. One strap of the skimpy, lace tank slips down, leaving plenty of room for exploration. My hands ball into fists as his caress trails from shoulder to wrist.

"Why do you try to deny the attraction between us?" Teeth graze the lobe of my ear. Hands circle my waist, deftly moving the thin shirt until there's skin on skin contact, before resting on my hips.

"Can you deny what you feel?" One hand moves from waist to belly and then lower. "Deep inside here?" It trails up the length of my torso until it rests it between my breasts. "Or here?"

I'm not sure what I feel, there may be something to what he says, but mostly I just feel lust.

"You were made for me, my dream come to life. A precious gift."

His words fling me onto the dance floor, another telling me I'm his dream. The vision dissipates as a hand skims down my thigh, his fingers playing with the hem of my miniskirt.

"You do not need to answer aloud." His hand slips between my legs. "Your body tells me everything I need to know."

It's then I realize I don't have anything on underneath. Any psychiatrist would tell me it's because I feel naked due to the circumstances of my life. I'd tell them it's my current circumstances making me want to get naked.

"Is it time to unwrap my present?"

Chapter 37

A strangled whimper escapes and he laughs stepping in front of me. "I'll take that as a yes."

He grasps the delicate fabric at my waist and I lift my arms, letting him slip it over my head. It flutters to the ground, the skirt following in a circle at my feet. Kneeling, he slides the sandals from my feet, tossing them aside.

Fear unfolds as his gaze roves over my body, then embarrassment as I remember his statement about breast size. Instinctively, I wrap my arms around myself. He stands and gently removes my makeshift shield, holding my arms out at my sides.

"My beautiful, little queen."

The ardent praise in his eyes triggers something I've never felt before, a new way of looking at my scrawny, ungainly body. I'm as beautiful as he claims. *Fool*, whispers that inner voice, but I push it away as he pulls me into his arms. This feels—right.

The garden disappears and I lay on a huge bed, firelight casting shadows over the curtains surrounding it, one shadow in particular drawing my attention. The clothing drops from his slender form, so like my own, with one large difference.

I shiver in anticipation as his silhouette turns to the side and his—I guess they're called trousers, drop to the floor.

Fool, screams that voice again. This feels so right, so perfect. Speaking of perfect, I gasp as he parts the curtains and climbs onto the bed. My desire to touch and be touched by anyone else is blown away. If I were an Un I'd swear I had the fever.

Vereinen lays propped on his side just staring at me, those features I found so harsh and sharp before, now softened, beautiful. His hand rests across my hip, mine against his cheek, we lay there like two marble statues perfectly posed. I don't know if I drew him down, or he moved of his own accord, but our lips meet. The kiss is water to my parched mouth. I want to drown as it deepens, until every part of me is drenched.

He breaks the kiss, my hand still locked behind his head. I should feel fear when those black eyes stare at me, but I only feel need. He smiles, thumb gliding across my cheekbone. I know my own eyes match that darkness.

The room grows dim, tendrils of darkness flitter across my skin. He tilts his head back, eyes closed, lips parted and I know I'm not the only one feeling it. Our Talents, feeding from, or into, our mounting passion. When he opens his eyes, they're flecked with tiny sparks of light and he buries his head against my chest. The warmth of his breath teases my nipple, sending a wave of pleasure through me. I feel him laugh and groan in response, my body undulating under his.

"Don't tease."

"I never tease." He captures my nipple between his teeth, tongue flicking across delicate nerve endings and I whimper.

My hand slides down his stomach, trapped in a vice before reaching its goal.

"Do not be so impatient."

Gently he takes my other hand and presses his lips against my palms before extending them above my head.

"Forget the light," he says, taking my hand in his. "Forget the dark; there are only shades of grey, my Shadow Queen." Tilting my head back, I see a silken scarf threaded through the headboard. He gently wraps one end around each of my wrists, looping the ends into my palms.

"And with me, you will always have a choice. No one will force you to say, or do anything you do not wish to do." He closes my fingers around the scarf, escape within my grasp.

He backs down the length of me on all fours, like some predatory cat, hair a curtain of sensation against my skin, stopping at my toes. Hands on my ankles gently spread my legs and that curtain retraces its journey, this time stopping just below the waist. Fingers stroke the insides of my thighs and that whimpering noise I struggle to squelch slips out, ignoring any command I try.

Laughter tickles my pelvis. "Why do you attempt to fight? Give in to your desires. Enjoy them. There is no penalty."

Even if I had an answer, I can't voice it. Coherent thought processes are not high on my list right now.

His hands slide under my legs, lifting, draping them over his shoulders. Those silken hands move up the back of my thighs until my lower cheeks rest in his palms. I suck in my breath and hold it as his smile disappears and his mouth makes full contact.

"Let go," he whispers against me.

And heavens help me, I do. I scream until my throat is raw and a haze descends across my eyes. But I'm not done and neither—thank the gods—is he. His tongue moves against me and all I can do is go back to whimpering, my throat too damn sore. Then that magical tongue slips inside me. My hips buck and attempt to twist, but he grabs them, holding steady. The haze thickens and my skin grows tight as sensations build.

No, echoes in my ears as blackness descends once again.

Chapter 38

Screaming, I thud against something soft. Voices murmur around me, distorted by the buzzing in my ears. The muscles in my arms and legs are killing me. I open one eye and then the other. My legs are bent at the knee, sticking up in the air. Arms extended above my head and hands clutching at nothing.

What the...? Slowly I lower my legs onto what I realize is *my* bed and push myself upward. And those voices in my head? They belong to those surrounding me.

"Wow, girl," says Nyssa, "that was some dream."

Rey wiggles his brow. "Was all that screaming passion, or pain?"

I just stare at them, not comprehending one word.

"You don't remember?" Rey's teasing turns to concern. "We were arguing about Jenny and you got pissed, your eyes turned all black, and then you passed out?"

"Don't talk to me like a child." My voice sounds like three packs a day since birth.

He moves away from me and I'm instantly

sorry. "I didn't mean—"

He waves it off and gets up. "No worries, I just thought you might like a glass of water."

Nyssa stays by the edge of the bed. Nibbling her lower lip and shooting sideways glances toward the door. While she's occupied contemplating slipping away, I take stock of the situation.

Mini and tank in place not naked, that's a plus. The whole thing must have been a dream. Vivid, erotic, but still a dream. No matter what Einen claims. But what if he's right? What if I did slip over the border? Better yet, what if he really can help me learn some control?

More muffled voices from the other room signals Rey's return with the promised water. I slurp it down like a desert survivor.

If Einen's right about the possibility of my Talent ripping me apart, this passing out thing might be a protective mechanism. Maybe it has something to do with his claims of border hopping. Either way it's an inconvenience, but better than attack of the killer shadows.

Nyssa has joined Rey in observing me at the foot of the bed. Nothing like being considered a freak of nature by others in the same category. Gingerly, I move myself off the bed, no need to worry about them following me to the living room.

I nod to Dara, hovering by the front door. Thankfully, someone was smart enough to make coffee. Grabbing a cup, I head over to the window. May as well check the circus below.

Mourning doves cluster on the outcroppings of the building and windowsills. When I was a child, I thought my constant companions were called morning doves and that was the reason they sounded so sad. I could relate, not being a morning person. Later, I learned it was mourning and as much as I love my little friends, it kind of creeps me out that they continue to hang around.

Across the street, Alric stands at one end of the block, Teiran at the other within sight of my building. Continuing their surveillance, NTF agents stand out in their black suits. The crowd below shouts my name. Subtract the not–so–flattering adjectives and it would be exhilarating. Like a monarch addressing her subjects. Letting the curtains drop before someone catches a glimpse of me, I turn to the room.

"Can someone fill me in on what I missed during my forced nap? Did anyone find Jenny?" I plant myself on the couch next to Rey.

"Nope, no one else saw her, it's like she just disappeared after she got out the door. Probably skittered off into the crowds of morons hanging around outside."

I nod. She wasn't the one they were waiting to get a glimpse of, or better yet get their hands on. That would be me. It doesn't matter that I'm not

The Collector, or that the attacks have ceased. That little fact actually plays into the public perception that I am what they think. Sick, but I almost wish he would attack again while I'm under surveillance.

Rey is the only one who's said more than one word to me. Makes a girl wonder when two of her best friends won't say boo to her. But they're still hanging around, that's something.

"What's with them?"

He shrugs, then looks over his shoulder into the kitchen. "No clue." He leans in closer to me. "What happened? I mean after you passed out."

I toy with my cup, unsure if I should, or want to tell him about Vereinen. I haven't told anyone about him. Partially because I don't want them to think I'm crazy chatting with what I thought was my imaginary childhood friend. I'm not so sure he's imaginary any more. Matter of fact, I'm almost positive he's very real. The first Schattenkind.

"Hey," says Rey softly, "you okay? I didn't mean to upset you, was just curious."

"It's okay. The last two weeks have just been a living hel."

"I know darlin'." Dropping a chaste kiss on the top of my head, he snags my cup and heads into the kitchen.

One freaky assed thing after another keeps dropping in my lap. I keep trying to wake up, but there's no hope, it's like being stuck in a nightmare loop. Turning, I watch the others congregated in the kitchen. My support team consists of people I want to trust. I'm just not sure if I can trust them.

Rey is, well...Rey, easygoing and smooth to a fault. I know he cares, but deep down I fear he'll do whatever it takes in the name of self–preservation. Nyssa is a sweetheart, but typical sprite behavior—trickiness, malice and vengeance—lurks in there somewhere. Dara has her own secrets and agenda, reaching far beyond the others. She refuses to answer, or deny anything, making it hard to confide in her.

Then there's Royd, Brand and Rand. Who knows with them? Something makes me want to trust Alric, but he's under Royd's thumb. Teiran Rand would prefer me served up on a platter; the hatred practically rolls off his skin. Then there's the Sun King—whatever the fuck that is—Var Royd. Indebted to him? Yes, in more ways than one. Trust him? Not in this, or any other lifetime.

I could run home to The Sisters—who, very likely aren't really my grandmother and aunts—and Annya, but that would only put them in danger. Not to mention, the NTF would follow and drag my ass back, probably tossing it in the pokey, or worse the C.U.

Vereinen. Seems my imaginary friend isn't so imaginary after all. After spending time with him, I know there's more to the story. If someone placed a block on my Talents as they began to emerge it could explain his *abandoning* me. Maybe it blocked him too. Which leads me to The Sisters, but why would they do something like that? He claimed love, or protection. Were they protecting me from my Talents, him, or something else? Aunt Liza said Royd was dangerous, evil even. Was that what they were protecting me from? And why did they lie to me about being my family and about what I am?

I feel a little like Alice in the Red Queen's court, waiting for the ax to drop. Confused and tired. Tired of the intrigue. Tired of being used. Tired of having to rely on those I'm not sure I should. Tired of worrying about everything I say and do.

I need some quiet alone time. Leaving my little group to discuss whatever it is they feel the need to leave me out of, I head to the office and grab a favorite book. Something to lift me out of reality, make it all go away, even if it's just for an hour, or two.

It seems CC has the same idea, curled up on the bed, ignoring life as only a cat can. I crawl in under the covers, for comfort not warmth. The June humidity takes care of that. His little motor starts up as I stroke his fur.

"Why couldn't I have been born a cat?"

He answers with a yawn as he stands and stretches before moving onto my lap.

"Yeah, I know you'd have to break someone new in to fill your bowel and dump your box."

A damp little nose nudges my hand. Taking the hint, I stroke him again. Maybe I just need some quality kitty napping. Leaning back against the pillows, book forgotten, Einen's silvery beauty paints my closed lids.

My heart thumps against my breastbone. I stand in a vaguely familiar room. I didn't realize this is where I wanted to be until I saw the glow of the fire and gigantic, curtained bed. Parting the curtains, I see what truly brought me here.

The paleness of his skin, enhanced by the deep red of the bedding, hair artistically spread across the pillows, sharp features softened in sleep. He's beautiful, not in the model perfect way of Var Royd, or the ruggedness of his elven spies. There's a delicateness to his features, slender, angular, yet graceful even when still.

Slipping onto the bed, I try not to disturb him. I curl myself against him and he stirs in his sleep, turning to drape a leg and arm around me.

"I did not know if you would come back," he whispers against the top of my head.

"I didn't know if I could."

"I'm glad you did. It is becoming more difficult

for me to come to you."

He tightens his hold on me drifting back to sleep. I sigh, listening to the steady rhythm of his heart. Without a doubt I can finally relax, at least until this nap is over.

Chapter 39

I wake back in my own bed, alone except for my furry friend, more refreshed than I have been in the past two weeks. I can't say it's love I'm feeling, but there's certainly a warm fuzzy spot in my heart for the man.

Glancing at the clock, I see I've only been out a couple of hours, yet it feels as if I slept eight. Talk about a rush. Sliding out of bed, I crack the door open and see the others gathered around the TV. My stomach growls when I smell the popcorn. Rey chuckles, nodding in my direction and the others turn to look.

"Nothing like hot buttered popcorn to bring sleeping beauty out of her slumber. Feeling better?"

I nod, joining him and Nyssa on the couch, groaning as I see the movie playing. "Who let Nys pick?"

"We had too. She wouldn't stop whining."

"It is actually not that bad," says Dara, legs swinging over the arm of the chair.

"Whoa, did I just hear that?" I pretend to clean my ears.

Rey's mouth hangs open, the handful of

popcorn he'd shoved in rolling down his shirt.

"Told you," Nyssa says, grinning like a fool.

Dara laughs, swinging around to face us. "Got you."

Nyssa's grin fades and her lower lip protrudes. "Okay, so I'm not in the Twilight Zone."

"Nope, just sitting in your apartment watching crappy chick flicks." Rey tosses a kernel at me, grinning. "That nap must have been what you needed. You're almost back to normal."

"Yeah, I know, as normal as I could ever hope to achieve," I say before they can and toss the piece of popcorn back at him.

"Any thoughts as to how you would like your hair done for Lorelei's party?" asks Dara.

"I don't even know if I'm going, let alone what I want done with my hair. I don't even know what I'd wear."

"You're going," says Nyssa, "Lorelei made us promise not to let you chicken out."

Dara shrugs. "I am sure we can find something in that bottomless closet of yours that will be appropriate."

"If all else fails," says Rey with a grin, "she can wear something of Nyssa's."

"No amount of rolled–up tube socks will help me fill one of Nyssa's dresses."

"And you're too tall," she says with a grin.

"You could raid Dara's closet, but this is a party

we're talking about, not a funeral, or a bloodbath."
Rey flings a handful of popcorn at Dara.

Casually she picks up the pieces that hit home and turns back to the movie. I try to decipher which mushy piece of crap Nys had to watch, until the over-spray of Rey's unswallowed beer clouds my vision. Nyssa laughs so hard she starts hiccuping, pointing at Dara. Turning, I see the last thing expected. She sits there blank—faced, hands held out and shoulders raised, kernels of popcorn attached to her fangs.

"Looks good," I say, trying and failing to contain the shock–induced laughter. "You should wear them to the party."

Rolling her eyes, she flicks them off with her tongue, pulling them into her mouth.

Rey shakes his head. "It's not a costume party."

Dara flips him something other than popcorn and he laughs.

Not normal by any means, but still better than it's been for a long time, more relaxed. Dare I say it? Fun?

⁂

Leaving the house to go shopping was pretty much out of the question. Going to the party without being hassled is going to be challenge enough. This leaves us with the great dress debate. Yes, my closet holds an abundance of items, but very few are of the formal variety.

I manage to find two bathing suits, a startling white bikini and a haltered one–piece the shade of a cloudy day. I don't think I've ever worn them. Heck, I don't even lay out. Flesh this pale and the sun don't a couple make, but this party is held by moonlight, so no worries.

I'm feeling a little guilty being excited about this party. Jenny's still missing and The Collector is still out there, leaving a big ol' target of blame on my back, but the fashion police told me not to worry about things I have no control over. I know they're right. Speaking of things I have no control over, what if my newly annoying Talent goes haywire and I end up sending people–eating shadows loose on Lorelei's boat? Or somehow raise the dead? What about Vereinen's warning about vamps?

"Huh?" I ask the three sets of eyes staring at me.

"That's what you will wear," says Nyssa.

"What?"

She waves a hand toward the pale grey one piece and a charcoal wrap skirt draped across my stylist chair. Rey holds a moonstone pendant and earrings. Dara dangles a pair of strappy silver and acrylic hooker heels from her fingers.

"Looks like you're set darlin'," says Rey, grinning at my fish impersonation.

"I can't wear those!" I point to the shoes.

"Why not? You obviously thought they were wearable when you bought them."

"I bought them for a Halloween party, years ago."

Dara shrugs. "So they will be going to another party. It is not as if you have never worn heels before."

I sigh, closing my eyes, no use fighting. Three against one is a losing battle. "Pole dancer heels, it is. Just don't make me look like a total slut when you do my hair."

"Would we do that?" she asks with a smile as she places the shoes in my hands.

"Do you really want me to answer that?"

"Clothing is decided, now it's time for your hair. Chop, chop."

"No chopping, Rey, just styling."

"Yeah, yeah, yeah, get a move on."

✦✦✦✦✦

"I ol you mot ta wa er air," says Rey, around the bobby pins held between his lips. Yeah, I know major code violation, but we're not open so I let it slide.

"Just apply more product," replies Dara, drying her newly bobbed locks, looking chicer than usual. The cropped back accentuating the longer sides jelled to curved points along her jaw leading to heart–shaped bangs, or fringe as our European counterparts call them. What can I say? I do good work.

Rey continues to mumble incoherently, nothing I probably want to understand. Between the acupuncture and the backcombing, I'm getting the mother of all headaches. He covers my face and the whoosh of spray fills the air. Just when I think it will never stop, he lifts his hand and stands back.

"Voilà," he says, handing me a mirror, but his smile is all I need to know about how it looks.

I position the hand mirror and he slowly swings the chair so I can see from every angle. A sleek French twist with a sweeping bang curving over the eye, ending at my jaw line. Very sophisticated and very Rey. Perfectly executed, making me glad he won the coin toss. Not that Dara would have done a bad job, but this is beautiful.

"Well?" asks Rey as the others join us.

"It's fabulous."

"Not bad, Fox."

"I love it, thank you."

He claps his hands. "Clothing, ladies, get a move on. Our ride will be here soon."

⚜⚜⚜

Giving myself a last once over in the full–length

mirror, the light dims, a halo of shadow manifesting behind me. I try to turn and teeter on the three-inch platforms.

"Shit, I knew these things would be trouble."

Something resembling laughter comes from behind.

"Einen?"

The air is still, yet artfully placed tendrils twitch against my neck. A whisper of pressure glides across my bare flesh, causing me to shiver in the most delightful way. I'm not asleep, but it's him. Isn't it? Could it be my own Talents? Is this a precursor of what could happen tonight on a boat loaded with Enchants? A not-so-pleasurable shiver ripples across my skin.

The door swings open to a chorus of, "It's time to go. The limo is here. Get a move on."

Impatient buggers, at least they knocked, if you can call the rapid cracks against the door as it opens knocking.

Yeah, I know, none of us have a steady job, but we decided a limo is the safest way to shuttle us to the party. Splitting the cost four ways helps and I actually get to enjoy the ride this time. Like Cinderella in her sparkly coach off to the ball that changed her life. Maybe by some wicked twist of fate mine will be transformed for the better.

Chapter 40

My stomach keeps pace with the scenery as it streams past the window. Rey steadies Nys as she balances on the seat to look out the moonroof when the car slows, entering the next town.

"The moron reporters are still following us." Nyssa giggles as she slips back inside.

"I could have told you that without climbing out of the car." Rey reaches over to adjust her windblown hair.

The reporters are the least of my worries. Most of my clients—supposedly loyal clients, now ex-clients—will be at this party. The minute this mess started, they abandoned me without question. I understand the fear, but that the thought would even enter their minds. Well, it pisses me off. There are plenty of *what ifs* tied to the scenario of seeing them. What if their reaction steps over the border of just snubbing me? What if anger triggers my new Talent and hungry shadow creatures attack? I don't want to ruin Lorelei's party. It would be a lousy payback for all she's done. Just when I think the short twenty-minute drive will never end, we pull into Saylorville Marina.

Lorelei hired taxis to take her guests out to Temptation, a fitting name for a boat owned by a Rhine maiden. Rey and the driver graciously attempt to help us board. Dara, true to form, ignores the outstretched hands, climbing aboard under her own power. I, on the other hand, grab both. Did I forget to mention I don't swim? I love the water and being on it, just not in it. Learning to swim wasn't a high priority in this Iowa girl's upbringing.

Lorelei's house looks like Fairy exploded, glowing with multitudes of tiny lights, flowers of every kind and pastel streamers. The decorators had been busy. That's just what's visible from the water. I can hardly wait to see the rest.

Dara and Nyssa slip off their shoes as we pull alongside and I copy with a groan, having forgotten we'd have to climb the ladder. Slipping the straps over her fingers to dangle from the back of her hand, Dara grabs the ladder and climbs with an easy grace I envy. Smart girl didn't bring a purse. I wonder where she's keeping her essentials, until the slit of her dress parts revealing a three-inch strap around her thigh. For the stylish assassin on the go, conceal your blade of choice in the attached sheath, and lipstick in the handy zipper compartment. Eeesh, the woman is a little too scary at times.

Nyssa follows, navigating upward without a hitch. I would have almost laid money on her charms getting stuck between the rungs, but somehow she makes it to the top without incident.

Rey gives me a little push, taking my shoes with a wink. Something tells me if I don't move fast enough, he's going to pinch my ass, or considering the light in his eyes bite it.

Twirling the opening of my skirt from side to front, allowing my legs to move freely, I grab the rung and not so gracefully hoist myself up. Two deck hands stand at the top and pull me aboard, motioning to the padded bench off to the side, where Nys and Dara sit putting on their shoes.

"Allow me." Rey kneels in front of me; hand firmly on my ankle, he slides on the first shoe.

"So it's true," says Lorelei from behind him, "you are a princess in disguise."

"Yeah," Rey grins as he stands. "We've been keeping her hidden in the tower until tonight."

"Ha, ha, ha, you guys are all sooo funny."

"Come, darlings, I have a party to oversee."

We follow our sashaying hostess to the stairs leading to the upper deck. A palette of sunset colors offset by filmy fabrics give the illusion of walking in the sky. An ice sculpture of a mermaid stands as focal point on a table containing finger foods, with no signs of melting even in this heat. Small groups of revelers seem to have staked their claims near the champagne fountain, barely leaving room for the help. I grab a glass from the tray held by a shirtless waiter who appreciatively looks me up and down.

"Yummy." Nyssa practically purrs as she gives him the same sort of look, taking it a step further with a finger down the chest.

Lorelei playfully swats at Nyssa's hand. "Now, now darling, it is going to be a long night. Pace yourself."

Bubbles find their way through my nose and I start coughing. Why is it people always wait until you take a drink before saying something funny, or shocking?

Lorelei floats off to mingle leaving our little outcast group stranded in a sea of icebergs. I expected a chilly reception, but the silence that descends when they see me is a little too unnerving. There are a lot of dropped jaws and whispers behind hands to go along with the staring. Rumors are flying, nearly tangible.

Then again, maybe I'm not the reason for their shock and silence. The crowd parts, spotlighting the two most beautiful people at the party. That's saying a lot considering all the pretties surrounding me. Unfortunately, I know one of them and he's the last person I wanted to deal with tonight. Okay, not the last. The Collector would be tops on that list, but Var Royd pulls a tight second. Making it worse, he and his companion are walking toward me. The smile on his face lets me know, he knows, I saw him. No escaping by pretending I didn't see them. Damn.

Chapter 41

His date is probably the most beautiful creature I've ever laid eyes on. The kind of beauty that inspires poetry, paintings, hate, jealousy, inadequacy and the desire to rip her face off. Ouch, where did that come from? It's not as if I want the man, do I? No time to dwell on it now.

"Mr. Royd," I say, trying to hold my composure in check as the golden couple approach. "I don't believe I've had the pleasure of meeting your lovely date."

His eyebrow shoots up and I could kick myself hearing the venom lacing my words. He so is going to misinterpret that.

"Miss Fey, let me introduce my sister, Vanadís." He might as well have said, *I win,* from the look in his eyes.

"A pleasure, Miss Royd," I say, wanting to wipe imagined filth from my hand—gods forbid I sully her perfection—before extending it to her.

Her laughter is like a million tiny bells as she takes my hand and pulls me into a tight embrace. Somehow, I manage to keep from spilling bubbly down her perfect back. The same *loved* feeling that

I got from Royd at our first meeting flows over me. "No one calls me, Miss Royd, it's Vana."

She releases me to the point of only holding my hand, perfect lips drawn into a frown as she gives me the once over. Talk about feeling like a bug under a microscope.

"You are not quite what I expected."

"Um...okay," I reply, not sure what to say, or if I should say anything at all.

"To hear him," she nods in Royd's direction, heat highlighting his cheekbones as he glares at her, "talk you are the most beautiful thing that walks the earth."

The silence is damn near as crushing as the weight of everyone's eyes on me as they wait for my response. Whether it's out of shock, or lack of quick wit, I manage to keep my mouth shut. I know I'm not beautiful, or even pretty. Exotic, or unusual might be better terms to describe me. Still, I can't help the bitterness that coats my tongue when this gorgeous woman reminds me.

"Not that you are not attractive, my dear, in your own way." She gives my hand a brief squeeze and smiles, like that's going to make it all better, before letting go.

Gods help me, but this woman stirs emotions like a blender, creating a smoothie combination no one in their right mind would order, but you drink it anyway. Worse yet, you like it and want another.

"You must forgive my sister's lack of," says Royd, glaring at his sister who smiles indulgently, "tact."

All I can do is shrug. What the hel can I do? Anything I say will make me look childish and catty. Dara and Nyssa flank me, Rey at my back, a comforting hand on my shoulder.

She laughs again. "Your friends are quite protective, are they not? Do not worry, I will not harm her." Something in her tone threatens a *much* at the end of that sentence.

Slender fingers toy with a chunk of raw amber that hangs from a golden chain. She lets it drop between breasts usually only seen after surgery. Tilting her head to one side, the corners of her generous lips curl upward ever so slightly.

I shiver, there's something cold and calculating in those pretty blue and gold eyes, almost predatory. Okay, no almost about it, I feel like the rabbit right before the raptor sweeps in with its nasty talons.

Giving myself a mental shake, I drag my eyes away from that all-encompassing stare, clearing my throat. "I don't want to keep you."

"Oh, you are not keeping me, darling, but there are others who demand my attentions. We shall speak again soon."

Wrapping her hand around Royd's arm, she bares perfect white teeth in what would seem a smile, but it's more like a challenge. A challenge for what I'm not sure. Hopefully, not the attentions of her brother. Eww, that thought is just too sick for words.

He gives me one last burning glance as she leads him away, sending shivers down my spine. Fear? Anticipation? Don't know, don't want to.

Dara motions to the pair's escorts; I'd been too blinded by the golden beauty to see earlier. Brand and Rand hanging just on the fringe turn to follow them. Brand acknowledges us with a brief nod; Rand gives his patented icy stare. I suppose having that kind of wealth means having bodyguards in public situations. Not my problem, the money that is, but they might come in handy fending off the stares that return with the departure of the golden twins.

"Screw it," I whisper, lifting my chin, staring right back at them.

This isn't high school and I'm not the *different* kid in the class anymore. So what if my Talents are scary? There are lots of others here with Talents just as scary. Gregori Falen stands not six feet away. What could be scarier than a vamp who writes children's books? What about Philip Monroe out there shaking his groove thing on the dance floor? Incubi can be fun, but there's always that nasty morning after affect.

Snagging another glass from a passing waiter, I head off to the buffet, friends trailing like little ducks. Let them stare. I was invited and I intend on having fun.

My mouth waters with all the artfully arranged temptation along the L–shaped table. Balancing glass and plate, I stalk my prey. Chocolate fountains and fruit, salmon and cream cheese pinwheels, delicate puff pastry with its crab filling and the pièce de résistance—stuffed mushrooms. The heavens are shining down on me and my obsession with edible fungus. I fight the urge to take nothing, but 'shrooms, after all there are so many tasty little treats that deserve a place on my plate.

During my little foraging excursion I end up separated from the others. Not sure how it happened, but it's not as if I need someone to feed me. I can handle that just fine on my own. Finding a quiet corner is next on the agenda. Not that the deck has any corners, but that doesn't stop me from finding a quiet spot where I can watch the party without everyone watching me stuff my face.

"How many times do I have to tell you darling, they are like mules, there will be no shadow spawn from their joining."

"Not always true. There have been instances where mules—"

"Too few to worry over."

What the...? The voices, Royd and his sister— or it sure sounds like them—filter through the giant potted palms to one side of the buffet. I know it's wrong, but it sounds like they're talking about me. I mean really, shadow spawn? Isn't it only fair I listen?

Whatever he says is too low for me to make out, leaving me wishing for vamp, or therian super hearing. Carefully balancing my plate and glass, I take a step closer to their ferny screen. Bending over the table to *examine* a few of the other delicacies in hopes no one blows my cover.

"What is the harm in her dallying with him, besides to your pride? Let them have their fun. She will lose interest when the desire to have a child takes her. After all, you fixed it so he will have more than a difficult time visiting her and I highly doubt she knows how to slip boundaries. If she does it, it's purely by accident. Problem solved."

As those words cause the floor to shift under my feet I almost miss my cue to vacate the premises, nearly spilling my hors d'oeuvres. Juggling, plate and glass, I continue the pretense of studying the table, but feel her eyes on me and slowly turn my head. She smiles before turning to follow her brother, letting *me* know *she* knows I heard.

What the hel did that exchange mean? Was she talking about Vereinen and me? How much did they know? What's up with the mule talk? And children?

Having children is not something I've ever had a desire to think about, let alone do, and I don't like having my reproductive system discussed as if I'm a brood mare.

I'm glad my companions have taken off for parts unknown and everyone else seems to be ignoring me. The last thing I'm in the mood for is conversation after what I just heard. Part of me wishes I could jump ship and another reminds me I can't swim. Gods, even my internal voices have a twisted sense of humor.

Along the rail, there's a padded bench and I decide it's as good a place as any to take up a solitary residence. Setting the glass at my feet, I concentrate on forgetting what I heard. No use ruining a perfectly lovely snack. Plucking the smallest of the mushrooms from the plate, I pop it into my mouth. Shroomy bliss envelops me and I lean back, closing my eyes to enjoy.

Something brushes the corner of my mouth and across my lower lip. Crystal tinkles and wetness splashes across my foot. The plate of yummy treasures is no longer on my lap, but splayed across the floor. My pole dancer heels slide to the right and I topple into a hard, strong arm that stops my descent to the floor. The low rumble of laughter emanates from the attached chest and I jerk upright.

Chapter 42

"Glad you find this funny. You not only made me waste a plate of food, but a glass of champagne. That's two crimes in one, alcohol abuse and the murder of perfectly innocent 'shrooms. Not to mention, the blow to what little dignity I have left."

Hiding behind the removal of splattered champagne and munchies that coat my skirt and legs from the knees down, I take a deep breath. So much for avoiding him.

"You were enjoying your treat so much I did not think you wished to waste any of it," says Royd, holding a cream–covered fingertip toward me.

He shrugs when I pull back and slips the finger between his lips. "Very tasty."

No need for a mirror, I know from the burning in my cheeks, my face is bright red. Snapping his fingers, three of the shirtless waiters appear. Two clean up my mess, another hands me a fresh glass.

"Thanks," I mumble. Quickly looking away, not wanting to fall into that gold and blue gaze and the thoughts I know lurk behind it.

He stands and holds his hand out. "Shall we walk?"

I ignore the offered hand and he lets it drop as I rise on jellified legs. Placing a hand at the small of my back, he steers me along the deck. Glancing over my shoulder, there's no sign of the recent crime, not even the tiniest of slivers have escaped the cleanup. Dang, wonder if those boys do salons.

"Are you enjoying the party?"

"I was, until you made me commit shroomacide."

Flips and flops in my stomach that have nothing to do with the motion of the water take up residence as he chuckles.

"I will fetch you another plate."

"I'm not hungry anymore."

We stop at the side of the deck and he grasps the rail, lowering his head. Taking a deep breath, he straightens and turns toward me. I try not to flinch and fail as he places a hand on either side of my face, forcing me to look him in the eye. "Sometimes, one must be cruel to be kind."

I don't know what prompted the statement, but it pretty much sums up the man. I swallow hard, waiting for the pressure of his hands to increase until my head pops. Instead, his head descends, catching me in a mind–whirling, knee–knocking, pulse–thumping lip lock.

"Get a room," says a familar and welcome voice from behind.

Royd frowns, only increasing my appreciation of Rey's timing. "What is it, Therian?"

"Brand requests your presence and I thought I'd keep an eye on Keely while you have your little powwow." He wiggles his brow and Royd glares at him.

"See that an eye is all you keep on her." Without a second glance, he stalks off, leaving me with a laughing hyena in fox's clothing.

"Um...how many have you had?"

"Aww, it was all in fun," he says, holding out his hand. "Let's join the party."

Rey is usually not so forward with his teasing, except with us, who know he's only joking. Chalking it up to one too many glasses of bubbly, I let him lead me into the throng of socializers.

"Having a good time?" he asks, snagging a couple of glasses from a passing tray.

I shrug, taking the offered drink. "As good as anyone would have, considering the circumstances."

His brow wrinkles, "What do you mean? Mr. High and Mighty giving you a hard time?"

"That doesn't help, but—"

Off to the side, I hear a familiar voice that stops me cold and I turn. Not more than twenty paces away from me stands Rey—my Rey—chatting with a blond bombshell. Mouth open, I look from one to the other.

"Who are you?"

The furrow in Rey number two's brow deepens and his eyes change from confusion to anger. He grabs my arm, sending the glass crashing to the floor. "Damn it."

I open my mouth, but before I can make a sound, he strokes his fingers across my lips and they clamp shut. Holding his arm around me like a vise, he pulls me toward the stern. I try dropping against him—dead weight is harder to move—but something compels me to keep walking upright.

"Stupid bitch," he says, leaning in close as he tugs me along. "Keep it up and I'll kill you right here."

Like that scares me. Kill me here, or kill me later, either way I'm dead. Here there's a chance of someone helping me. Seeing as the little bastard took away my power of speech, I try grabbing anyone within range, but I can barely move a finger, let alone lift my hand.

He mutters something under his breath and sneers at me. I don't know what he did, but everyone looks right through me, as if I were made of glass, or worse I don't exist.

Between the compulsions and what I suspect is a cloaking spell, I'm screwed. About the only thing that can save me now is if I were telepathic. I remember that night on the dance floor when Brand touched my mind. Was it a fluke? Only one way to find out.

I concentrate on one word. Help! Hoping someone, anyone hears me. The party continues around me without even a ruffle, leaving me empty, desperate and terrified.

Once we're away from the others, he drops the glamour used to impersonate Rey, probably the Talent stolen from the morph. How in Hel's Realm is he able to use it?

He gives me a shove and luckily, some of my muscle control has returned. I land painfully against the rail, clutching at it as I look over the edge into the deep, dark lake. The lesser of two evils—psycho, drowning, psycho, drowning—which do I choose? Not an easy decision, or one I'm prepared to make.

Taking a deep breath, I turn to face possibly the last person I'll ever see. Not a pleasant thought. His skin is pale and not in a good way. It has an almost yellowish hue, like someone who's been, or is sick.

We already knew he was sick in the head, but this adds something new to the equation. Maybe I can use it to my advantage, not that I have much of one at present.

There's something familiar about him, but I just can't put two and two together and come up with a coherent answer. Who can blame my brain for not focusing on anything except being scared shitless?

"What do you want?" Not original I know, but like I said I'm not firing on all cylinders.

"What do I want? What do I want?" he asks,

while pacing back and forth in front of me. Who does this guy think he is? De Niro?

"I want what was denied me by my loving parents."

He stops just inches from me, the heat and wretched smell of his breath against my face. The smell, like the sallow tinge to his skin, isn't right. I notice the dark shadows beneath his eyes and a rash along his neck and cheeks. Without doubt, there's something physically as well as mentally wrong with this guy. I don't have to be a doctor to see that much.

Swallowing back the bile that climbs its way up my throat, I stand up straight, lift my chin and stare him in the eye. I may be terrified, but I'm not just going to roll over and let him do whatever it is he has planned for me.

He shakes his head and laughs. "I should thank you. Not only did your salon supply the missing element, but it drew attention away from me on to you."

I bite my lower lip, holding back any comments that might leak out.

"Sure, at first I was pissed off that the cops thought a stupid hairdresser could pull off something so complex." He pauses, watching as my jaw tightens. "Oh, don't be angry about it, we both know you never could have come up with a way to gain and use the Talents of others."

"Whatever." It slips out before I can stop myself.

He laughs and begins his pacing again. "Then I realized with their attention on you, I was free to do as I pleased as long as everything pointed to you."

"Explains why you kept choosing clients from my salon, and stole the pages from the appointment book."

"Ooo, you are smarter than you look."

The sarcasm in his tone is undeniable and pissing me off.

"But your free ride ended when my salon got closed down. Too bad, so sad."

His hand connects with my face and my head snaps back. That's going to leave a mark. I've got to learn to keep my mouth shut. Fortunately, it was an open handed slap instead of a punch, or I'd be on my knees, or over the side.

"Doesn't explain why you tried to break into my apartment."

"Would have succeeded if that bitch vamp would have stayed asleep like she was supposed to."

"But why?" I try to keep him talking, hoping one of those wandering couples will stroll over this way.

He shrugs, reaching up to scratch at his neck and face. "The challenge. Your salon was already my playground, I just extended it to include your home. I wasn't interested in your Talents." A sinister little smile plays at his lips, sending a chill down my spine. "At the time."

A pendant swings free from his shirt, triggering how I know him. The coffee shop with Jenny, the greasy little scumbag I thought might be her pimp. Jenny was in on it, I remember her wearing the same necklace. I feel the floor move under me, or maybe it's just the boat rocking in the waves.

He reaches out and strokes the cheek he'd abused just moments ago. I yank my head to the side.

"Oh, don't be that way, I've seen the men come and go from your place. Did you have to make a little cash on the side after your salon got closed down?"

That does it, he pushed me too far, I spit in his face, but my aim is a little off, it lands on his chest. Having never done that before I'm rather pleased, I manage to hit him. I brace myself waiting for another hand to the face, but he just laughs.

"Is that the best you can do? I'm about to tear you to shreds so I can have your Talents and you spit at me? Guess the rumors were right. You don't have control over your power."

He was right. I can't just turn it off and on, I don't know how. Concentration is the key and right now, there's no time to give it the old college try. Glancing over my shoulder as he takes a step, reaching for me, I make my decision about the lesser of two evils. Swinging myself over the rail, he makes a move to grab me. Luckily, he misses. Or not.

Chapter 43

When I finally hit it, the water feels like cement. Pain radiates from every pore. The cold steals my breath. Gasping for air, I only manage to suck in mouthfuls of water. Gagging and choking, I flounder around, trying to remember what Nys said about treading water.

Relax was rule number one, but it seems I've broken it and as punishment, I'm pulled under.

Something soft and warm crushed against my lips, held tight against something silky smooth and firm, rocking back and forth. I hear words, but they don't register, again, something crosses my lips. Stroking, I don't want it to stop, I try to tell it not to, but it does. Words again, this time one stands out.

Keely.

That's me, I'm Keely. I giggle and end up choking. I try and lift my hands reaching for that warm, firm... Body?

My eyelids feel like they weigh a ton. I manage to open them to a curtain of silver. Sharp, ashen features come into view, pain and fear in virtually colorless eyes. Sensuous lips curl upward in a smile and I try to lift my head to kiss them.

"I thought I'd lost you, but there's still a chance. You need to wake up."

My dream lover, Vereinen. If I wake up, he'll be gone. "I don't want to."

"You have to, if you do not, you will drown."

"Drown?" I giggle. "How can I drown if I'm here with you?"

"You are asleep, remember?"

"I don't care. I want to stay with you." My brain is a fuzzy mess, I can't concentrate on anything.

"You can come another time, preferably when you are on dry land. Now wake up, Keely, and swim."

"Don't know how."

"Damn."

I reach out and stroke his smooth hairless chest. He gently removes my hand.

"There is no time for that."

"Dere's always ime fer dat," my words become slurred and movements slow motion. The fuzziness thickens and my ears ring something awful.

"Damn it, wake up," he shouts, shaking me. "Concentrate on the shadows lifting you to the surface."

"Dere's no shadows uner da water."

"There are shadows everywhere light and dark meet, now concentrate. I cannot help you if you do not try."

Sighing, I picture shadowy hands along my body, caressing, stroking.

"Lifting, Keely!"

Slowly the hands take hold and drag me upward. He says something as I'm pulled away, but I don't catch it. The hands move too fast.

Air, cold and clean slaps me in the face. The waves pushed me toward the shore far enough, I can touch the bottom. With jelly for legs standing isn't an option. I claw and scratch my way onto the beach, heaving the water from my lungs.

Lying in the wet sand, what would have been the last moments of my life flash behind my lids. What in Hel's Realm, had I been thinking, jumping in the lake? Obviously, I hadn't been. Thinking that is. I'd definitely jumped. Sure, I'd averted becoming the next piece in the collection, but I'd almost drowned. If it hadn't been for Einen, I'd be fish food right now.

This is starting to become a very bad pattern, of playing the damsel in distress while someone rushes in to save me. Hel's Realm, even my cat has saved me. Guess it stops here. I slowly rise to a semi-reclining position. None of my hunky men, friends, or even the cat, are going to get me off this beach. It's just little ol' me. Take that back, little ol' me and a lone figure walking this way. One whose posture and rate of movement doesn't look exactly friendly, or helpful.

"You fucking bitch!"

Nope, not friendly, or helpful. How did he find me? I mean really, what are the chances he'd find me? As he closes in, I see his clothes, hanging from that spindly form like wet rags. That's how. The idiot jumped in after me, so obviously not as smart as he thinks he is. He may not be a genius, but he's still dangerous. Out to kill me dangerous.

Jelly legs still aren't cooperating, but adrenaline forces me to try anyway, and fail. I slip and fall with a bone–jarring thud, grabbing sloppy handfuls of sand propelling myself forward. Just not fast enough. My head jerks back as his fingers tangle in the sticky remains of my 'do. Damn that hurts, but it's nothing compared to what he has in mind.

Wet sand scrapes along my skin and ends up in the most inconvenient places. On the bright side, he's digging a nice trench. I just disapprove of his choice of tools. The body isn't meant to be a tool for excavation, and hair isn't made for being used as a handle either. I'm surprised I have any left. Wait a minute, not that I have one, but I do have an idea.

Long ago in a time far, far away—high school to be exact—I'd been angry with a girl, something about a boy, but that's not important. The big picture is I made her hair fall out, now if I can just do that to myself.

First step is forcing myself to let go of his wrist, easier said than done. It's the only thing lessening the pain of his grip, but I don't want to be holding on to him if this works. Taking a deep breath I let my hands fall to the ground, tears take their cue and spring to my eyes.

Damn that hurts! I begin to doubt I can pull this off. Concentrating through this much pain is not something I've done before, but I'm running out of options. Not having the physical strength, or know how, I'd lose an all-out fight. As much as I resent my new Talents, right now they'd come in handy, but I have less than a thread of control. The only thing I can count on is the hair and nail Talent and fear is a great motivator.

Pushing my way through the tears and pain, I look for that little place deep inside. I visualize the hair shaft, from tip to root. Coaxing it up and out, watching it lengthen. A vicious tug snaps me back to the real world as he entrenches his hand further into my hair. Sobbing, I work at keeping up the growth, seeing the shaft come to the end of its span.

Hair falls out all the time, approximately one hundred eighty a day. I'm just quickening the process and the count. The tension on my scalp lessens and the scrap of sand slows until it stops.

I'm lying in the sand, half–bald, but that's the least of my worries. Coming at me is a pissed off psycho holding a handful of hair. It would be comical if I was watching it on the big screen, but I'm living it, so funny goes out the window.

Scrambling to my feet I head the other direction, zig–zagging until I've switched positions with him. Not an easy feat in these stinking heels, why hadn't I taken them off? Talk about stereotypes, stupid blond running away from a psychotic killer wearing three–inch heels.

Do I stop and take them off, or keep running? Either could give him an advantage. Doesn't matter. I'm face down, my back feeling snapped in two. While I'd been debating, he decided to play football. Guess I had the ball and didn't know it. Straddling my hips, he rolls me over.

"I've had enough, cunt." He lands a punch any heavyweight would be proud of.

Chapter 44

This is it. I'm done for. My life flutters before my eyes. It seems so short when you really think about it, but even with death lurking, I'm not admitting exact numbers. I'd use my standard, old–enough–to–know–better–but–still–too–young–to–care, but it doesn't apply. Obviously, I care.

Gods, how I hate duct tape! This will be the second time tonight I've been denied proper amounts of oxygen. I'll give him credit for using my skirt to somewhat cushion my head, but don't get me started on the mode of transportation. Trunks are for inanimate objects, not people!

I suppose the exhaust leak doesn't matter since he's going to kill me anyway. More merciful than what he has planned. Did you know giggling against duct tape vibrates your lips? I'll chalk that informative little bit up to inhaling fumes.

The hair growing thingy didn't work out, at least not the way I wanted, so what's next? I've already played your run–of–the–mill heroine, wearing heels and running screaming right into the villain's arms. Okay, so he tackled me from behind, not a lot of difference in the outcome. If I follow the script, I lay there and whimper, pleading with him not to hurt me. As if that's going to work. I highly doubt he'll suddenly want to be friends.

I could try calling up the shadows again, it worked in the lake, but I'd had Vereinen to help. Letting down the wall would unleash the dead things, but the last time that happened, I ended up with the short end. At best they'd take him too, at worst I just helped him.

That I'm not a telepath was proven on the boat. The only person I could possibly communicate with would be Einen, but then I'd be asleep. Trussed up like Sunday dinner in the trunk of a car and I can't think of a single thing.

My chariot slows down, changing direction. We go from semi–smooth pavement to off–road adventure. Great, he's going to butcher me in the woods, or better yet, a cornfield. It loses some of its charm, this early in the season, unless you're a munchkin.

What a day, first I almost drown, and then I'm knocked out, now I'm being subjected to exhaust poisoning. I still have mutilation and murder on the agenda. Can a girl get a break?

I'll take that as a no, since the joyride from hel comes to an end.

The trunk pops open and he hauls me out like a bag of dirty laundry. Bracing me against the bumper, he slits the duct tape holding my ankles together. Running is out of the question as he stands me upright. I don't recommend wearing pole dancer heels on uneven ground. The only thing keeping me off my knees is his grip. From what I can see, I didn't end up in a cornfield, but it's still pretty dark.

He starts pulling me forward and I stumble again, twisting an ankle. Not expecting the slightest interest in my welfare, it's a bit unnerving when he stops and none-too-gently removes my shoes.

The pause allows me to check out the scenery, trees and lots of rock. At least I have an idea of where I am, somehow, the bastard managed to avoid the flooded areas. We're at Ledges. I can feel the power roll over my skin. It's one of Iowa's first national parks and like other national parks, a nexus, or place of power. Not every nexus is a national park, but every national park is a nexus.

Think about the last time you visited one. The extraordinary beauty, or those little tingles you get stepping inside the boundary. Those little tingles are power, raw and untamed. Even Uns can feel it, to a lesser degree. Now if I could just use it to my advantage.

Shoes gone, the dragging commences yet again. I'm starting to feel like a rag doll, and maybe losing the shoes wasn't such a blessing. Stones, twigs and other painful objects find the bottoms of my feet the preferable place to lodge themselves, matching my bloody kneecaps embedded with sand and other debris. Not that it'll matter after he dismembers me.

Speaking of which, we come to a stop under what looks like Table Rock. Can this guy get any more cliché? I mean really, the whole virgin—or in my case, not so virginal—on the altar thing is so predictable.

This is the first place anyone would look for a diabolical killer in the park. He really needs to work on the originality to maintain that evil genius status he's so fond of. Maybe I'm wrong. It's so predictable that everyone will assume he won't use it.

Either way I'm not looking forward to the climb, a swimsuit and bare feet are hardly proper hiking attire. My body shakes as laughter bubbles up, a weird muffled sound behind the tape, but I can't get enough air to really let loose. Tears well in my eyes from both the laughter and the cuff to the side of the head it brings.

"What the fuck are you laughing at, bitch?"

"You," I say behind my gag, but it comes out more like moo.

My face is on fire as he rips off the tape and the pent-up tears flow freely. The temptation is there to thank him for the wax job, but all I can do is gasp for breath. I flinch, running my tongue over my lips. With as tender and swelled as they are, I'll be giving Angelina a little competition.

"You can't be serious," I say, nodding in the direction of the sandstone wall.

There's a moment of confusion as he looks from me to the wall and back.

"I'll never make it up that." I lift one of my feet, reminding him of my lack of shoes. "Might as well just kill me now."

This earns me yet another open handed smack to the side of the head, just hard enough to shake my balance. You'd think I'd learn. Don't poke the bear. Especially when the bear's going to eat you, but it's that, or fall in a whimpering mass at his feet. Sarcasm as a shield, not the best, but the only defense I have at the moment. If I can buy a little time, maybe the others can track me down, or I can catch him off guard and slip away.

"I'll kill you when I'm damn good and ready, so shut up."

"Why? Like you said you're going to kill me anyway, what's the point?"

This time he lands a right hook against my jaw. My knees crumble and I tumble sideways. Without hands to catch myself, hip and then shoulder strike the rocky ground, my head the last thing to make contact. Lights flash as the pain explodes through my skull and all those delightful appetizers try to make a hasty exit. I swallow another wave of serious nausea and my vision blurs as something jostles me.

Go to sleep, says something in the back of my abused brain. I need the ground to stop shifting. The throbbing in my head worsens with each movement. Go to sleep, the voice says again, and this time I don't fight. What does it matter if I don't wake up? I'm dead anyway. I've heard dying in your sleep is the best way to go.

Chapter 45

I'm cold and sore beyond belief, but the pain in my head has lessened to a dull throb. Cracking my eyes open I see nothing, except the palest glow illuminating my surroundings. Rock, lots of rock. Under me, over me, around me, nothing, but rock.

Ledges, I'm at Ledges, but there aren't any caves. Unless the bastard moved me somewhere else, but I doubt I was out that long. Wincing, I lift my head, trying to get a better view. Bad move, the dull throb intensifies trying to beat its way out of my skull. I gently lay it back down on my concrete pillow, trying not to shiver as the chilly ground leaches away my body heat.

Distant shuffling noises become footsteps. As they come closer a sickly sweet smell, I know all too intimately, looms over me.

"I know you're awake."

He gives me a pull and I roll over, staring at my captor. In the dimness, his appearance is all the scarier. That nasty rash on his cheek, shiny with dark streaks, blank voids where his eyes should be and pinched features sharpened by shadow.

He looks every bit the monster I know him

to be and frankly, I'm scared. Not that I wasn't before, but as he stares at me like the cherry on top of the sundae, it registers that this is the end. There's nowhere to run to and no one to help me.

"Where are we?" I ask, little more than a whisper. I keep telling myself I won't go out like a whimpering fool. Easier said than done.

"At Ledges, or more precisely in Ledges."

"There aren't any caves at Ledges," I say looking around.

"None that can be seen," he says, chest puffed with pride.

What the...? Did he actually breach The Veil? He'd have to have taken the power of an En who had mythical blood, such as a fairy, or an elf to open a doorway.

The thought of him holding that kind of power terrifies me more that losing my own life. The havoc he could cause in these realms would be catastrophic. Not only the losses to the magical community, but he could use doorways to evade capture.

The Holden and Unholden courts, as well as the Seelie and Unseelie, might take it as a sign of invasion. It might even start an all-out war. Like the floods of '93, or the tornadoes of '05, there would be devastation everywhere. If I'm right, this dipshit has no idea what he's done and probably doesn't care. Gods, please let me be wrong.

An amulet slips from his shirt, dangles over me. "I saw Jenny wearing that."

His fingers slide over it lovingly, a twisted smile growing as he clutches it.

"That wasn't Jenny you chatted with that night."

"You?" I ask, barely able to voice that single word as my thoughts drift to the shape–shifting actor. This bastard had used those Talents to become Jenny for the night.

He taps the bright red stone and nods.

"Is that how you hold the Talents you've taken?"

He nods again, sitting down beside me like an eager puppy awaiting praise. Praise he doesn't deserve, but I get the feeling he's starved for attention. And all criminal masterminds want the world to see their accomplishments, right? I'll play along, anything to prolong my pitiful existence.

"The knot work is a spell?"

"Yes."

"And the stones?"

"They are true power."

"So somehow you manipulated the stolen Talents into the stones and the knot holds them together."

He claps. "Very good. You aren't as stupid as I thought."

"How did you get the stones to contain the power? I mean, it's not as if I'll be telling anyone your secret."

"I suppose there's no harm in telling you. As you pointed out, you'll be taking it to the grave." His words and laughter reminiscent of the villain in any cheesy movie.

Rule number one; make the client feel like the most important person in the world. Easiest way to do that is to get them talking about their favorite subject. Themselves.

Having nothing to lose I struggle to sit up, exaggerating how the binding of my arms hampers me. He's so excited about telling someone about his accomplishments I might as well push my luck.

"Considering you've repeatedly pointed out I'm not leaving here alive, could you possibly undo my arms, or at least tie them in front of me? I promise to stay put while you tell me everything."

He shrugs, flipping open a pocketknife and cuts me free. Who looks stupid now? Every muscle protests as I prop myself against the wall. His agitation pronounced as he jostles my body up and back. The last thing I want to do is screw it up, now that I've come this far. Pretending to be interested—I know I should, it might lead to something important—is more difficult than imaginable.

My broken body settled, he sits a little too close for comfort, legs crossed and hands resting on his knees. Leaning forward, his face is animated with something other than anger. I can practically feel the internal struggle between his desire to tell me everything and caution.

It's so childlike, the need for acceptance and praise. For a brief moment, I feel sorry for him, but it's wiped away when I think of the ruin his actions have left my life.

Hold on to your anger, keep him distracted. If he's busy talking, he isn't killing me, and maybe, just maybe my luck will change. I might find a way out of here, or help could show up. Not going to hold my breath over that last thought, but it's possible if we have crossed through The Veil. Maybe Einen can find me. No matter how slight the chance, I have to have something to hold.

"So, how did you trap the power in the stones?" I ask, not wanting to let the window I opened close.

He literally giggles. Like a teenager, proud of how he's deceived the adults. "Believe it, or not the answer was on the Web."

"The web?"

He gives an overly exaggerated sigh and rolls his eyes.

"The Web—the Internet—you have heard of it, right?"

I nod, not trusting my response to come out without the sarcasm, I taste on the tip of my tongue.

"There was this site—I came across it by accident—talking about preserving your loved ones as gemstones. With the correct pressure and heat, cremated remains can be changed into jewels."

I suppress my revulsion—twisting something meant to be a tribute into something so disgusting.

"How were you able to find the equipment, to pull this off?

He laughs.

"Weren't you listening? I found a company on the web that specializes in doing it, all I had to do was collect what I needed and cremate them."

"So you used the hair from my salon to trap your victims, cut out their Talents, burned them and sent them to this company?" I'd always wondered about that saying, 'I just threw up a little in my mouth,' now I know.

He nods gleefully. The only thing that could top this would be if he clapped his hands.

"It was perfect." His face clouds over. "And would have continued to be, if you hadn't brought Royd into it."

"Hey, whoa, you can't blame me for that. You're the one who threw me into his crosshairs. I didn't even know the guy until the police put two and two together and got victims equals clients. If you hadn't used my salon as your personal shopping ground, he wouldn't have even bothered to enter the equation."

"If you believe that you're a bigger fool than I thought. You're the reason he took such an interest in the case, why do you think he sent The Sword and Shield to watch you?"

"Huh?" Damn. *His Shield will protect and his Sword will cut.* I was right—The Sisters' warning—Alric and Teiran are this Sword and Shield.

"I take that back about you not being as stupid as you look. You don't even know your own history. My parents may have denied me my natural Talent, but they at least taught me history."

His growing anger and disdain feeds my own.

"Kind of hard to have parents who abandoned me at birth teach me anything."

He makes a little clicking sound with his tongue.

"Poor Keely. That doesn't excuse you. You could have taken the time to find out on your own."

"Whatever."

"Look at everything I found out on my own."

"Your parents must be so proud."

"Oh, I'm sure they are." A chilling smile snakes its way across his face as he touches two of the stones in the amulet.

Oh gods, he killed his own parents, really shouldn't be any big surprise. If he's willing to do that, what chance do I have? Zilch, zero, nada would be my guess, but a girl has to try.

"Why my salon? There are plenty of salons that cater to Ens."

"Why?"

"That's what I asked." I drop the asshole before it slips out. Insults are not helpful when you're trying to stay alive a few minutes more.

"Why not? You had everything I needed. A large and important clientele, a small staff, and face it, Keely, you're a sucker. You may be a respected business woman," he laughs, "or used to be, but you're a soft touch. Look at the misfits you take in as staff."

"What's that supposed to mean? They're all good at what they do."

His grin widens. "Yes, yes they are."

"Speaking of my staff, I don't suppose you had anything to do with Jenny's disappearance."

His jaw hinges guppy–like then slams shut. The cold gleam in his eyes tells me everything I need to, but don't want to know. A chill flows over me and the oxygen is sucked from my lungs. I doubt there's a gemstone immortalizing her in that thing around his neck. She wouldn't have anything he wanted besides what she'd already given him.

"It was her own fault."

His muffled voice continues on, but I've had all I can take. I try to shut him out, it's no use. My hands are pulled away from my ears and the strange combination of his laughter and my chanting enough, assaults me.

"Now, now, you wanted to hear everything, remember?"

Nothing like being forced to eat your own words. Next thing you know, he'll expect me to keep my promise to stay put. That ain't going to happen, not after everything he's done and what he's about to do. Bringing my feet up I plant them in his chest, thrusting with what little strength I have. Surprisingly, more than I expected as he lands with a satisfying thud. Scrambling to my feet, I run, not caring where to as long as it's away from him.

He shouts something, followed by that maniacal laughter, but I'm beyond caring. I just run, stumbling along until I hit my first roadblock. Wouldn't you know it, there's a fork in the road, another choice. Damn The Sisters and their prophecies.

There's no time to weigh out the options so I head right, my lousy sense of direction amplified by the lack of visual difference in my surroundings. I discover the glow I thought came from something he was doing emanates from the rock itself. It gives me enough light to navigate the unfamiliar paths. Problem is, he also has light.

The once-distant footfalls are closing as I lose steam. Nearly drowning, tossed in a trunk and being beaten takes a toll on a body. My muscles scream in protest, but nowhere close to as loud as my instinct to live.

Using the wall as a crutch, I continue my faltering gait searching for a place to hole up until he passes. Hoping and praying to whatever god might be listening that tracking isn't one of the Talents he's acquired. Had I been thinking clearly I'd have snagged that horrid piece of bling he's so proud of. To think I'd thought it pretty when Jenny, excuse me, fake Jenny was wearing it.

Stubbing my toe against a jutting piece of stone, I silently curse not only my own stupidity, but also my guardians for not teaching me how to border hop. Even if all the blame can't be laid at their feet, the pain in mine wants to. My snail's pace slows even more as a sharp edge slices across my palm. Here come the tears again. Doesn't matter if it's fear, pain, or just plain exhaustion. I don't have time for them. A trail of blood streaks the wall behind me. Can I make this any easier for him? I pull my hand away, but not fast enough. My arm is sucked into the stone, but the sound of his footsteps closing in, making yet another choice for me. Lesser of two evils again? I guess we'll find out.

Chapter 46

The last time I had to make a choice like this my lungs filled with water, this time it's dust. Would what waits for me on the other side be as helpful as Einen, or something far worse than The Collector?

Millions of voices reverberate and I cover my ears against the constant ooommm, but it doesn't even muffle the noise. Motion slows to a crawl, like pushing through a wall of molasses, only cool and dry instead of sticky. Reaching the other side leaves me gasping, trying to focus in virtually total darkness. Having claustrophobia could become an issue when jumping between worlds. I'm glad being in close spaces doesn't bother me and if it did, the alternative would cure me.

Blinking away the grit, my eyes slowly adjust to the difference in lighting. Still a soft glow, but the rocky walls are an iridescent silvery blue instead of warm gold. The drop in temperature prickles across my skin and foggy puffs of breath obscure my sight. One of the more colorful old timer's sayings comes to mind, *colder than a witch's tit*, not that I've ever tested that theory. Not high on my list of things to do.

I'd give anything to ditch the swimsuit for a parka, my teeth chattering so hard what's left of my brains rattle. The wall behind me begins to hum, the glow brightening, a body slowly emerging. Okay, not anything.

Limping my sorry ass away from the arm and now leg sticking out of the wall, I bite my lower lip to keep from whimpering. Those of you who think heels kill are in for a rude awakening when you try barefoot on stone. Icy, cold stone to boot. The only saving grace, it's not slick.

Pain slows my movements and the fear of more pushes me forward. Sharp edges bite into tender soles, leaving a bloody trail of prints. Every muscle throbs including my heart, beating in my ears so loud it almost drowns out the tapping crunch of his shoes.

Tears flow freely as my big toe connects with an unseen protrusion. Flailing limbs take the brunt of the impact hitting the ground with a snap. That can't be good, I hear the inner voice of reason mutter, followed by a flash of pain so intense my stomach heaves.

Laying there on my face, sobbing, I see my left hand at an odd angle, something protruding from the wrist. The light—what little there is—nearly goes out as I realize it's not a foreign object. That pale thing sticking out is bone, the streaks of dark running down my hand onto the ground, blood.

Stomach muscles twist and squeeze, but there's nothing left to give.

I want to curl into the fetal position and cry. I want to pass out. I need to hide, because I don't want to die. Half crawling, half dragging myself behind an outcropping of stone, I sit, willing myself to fade into the rock. Cradling my broken wrist, silent sobs wrack my body, a never-ending cycle of quaking pain.

"Hiding won't do you any good, especially when you've left me such convenient clues."

His garbled words find their way through the maddening static in my ears. Who knew pain had sound? Salty-sweet copper dribbles over my tongue as teeth gnaw their way through my lower lip. At this rate, maybe I'll bleed out before he has a chance to slice and dice me.

If the smell of rotting meat was the first clue he'd found me, my head connecting with rock is the last. He grabs what little hair I have left and drags me into the open.

My body screams in protest as knife-like objects rake across abraded skin and so do I when my hand smacks the ground. Flesh feeling like hamburger, a Kaleidoscope of color flashing, my empty stomach convulses. Had there been anything left inside I would have choked.

"Look what you've done to yourself, Keely. Had I let your little game of hide and seek continue there's no telling what other damage you would have inflicted. As I was telling you before you so rudely kicked me, I need your Talents to fix my mistake."

Fix his mistake? The words cut through the pain long enough for me to put two and two together.

"Sometimes we punish the ones we love. When I bring her back, I can explain everything,"

"You really think she'll believe you love her after you killed her?" My voice sounds like my throat feels, dry and damaged. Like acid was poured down it, or in my case up, as in stomach acid.

"I'll make her," he says then shrugs. "If she doesn't, I can always just kill her again."

What does he think this is? A video game? You can't just reboot a person after you kill them. Take that back, vamps, zombies and other undead types count, but the thought of Jenny forcibly reanimated. A shiver races through me and I groan.

Someone has to stop this insanity and considering I'm all alone, I guess that would be me. The idea of me stopping him brings my own sanity into question. Maybe that's not such a bad thing, a little crazy might go a long way.

Reaching up with my good hand, I tangle my fingers in the chain dangling over my face and give it a tug. He loses his balance, ending up on his hands and knees.

"Listen, asshole," I manage to croak. "It isn't

going to happen. You're not using me to bring Jenny back."

He lets out a slow, long breath, closing his eyes. "Keely, Keely, Keely, you really are dense, aren't you?"

I twist my fingers tighter in the chain. "Maybe, but then again, maybe not," I say, giving it a swift yank. Damn. I try again, using the weight of my body and roll. In a perfect world, that chain would have snapped, just like in the movies. If you want to get technical, in a perfect world, there wouldn't be any need for that chain to snap. In this world, I succeed in screaming in pain as he lands on top of me.

Righting himself, he clicks his tongue and untangles my fingers from the chain. A little tremor of fear tickles the base of my spine as his thumb gently wipes my tears.

"It's a pity I can't keep you as a pet. You really do amuse me, but that's just not in the cards."

Twice tonight I thought, this is the end, I'm a goner, but I'd been wrong. Guess three times is a charm because I'm pretty sure this is it and it makes me sad. It's so unfair. I don't get the whole life flashing before your eyes experience. Instead, my last sight will be his raw, oozing face.

Sadness flitters away, leaving fear and with fear comes what? Laughter, starting out as muffled giggles and building as pain screams through my body. For some sick reason nature has given me the most useless of defense mechanisms. The more pain, or fear I feel, the more I laugh.

The creases between his brows tighten and his jaw flops like a fish. My head swings to one side as his hand connects with my cheek. I laugh all the harder, tears streaming down my cheeks.

"Stop it."

"Stop it," I repeat.

"I said stop it."

"I said stop it," I say, continuing the childish game.

He grasps my shoulders, giving me a bone-jarring shake, my head bobbing.

"Stop it right this minute."

"Stop it right this minute," I reply between hiccuping laughter. I know I'm pushing my luck, but caring has flown the coop.

He shakes me again, this time hard enough for my head to bounce against the floor. The laughter stops as bursts of light flare, but the tears continue to flow. It's bad enough he's going to kill me, but does he have to give me the mother of all headaches? Apparently, that's the plan, or he intends on shoving me through the earth. Funny in a warped sort of way, considering that's what I was trying to do earlier.

Bright light flashes when my damaged hand slams against the ground. All my pain condensed into one small place. The howl of an injured animal shatters the silence. Brightness fades to red as all that concentrated pain reaches my brain, the receptors all too receptive. My surroundings disappear, there's nothing, but color, white noise and pain. The noise intensifies and blackness squeezes around the color, every nerve screaming as my body shifts against the serrated earth.

Why not give into the darkness, let it swallow me? There's no use fighting, he's going to kill me anyway. No one's body is meant to take this much pain. Nor is the mind capable of processing it. It shuts down, but not before I feel the ground give away below me.

Chapter 47

The world spins as millions, no zillions of whispers thrum in my ears. Unseen fingers caress my skin, cold like a winter breeze. Exhausted, terrified and hurting, to the point of not caring, I ride along the silken darkness.

When the spinning stops, I play rabbit. If I don't move, he can't see me. Not that it should matter, I'm dead right?

"What do you want, little Schattenkind?"

Crap, there's that name again. The voice is torn and ragged, mingled with an enticingly seductive quality. Like two in one, similar to The Sisters with their surround sound.

Turning my head toward the voice, hesitantly I open my eyes. Posed in profile, sits a woman on a dark throne. If she hadn't spoken I would have thought it was a statue. A rendition of perfection meticulously carved in luminous stone. Her profile is so stunning I'd have to vote her top of the beauty food chain. Okay, so Royd's sister ranks up there if you like the Malibu Barbie type. I guess you could call it a tie. What can I say? In my profession, you notice these things.

"Your lack of answer is yet another rudeness, I must tolerate, Schattenkind." Her tone brings the mask of calm she wears into question.

"What did you call—I'm sorry." My hashed throat barely manages a whisper that sounds almost as ragged as half her stereophonic voice.

"I called you Schattenkind for it is what you are and shall accept your pathetic apology if you tell me why you are in my domain."

Somehow, I manage to roll over and push myself up onto all threes. Sweat breaks across my forehead and upper lip, intense pounding in my head and ears nearly knocking me flat. My hand and wrist throb with a life of their own as I attempt to keep the arm tucked against my body. Swallowing, I raise my upper body, cradling one arm in the other, hissing as my hand flops to one side. This is going to make my job near impossible if it doesn't heal correctly. What am I saying? I highly doubt I'll be doing hair in the afterlife. Wait a minute.

I'm dead, right? That would make her... That elegant profile turns toward me before I can even think her name. Like a freakish Halloween costume splitting a person down the center, the other half of that perfect alabaster profile wavers between a mirror in onyx and cadaverous remains. The Mistress of the Dead. The goddess, Hel.

After nodding in respect, I fix my attention

on the attractive side. Not trusting my reaction to the other, the last thing I want to do is insult her. Seems I've already pushed the boundaries of politeness.

"Um…I'm dead, aren't I?"

Her laughter is like crystal drug over gravel. "Now, if you were I would not be asking why you are here." Eyes, one frost-colored, the other empty darkness, rove over my broken form. "From the look of you, it is a distinct possibility, if you do not see a healer."

Advice I don't really need, I know I'm in a bad way. Battered, bloody and severely dehydrated.

"I don't suppose you have one of those down here?" Stupid question, but it gets her to laugh. Laughter is better than the alternative, whatever that might be.

"If I did you this favor what would you give in return?"

Damn, there's always a catch when it comes to dealing with gods. Scratch that, it doesn't matter who you're dealing with, there's always a catch. What could I offer that is comparable? Free haircut, manicure, how about a facial? I shiver at the thought of touching her and it reminds me how important it is I find a healer ASAP.

Clearing my tortured throat, I end up coughing, finally managing to spit out, "What do you want?"

Her smile is downright nasty. "A boon of my

choosing, at a time of my choosing."

"Like what?"

"As I said, of my choice, when I choose it to be so."

Not a good idea to bargain with the ruler of hel, especially when I don't know what I'm bargaining with, but what choice do I have?

"Well? Do we have an agreement?"

Pain and the fear of what awaits me on the other side push me to a decision, and I nod.

"I will instruct my personal healer to do what he can."

"One small problem with that."

"You do not agree to the terms?"

"It's not that I don't agree. If I'm bargaining with the unknown, I'd like to add a term of my own. I need help getting back home."

I can feel the exasperation in her sigh. I'm not pushing my luck on purpose I really don't know how to get back. I don't remember how I got here. Something about wishing the earth would swallow me. It's all static and fuzzy pictures.

"I will assign someone to take you to the edge of my kingdom and from there you will be on your own."

The giant lump of fear in my throat grates as I swallow. I'm not going to get a better deal. I'm lucky she's offering this much and probably luckier that she hasn't squashed me like a bug.

"Thank you."

"Do not thank me, just honor the agreement. At a time of my choosing, you shall deliver what I ask."

❦❦❦❦❦

I figured the healing would hurt, but I'd forgotten one little hitch. My Talents and the whole dead thing. Duh, her healer would be a dead guy, it only makes sense.

The minute he enters the room the situation begins to spiral and by the time he touches me it's out of control.

Unlike in the mortal realm, shadows don't slink in, they bum rush me. Piles of bricks restraining my Talent quiver and rock before shattering, leaving a cloud of dust and me open to death's influence.

Pain in my throat tells me I'm screaming, but I can't hear it over the choir echoing around me. Being in hel is a bad, bad thing for someone like me when it comes to control. The slender grip I had on my control slips through my fingers and I'm too weak and tired to get it back.

Cold hands grip the sides of my head, muffling the voices. I hear Hel tell her healer to work faster and me to shut up. Then blissful darkness.

❦❦❦❦❦

"Since I cannot trust you near my subjects, I am forced to escort you."

The Queen of the Dead has a soft spot no matter how she tries to hide it, one that gives warm cloaks and shoes. I don't think she hates me as much as fears what would happen if someone with my Talents were to stay. Can't say I blame her. I'd be a bit peeved if a stylist that could do what I do moved into my salon.

Try as I might, I can't keep up. Even in peak condition, it would be near impossible. My healing didn't go as well as I'd hoped. My wrist and hand bound in a crude splint, bruises and scrapes faded, pain factor dulled to somewhere between five and six on a scale of ten. I still look and feel like crap.

Surprise, surprise the dead can't heal the living, but I'm able to move and my head is clearer. If anything, the healer looked better when he was done. I have a feeling the total adoration in his eyes when he looked at me is going to be a problem later.

She grabs my arm and pulls me along. The contact makes it easier to focus on not only my surroundings—not that there's much to see besides barren trees and rock—but her as well. The constant shimmering between death and beauty stabilizes leaving only the beauty part.

At the edge of the stereotypical spooky forest, she stops, yanking me back. The rest of me feels lighter than a kite as my heart plummets. Exactly what I would have done had I taken that last step. Pebbles roll from under my toes as I teeter on what looks like the edge of the world.

"I take it this is it."

She nods staring at the obsidian perfection of the hand resting on my arm. Raising the other, she studies its crystalline beauty, her features soften and longing fills her eyes. By touching me, she's become an exquisite otherworldly work of art made of two glassy stones.

Swallowing back fear that threatens to choke and fighting the urge to pull away, I almost feel sorry for her. It's definitely time to go before she changes her mind about me staying. I'm in the business of making others look good, but spending eternity in hel playing personal stylist to a goddess isn't what I had in mind.

She pulls away quickly, power and prestige, winning out over vanity, and the dizzying cycle of beauty and the beast resumes.

"Yes," she says the faintest touch of regret in that gravelly tone. "From here, you go on alone."

The ground continues crumbling in front of my feet, the debris falling so far I can't hear it hit the bottom. "So I just jump?"

She shrugs. "If you wish, but one step is all you need."

One step sounds simple enough, but it's a long way down. I'm not afraid of heights, I'm afraid of falling and the big splat I'm going to make when I find the bottom.

"What is this place?" I ask, nodding in the direction of the nothingness on the other side of the line.

"The Between."

"Between? As in, between worlds?"

She nods.

A race to the top of my spine starts as I remember what little I know of The Between. It's nothing, except unfiltered chaos. The possibilities of what can happen when you are there are endless. I could end up sitting on my couch eating Moocha Java, or in an endless loop of dealing with past complaining clients. At the very worst, the beings that live there could rip me to shreds. The longer you're there, the greater the chances of you ending up in the nut house if you make it back. Navigating The Between is no easy task for those who know how. For me, it's going to be near impossible.

Chewing on my lower lip, I glance from her to the chasm of nothingness below and back. Maybe staying wouldn't be such a bad thing. I mean really, how taxing would being her personal stylist be? I'm tired, but that could be from all the walking and my physical condition, not from her zapping the life out of me, right?

Turning to ask if we could come to some sort of compromise, I see her hands extend toward me. The force of her blow sends me over the edge. Guess that would be a no.

Chapter 48

I'm running, to something, no from something. The rational part of my brain tells me I'm dreaming, but fear doesn't seem to care. It's too real.

Shadows spread across the bleak landscape. I'm being pursued. I don't know by who. Only that they want me and if they catch me, it will be bad with a capital B.

That little voice of reason again tells me it's not real, but others soon drown it out. Maybe they're just the reaction of an overly vivid imagination, but they sound real. Real scary and real threatening.

Run is the only thing I can do. Stay ahead of whatever hunts me. That's the only thing that matters, keeping one-step ahead.

Waist high, grass slaps and slices. Adding insult to injury, I'm naked. My legs hurt and my lungs are on fire, but it doesn't matter. Something's out there and if I slow down—or gods forbid, stop—it'll get me.

I stumble, ground cover tangling around ankles that twist painfully. Tears sting my face and blur what little vision I have in the encroaching darkness.

Something screeches in the distance followed by howls and something that sounds like laughter a lot closer. My body protests as I misstep and tumble to the ground. Clawing at the grass, I pull myself a little further, then collapse.

I lay there in the fetal position, shaking with silent sobs. Unseen fingers caress my skin, cold like a winter breeze. The world spins as whispers thrum in my ears. Exhausted, terrified, humiliated, to the point of not caring anymore, I squeeze my eyes shut. *Let them take me, just let it be quick and as painless as possible.*

Silvery light blossoms behind my eyelids, chasing away the darkness, sending the voices and hands with it. Slowly I open one eye, then the other and push myself up. I'm alone. Even the grass is gone. No sky, no land. No ceiling, no floor, no walls. There's nothing, nothing, but the light. Soft and silvery.

The fear of being pursued and hunted is replaced by another kind of fear. Being alone. Utterly and completely alone in this vast nothingness. It sounds silly, being afraid of nothing, but I am.

My poor, tired brain runs in all directions at once and nothing becomes something. Something even more horrifying. Nothing is exactly what everything I've worked for has become. In the blink of an eye my world, once so full became empty. Stripped naked, just like my body.

No, not taken, just changed.

"No, he took it. Destroyed it. Everything I ever wanted gone. Poof!"

The important things are still there.

"Like what?"

Your friends. Your family. Your self–respect.

"Ha, my family hid things from me and my friends want to use me," I say feeling the unwanted guest of guilt creeping in.

Your family did what they thought best, and there is no proof your friends wish to use you.

I don't want to feel guilty, I want to pout and feel sorry for myself. I don't want to think about the good things in my life. I want someone to blame other than myself. I want to rail at the world for everything that's happened. Most of all, I want to take the easy way out. Like the rest of society, I want to ignore it and pretend it will go away.

You can fix this.

"No, I can't!"

You can, and what's more, you know you can.

I scream, covering my ears with my hands.

Oh gods, I've finally stepped over the edge. Trapped in my own mind, doomed to hold pointless conversations for eternity.

Stop being a whiny little bitch and do something for a change!

Damn, now I've done it. I've gone and made myself mad at me. I snicker and that turns to giggling, then a full–blown rolling–in–the–nothingness belly laugh. I really have gone mad—ooops, make that crazy.

Keely.

"Yeah?" *My* voice, is suddenly deeper and very sexy. The giggling intensifies until tears are streaming down my face.

Keely!

"What?"

Come back.

"Come back where? Reality? Sorry, no can do." I've become a Tickle Me Keely doll, the slightest thing setting off the laughter. Even things that aren't funny, like my slender hold on sanity.

Come to me.

"If I knew who you were, I might think about it."

Do not think about it, do it. I refuse to lose you.

"You lose me? Hel, I've lost myself."

My giggles come to an abrupt stop with the hot stinging pain in my cheek.

Forgive me.

I lay my hand gingerly on my throbbing flesh, the tears in my eyes no longer from laughter. Is this what they mean by a danger to yourself? Will the *others* part come later, because I'd sure like a crack at the owner of that invisible hand. Wait, it's me. My psyche is taking arguing with yourself to a whole new level.

"Fuck you," I scream, cradling my aching face. "Just go away and let me be."

Curling into a ball I lay there choking on my own tears. Wave after wave of emotion wracks my body—anger, fear, hopelessness. I've reached the point of not caring what happens, showing just how pitiful I truly am.

Invisible hands grip my arms, squeezing until my sobs become whimpers. Jerking me upright, shaking me like a naughty child in the toy aisle.

You are acting like a foolish child, not the capable woman I know.

"Ha, then you don't know me very well."

I try pushing the hands away, but there's nothing there, just the painful tightening around my forearms. Another lovely illusion brought to you by the cracked mind of Keely Fey.

I know you and what you are going through better than you think.

"Whatever." My lower lip protrudes and I feel the urge to say, *you could never understand what I'm going through.* Amazing how a woman of my years can be reduced to adolescent angst.

I gasp as the grip on my arms tightens. Red imprints flush to the surface, amplifying the intensity of my delusion.

Stop.

"Stop what? I've already teetered off that tiny ledge of reality. It's too late, so just leave me be."

I give up struggling and just hang limply. It's too late.

Self-pity is the only pity, you will receive.

Apparently, the contempt I feel for myself is out in the open. Even I can't stand me when I'm sitting on the pity pot.

"Fine, I didn't ask for anything from you. Just go away. I don't want to fight anymore."

All I want to do is lay down and close my eyes. I'm tired. Tired of things I can't do anything about. Tired of the intrigue. Tired of the lies and half–truths. Tired of being placed under a microscope. Tired of everyone thinking I'm something I'm not. Tired of being used. On top of that I'm just plain tired, physically and mentally. Like that's not evident considering I'm chatting with and physically abusing myself.

"Just go away and let me sleep."

The voice starts to recede as I pull inward, drifting off. In my dream inside the dream, I'm standing at my wall. That lovely shield that stands between me and everything else. I begin piling brick on brick, walling off that part of myself, just like the dead. Why didn't I think of this sooner? Three more walls, and I'll finally be alone.

The voice keeps rambling, but I've given up listening, substituting an internal radio station. Humming along with my favorite band I move to wall number two, three if you count the one previously installed. It's hard work, but it helps. Keeping my hands busy seems to cloud the echoing drone of that voice I've come to think of as my male side.

What? Women are always claiming they want to see the feminine side of men—problem is when we do, we usually want to toss it back in the closet—it's time we admit we have a male side.

Before I can slam the last brick into place, something clamps down on my shoulder spinning me around. I let out a yelp. If I had panties on, they'd probably be wet right now. The familiar white gold hair and silvered skin lets the air out of my tires.

"What are you doing here? How did you get in?"

"I've come to find you. Have you forgotten The Between is where we always meet? The only place we can meet?"

Images of our last meeting float across the big screen of my mind, accented by the hand that strokes my arm. My pulse flitters like a captured butterfly.

The desire to touch and be touched by him is there, but different. Not the rightness of interlocking puzzle pieces that need to be together. Plain old, *I've had a couple of drinks and want to take you home*, thinking with your crotch. Nothing *special*. Nothing I can't shake off, or ignore.

"Well, you found me. Now leave. I know misery supposedly loves company, but I want to enjoy it alone."

"Nope, don't think so."

I open my mouth to tell him to take a hike then snap it shut. Wait.

"What did you say?"

"You heard me. I said I don't think so."

There's none of the softness of our last time together in his harsh features. Or even the animal hunger he tries to keep hidden. Something twisted, not right about the set of his lips.

The speech pattern and tone, so not right. Vereinen uses proper, old fashioned English, no conjunctions, or slang. Eyes are just wrong, size, shape and color. Vereinen's are pale like mine with just a hint of silvery grey to distinguish them from the white. These eyes are grey, too dark, too small and even though narrowed, too round.

The more I study the face in front of mine, the more I notice the *wrongness*. Too full and round, no prominent cheekbones, nose too broad, lips too thin. Height is next, I'm looking him right in the eye. His frame is too wide and squat. The hand that holds my arm is rough, calloused.

Not Vereinen. My first clue should have been that he didn't try to pull me into his arms. Obviously, I don't pay attention to clues. My second should have been him insisting we meet in The Between. Whoever this is, he's not Einen. I don't know what kind of cruel joke my addled mind is playing, but I've had enough.

"I don't know who, or what you are, don't care, but it's time for you to leave."

I try to pull away, but no luck. He only tightens his hold.

"Look, this is my dream, I told you get out."

He starts to laugh. "Dream? You think this is a dream?"

That laugh sends familiar shivers racing across my bare skin. I should be scared and it creeps along the edges of my mind, but I ignore that little inner warning.

"I don't think, I know. Now get out and let me finish."

"Too bad you weren't faster. This might have been avoided."

"What in hel are you talking about?"

"The walls. If you'd have finished, I wouldn't have been able to get in."

"Whatever. You're a figment of my imagination, so the walls wouldn't have made a difference."

"If I really am a figment of your imagination, why can't you banish me?"

"If you haven't noticed, my brain is cracked, not exactly taking orders at the moment. If it were fully functioning, neither of us would be here."

My hand against his chest, intending to give

him a push toward the opening where my last wall will stand, I feel something cold and hard. Sliding my hand to the side, the opening of his shirt widens. Glittering against his chest is a mass of twisted knot-work, studded with ghastly jewels.

Chapter 49

A slow smile stretches across his face. "Still think you're dreaming, Keely?"

I let my hand drop, tightening my grip on the brick and look at the first of the walls. It exists only in my head. A shield guarding me from the monsters my renegade Talent can call up. I put it there, so I should know where it resides. Right?

"It has to be."

"I told you we are in The Between."

I shake my head, staring at his disgusting talisman. That one word keeps reverberating through the cracks in my mind, between. Finally, it dawns on me. The Between, that's where Hel left me. I'm not dreaming. I'm stuck in The Between. Even better, I'm stuck in The Between with the asshole who's trying to kill me.

He's also the reason my life is total shit.

Anger trumps fear. With a full body swing, the brick in my hand makes contact with the side of his head, face, whatever. I don't wait around to find out. Letting the momentum carry me, I stumble, drop and roll away, biting back a cry of pain as I come to a stop. My makeshift splint is no match for a body weight and stone sandwich.

"Ouch." I hear him.

He sits across from me, laughing as blood trickles into his eye and down the side of his face. My weapon lies at the half way mark, no way I can get there before he does.

"That's the best you've got?"

He giggles as if I'd tickled him instead of smacking him upside the head with a brick. I may be wiry, but there was still enough force behind that swing to land him on his ass. It pisses me off that he has the nerve to sit there laughing when that should have hurt.

Pushing myself up into a crouch I stare at the reason my life is in the shitter. Throwing my energy into my anger, a familiar slow itch creeps across my flesh. The faces of those he's hurt flashing in my mind's eye. The lives he's destroyed. The lives he took. Like Jenny.

I kick at the metaphorical wall in my head. I couldn't protect her when she needed it, but I can do something now. There is no way I'm going to let him use me to bring her back.

He's on his feet now, looking nervously at the wall as it shivers, shedding dust.

The smile on my face must not hold much in the way of comfort his Adam's apple rises and falls in quick succession. I give the mental wall another kick, delighting in how the one around us shakes.

He scrambles, digging in his pocket, pulling out what looks like silver threads.

"Your hair," he says, brandishing a lighter in the other hand.

I hesitate, remembering my little hair loss trick. Guess it backfired. Lousy bastard kept some of it.

"So?"

"You know what will happen. You'll be powerless just like the others." He suspends the tuft of hair over the ignited flame.

All I have to do is get to him before he finishes the spell. I take a step toward him. He raises the flame until it licks at the bottom of the strands and the beginnings of a noxious smell coats my nostrils and tongue. Damn it! I hate the smell of burning En hair, especially mine. That slow itch now prickles with joyous pain from head to toe.

"You'll never make it in time."

"Seems you missed the memo," I say, letting the power flow across my skin and outward. "*I* don't need to make it at all."

Thrusting my hands toward him, I feel the power tingle along my body. Unlike when I use my regenerative Talent on a client, it doesn't gather in my fingertips, but flows from every pore. I release it, keeping my focus exclusively on him, and feel instant pleasure. Urge and need—like a building climax during really good sex—fill me as I manipulate the shadows cast by the walls.

They converge on him, slithering across the floor and up his legs, binding him. Panicked, he waves the lighter at them. I'm not sure if it's the encroaching darkness, or the breeze he created, but the flame extinguishes. His frantic search for a way out only heightens my pleasure. He's mine to do with what I want and he knows it.

Taking my time—I have all the time in the world—I walk toward him. There's nothing, but him, me, and justice. I'm standing so close I can feel his panting, smell the stench of fear and hear the throbbing of his heart. My own pulse echoes that fear with excitement. I reach out, grabbing the twisted magic around his neck.

"It's mine," he cries.

"It was never yours," I say giving a savage pull. This time it breaks like a single strand of hair. Teasingly, I dangle it before his face, snatching it away as he attempts to grab it, laughing at his childish whimpers.

Looking at the wall that holds death at bay, beckoning with my finger, a brick slips and then another. With each brick, currents of air whip my body, lashing my flesh until it becomes numb. The howling of those trapped behind becomes a glorious symphony of vengeance to my ears. I want him punished for everything he's done. What would be more poetic than to let his victims extract their revenge? His screaming pretty much tells me he knows what's coming for him as the bricks slowly fall.

They move at an achingly slow pace and I watch as he struggles against the shadows that bind him. I step back as they reach their target, laughing as he begs and pleads. There isn't a doubt in my mind that he did the same with his captives.

My little army of dead surrounds him, pulling him down until all I see is his hand above the swarm of ragged bodies. One of the dead turns toward me, body still fresh, tears streaming, a sad smile as my name tumbles from her lips. For a brief second I see the girl I knew.

Jenny fingers the blackened marks around her neck and that sad little smile disappears. She bares her teeth in a feral grin and turns her attention to the writhing mass on the floor.

A raging headache rips through me, splits me in two. One side urging me on, enjoying my victim's tortured screams, consequences be damned. The other repulsed, ashamed that I would even think of using my Talents in such a way that makes me no better than my prey.

I stand there sobbing, grasping my head, trying to push the two halves back together. This is no time to have second thoughts. It's too late for second thoughts.

The power reels back against me with the force of an F5 tornado, landing me flat on my back, gasping for breath. Slowly I roll over and crawl on my elbows and knees toward where he'd been standing. Nothing, not even a grease spot where he should have been. Reality slaps me. Not relief at being safe, but what have I done?

Kneeling, I wipe my brow, the grisly *collection* of Talent banging against my nose. Giving it my best girly throw ever, it lands in the rubble of what's left of my wall. Doubled over clutching my stomach, wave after wave of nausea hits me until there's nothing left, but dry heaves. I'm not sure if it's because of that thing, or what I've done. Probably a combination of both.

I lay in the fetal position, whimpering, something's broken and a splint isn't going to make it all better. A familiar scent and touch wraps itself around me.

Keely, you must get up.

I shake my head.

You must leave.

"Einen?" Little more than a whisper.

Yes, now you must get up and leave this place.

"I can't. Come get me."

I cannot, they are coming.

"Who?"

Keely! Hide, they are there!

My brain is a tangled mess of regret, fear, and perverse pleasure. My sense of right and wrong is tattered and torn. My spirit, severely bruised. My body, feeling the effects of massive withdrawal and the backlash of overextended use, tempered with climatic release. To put it in a nutshell, I don't care. About anything, living, dying, the whole shebang. I just want to sleep. Sleep and forget. Perhaps, if I sleep, I can find Einen.

Just before consciousness slips away, I feel strong familiar arms lift and cradle me against a familiar body.

"I am too late." Whispered against the top of my head.

Chapter 50

I don't need to open my eyes to confirm the incessant hum and flicker behind my lids belong to fluorescent lights, but I do. Mistake number one.

Jerking my head to the side to avoid the glare. Mistake number two. The polite knocking in my head becomes a battering ram.

Bits and pieces of my *adventure* scatter, then come together in a nightmarish mishmash. Bile rises and I try to roll to the side. Mistake number three. Every muscle screams in protest. I can feel the sizzling zap of the restraints around my wrists and ankles lessen to a tingle as I relax against the bed.

Slowly, I lift my head, squinting against the too bright light. Not my room, obviously. I would never decorate with harsh fluorescents and dingy white. Nor do I own a mattress designed with torture in mind. From my vantage point, I can't tell if there's anything else in the room besides the bed, a crappy institutional chair and me. The only window, a tiny square of glass sandwiching a wire mesh in the door.

I'm definitely not in The Between, unless my

cracked brain is still screwing with me. Which, in The Between, is possible. Testing the theory, I close my eyes and take a deep breath. I should be able to start building my wall again. Nothing. No wall. No crazy illusions. Not even the spark of my Talent. It's gone. Tears leak down the sides of my face with the slow build of hiccuping sobs. Instinctively moving to wipe them away, my body convulses in pain, radiating from the restraints.

There's no way to measure how long the nasty shock treatment lasted. I passed out. It's pretty safe to say I'm not in The Between. Now I understand why Einen told me to hide.

I'm in the Enchant Containment Unit.

Acknowledgments

They say writing a book is a lonely thing, something you must do alone. Quite the contrary, I alone pounded the keyboard, but was far from lonely.

I had the support of friends and family. My writers group, The Saturday Writers. My most excellent husband, The Breadwinner, and let's not forget the cast of Disenchanted. Without all of whom this book would have never seen the light of day.

Special thanks goes out to my beta readers, Tracey and Melissa, who read the first few drafts and wouldn't let me quit. My critique partners, Cheryl and Malynda, who pointed out all my little faux pas. I also need to thank Donna, Maggie, and John, who went above and beyond in the inspiration department.

About the Author

A.R. Miller writes urban fantasy for grown-ass women (and men) who are still too young to care.

She lives in Iowa with an accommodating husband and their four-footed companions. When not testing the patience of readers with cliffhanger endings, you might find her wielding a makeup brush or curling iron as a freelance stylist.

To find out more about A.R. or the Fey Creations series, visit www.feycreations.com.